MOTION TO DISMISS

"Jacobs is a master storyteller. Her plot is intricate and compelling." —*The Piedmont Post*

"If you haven't read the earlier Kali O'Brien books, I recommend them, until you can get your hands on a copy of this one." Linda Fairstein, author of *Cold Hit*

"A must read for legal thriller fans and those who have enjoyed

...*oklist*

"A confident, classic whodunit with a smart sleuth." —*San Jose Mercury News*

An excellent plot . . . an astonishing conclusion." —*Kate's Mystery Books*

SHADOW OF DOUBT

"Jacobs writes with a sure sense of character." —*Publishers Weekly*

"Charming, witty and stylish." —*Grounds for Murder*

Books by Jonnie Jacobs

Kali O'Brien Novels of Legal Suspense

SHADOW OF DOUBT

EVIDENCE OF GUILT

MOTION TO DISMISS

WITNESS FOR THE DEFENSE

The Kate Austen Mysteries

MURDER AMONG NEIGHBORS

MURDER AMONG FRIENDS

MURDER AMONG US

MURDER AMONG STRANGERS

Published by Kensington Publishing Corporation

Shadow of Doubt

A Kali O'Brien Mystery

JONNIE JACOBS

KENSINGTON BOOKS
KENSINGTON PUBLISHING CORP.
http://www.kensingtonbooks.com

For my parents, with affection and gratitude

ACKNOWLEDGMENTS

I'd like to thank the following people for their advice and guidance: Charlotte Cook, Sandy Lauren, Lynn Mac-Donald, and Prudence Poppink. I'd also like to thank Tom McBroom, Senior Vice President at World Savings and Loan for the mini-course in banking transactions. And once again, a special thanks to my husband and sons, for so many things.

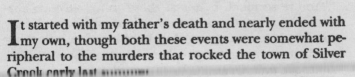

It started with my father's death and nearly ended with my own, though both these events were somewhat peripheral to the murders that rocked the town of Silver Creek early last summer.

It was my father's funeral that brought me home in the first place. When I left Silver Creek twelve years ago to attend college, I vowed I'd put as much distance between the town and myself as possible. And while I ultimately ended up less than four hours away in driving time, my life in San Francisco was light years away in other respects. I was a senior associate in one of the city's small, but notable, law firms; I owned my own architecturally significant (albeit heavily mortgaged) house in the Berkeley hills; and I was in the early stages of what I hoped might become a fairly serious relationship with the firm's star litigator, Ken Levitt. If you had asked me, I'd have said that I'd finally brushed the last of Silver Creek's dust from my shoes. Which goes to show just how wrong a person can be.

My father and I had one of those relationships which improve with distance. Although I was diligent about calling on alternate Sundays, my visits home were infrequent and usually quite brief, sometimes lasting only an hour or so as I drove through town on my way to some more glamorous destination. I would have liked my stay that June to have been as abbreviated. To drop in for the funeral, the way Sabrina did, and then out again less than forty-eight hours later, leaving the loose ends of an emptied out life for others to deal with. But Sabrina had children, a husband, and several thoroughbred horses, all of whom needed her at home, while I had not so much as a single house plant that required my attention.

"You're so much better at these things anyway," Sabrina told me as she slid into the airport limo that Friday morning. It was no use arguing, but I knew the only thing I was better at was getting suckered into taking on responsibility she didn't want. It had been like that as long as I could remember. Of course, Sabrina had at least shown up, which is more than could be said for our brother, John, who pleaded an inflexible schedule and sent an ostentatious arrangement of lilies instead.

The patterns of our childhood, it seemed, hadn't changed much. As the oldest, and only boy, John had more or less assumed a posture of aloofness, deigning to mix in family matters only on those occasions when it suited him. And my parents, knowingly or not, had encouraged his behavior by treating John as someone whose affection was to be wooed. Sabrina, on the other hand, had cast herself in the leading role at every opportunity. Two years my senior, she was very much like our mother—bubbly, fun-loving, and conveniently helpless when it came to anything tedious. Growing up, the three of us had been like the points of a triangle, each pulling in a different direction. I couldn't say we'd worked out our differences really, but over time we'd come to accept them.

Which isn't to say I wouldn't have liked a little help in winding up my father's affairs.

Still, I was managing just fine until the day after the burial when I found myself alone with my father's springer spaniel, Loretta, and a houseful of memories I never knew existed. I hadn't counted on that. I'd figured I could sweep through the house fairly quickly, tossing most of what was there into the big Goodwill boxes I'd brought with me, and the remainder of the stuff into the trash. But I'd been at it since seven that morning, and I wasn't even half through with the kitchen. I simply couldn't decide what belonged in which pile. I'd even started a third pile, things I might want to hold onto. And while it wasn't yet large, its very presence confused me more than I cared to admit.

By late afternoon I'd had it. I picked up the phone and tried calling Ken, whose own world fell so easily into neat little piles it sometimes scared me. As usual, he was in conference and couldn't be disturbed. This could mean anything from a heavy negotiating session to a late lunch, and his secretary, a stern old-school type who didn't approve of women attorneys, wasn't about to clarify the issue for me. "I'll tell him you called," she sniffed, then added with emphasis, *"again.* I'm sure you realize what a terribly busy man Mr. Levitt is." I did, although I was still a trifle peeved that he hadn't come with me to the funeral.

"It's not like I knew your father," he'd explained before I left.

"You've met him," I countered, "and besides, you know *me.*"

"I'm sorry, Kali, but the timing's terrible. I'm swamped with work. And the partner's retreat is that weekend."

Reluctantly, I'd conceded the logic of his argument, but that didn't stop me from feeling put out. And the fact that he'd been tied up in meetings the last two times I'd called hadn't helped matters.

I went back to packing, but didn't make it past the lumpily woven pot holder I'd made my mother one Christmas years ago. It was stuck in the back of a drawer filled with her homemade aprons and hand-embroidered dish towels. Like a sudden nighttime fever, the past swept over me and filled me with longing. There I was, Ms. Cool-Headed Efficiency, propped against my father's greasy old stove, blinking hard at the worn linoleum floor in an effort to contain the rush of tears.

Which all goes to explain why, when Jannine Marrero called and invited me to a barbecue that evening, I accepted without a moment's hesitation.

"I hope you don't think it's rude, inviting you at the last minute like this, and so soon after your father's passing. Eddie says it's downright insulting, but I figured you might be ready for a little diversion by now."

Jannine's voice has a kind of twang to it which I've always found comforting. We were best friends all through high school but somehow, without meaning to, we'd drifted apart after graduation. Although we exchanged Christmas cards and occasional phone calls, I hadn't seen her in five or six years.

"I'm not insulted at all," I told her truthfully, "and I'd love to come."

"There won't be many people you know, mostly other

teachers from the school and stuff, but now that I know you'll be there, I'll see if I can't get some of old gang to drop by, too." She paused to take a breath. "Gosh, Kali, it's going to be good to see you again."

I didn't know about that. I thought there was a good chance we would run out of things to say to one another very quickly, but I was pretty sure I couldn't stand my own company for the whole night either.

Jannine greeted me at the door with an expansive hug. "Shoot, Kali, you don't look a day older than you did when you left home. Or a pound heavier. Must be that big city drinking water or something. Maybe I ought to try a jug or two myself."

We looked each other over, discreetly at first, then much more candidly. Jannine, who had always been a little plump, was now a good thirty pounds overweight. Her overly permed hair hung at odd angles, forming a shapeless mass around her face. But she had always been one of those people blessed with true inner beauty, and that had not diminished. When she smiled, her whole face lit up with an honest, down—to—earth pleasure that caught you up in it, willing or not.

"It's good to see you, too," I told her, surprised to discover I truly meant it.

She squeezed me again, then clasped my hand as though I were an errant child and dragged me into the back yard. "Eddie, come look who's here."

From across the yard, Eddie turned and gave me one of his prize smiles. It hit me in the stomach just the way it had in high school. He had been handsome then, the stuff girl's dreams are made of, and if anything, he'd grown better looking over the years. Curly black hair, dark eyes and straight white teeth. Even the slightly thicker middle looked good on him. "Hey, kiddo, long time no see."

I gave a self-conscious laugh. "Well, here I am."

"She looks terrific, doesn't she, Eddie?"

He slapped Jannine playfully on the fanny. "Damn sight better than you, sweetheart, that's for sure."

"Jannine looks wonderful," I protested, but she'd already given him a solid jab in the ribs with her elbow. This was apparently an old argument.

"I'd like to see what you'd look like after four babies and two miscarriages."

Eddie raised his arms to fend off an imaginary blow. "Jesus, don't go pulling that woman stuff on me again." He reached into the ice chest and dug out a beer. "Want a drink?"

"Sure." I took the can, then looked at Jannine.

"Nah, Jannine doesn't want any," Eddie said, with a laugh. He draped an arm loosely around his wife's shoulder. "It addles her brain. Doesn't it, sweetheart?"

Jannine laughed too, though not quite so heartily. "My brain's always addled."

"How's life in the big city?" Eddie asked, turning his attention back my way. "You rich and famous yet?"

"A long way from both."

I'd gone into law initially with the intention of righting wrongs, of tipping the scales of justice in the direction of fairness and decency, but I'd discovered that people with sizable student loans couldn't afford such lofty principles. Although my five years at Goldman & Latham hadn't done much for the general good of humanity, it had made a fair dent in the size of my indebtedness. Still,

I wasn't rich and I wasn't famous. Sometimes I wondered if I was even happy.

Eddie took a long slug of beer. "I'm working on my M.B.A. now," he said. "Did Jannine tell you?"

"She hasn't had a chance to tell me much of anything yet."

"I've got plans. Someday I'm going to be a hotshot myself, just like you."

"Eddie Marrero," I said, in a tone which was only half-playful, "you've always been a hotshot. It was you they had in mind when they coined the phrase."

Eddie grinned, cocking his chin and shoulders like Jose Canseco stepping up to bat.

"Hey, Marrero," a voice called from the porch.

Eddie turned and waved. He tossed a pretzel into the air and caught it in his mouth. "Catch you later, Kali, I got to go check the grill."

Jannine shook her head. "To listen to him, you'd think he was headed for the big time." She grabbed a beer and popped the tab. "Come on into the house for a minute while I finish up with the salads. A high school girl was supposed to come over and help, but she had to cancel at the last minute so I'm kind of behind schedule."

We moved into the kitchen, where Jannine began pulling plastic baggies of vegetables from the refrigerator. A minute later a lank, freckle-faced girl slid past Jannine and reached for a Diet Coke from the refrigerator.

"Erin, honey," Jannine said, draping an arm around her daughter, "this my friend Kali, the one I've been telling you about."

Erin offered me a weak smile.

"She was just a toddler the last time you saw her," Jannine said, beaming. "Now she's eleven. Eleven, going on sixteen." Erin gave her mother one of those icy glares girls her age are so good at, but Jannine let it slide right past. "You want some chips, too? You can take a bowl up to your room if you'd like."

"Mom!" Erin made it a two syllable word.

"Skinny as a rail," Jannine said, as Erin scooted past us on her way out the door, "and she thinks she's overweight. Won't eat anything but rabbit food. If only I had that kind of willpower." Jannine blew an affectionate kiss, which Erin, surprisingly, returned. Then she wiped her hands on her apron and dug out a big plastic salad bowl. "I was sorry to hear about your father," she said, turning to face me. Her voice was soft, weighted with things left unspoken.

I shrugged. The father I missed was not the reclusive shell of a man who had died of a stroke four days earlier, but the gentle, even-tempered man who had slowly withered away following my mother's suicide my freshman year in high school. I didn't need to explain, though; Jannine understood as well as anyone. She had lived through those years with me almost by the hour. Her family had, in fact, become my own.

"We sent a donation to the hospital in his name," she said. "Since there was no funeral, we didn't know what else to do."

By my father's own request we'd had a simple, private burial. Whatever sense of loss accompanied his death was also borne privately. It was a marked contrast to my mother's funeral years earlier and the emotional fallout that followed. I hadn't realized until she was gone how strong a force she'd been in our lives, and how much my father had relied on her energy and strength.

Of the three children, I bore the brunt of it. John was

away at college by then, in a world where even living parents rarely made an appearance. And Sabrina had her boyfriends, an ever–changing parade of star quarterbacks and prom trotters who were more than willing to offer comfort. The only person I knew to look to for comfort was my father, and he couldn't provide it. I've never truly forgiven him that, nor my mother for being the cause of it.

"We didn't see each other all that often," I said. "It's like he's been gone for years."

"Still, death is so final." She began tearing lettuce into a bowl. "So what are you going to do?" she asked, after a moment.

"Do?"

"With the house and everything."

"Sell the house, if anyone will buy it. There isn't much else."

She grabbed a handful of chips and munched as she worked. "I wouldn't worry about the house, I bet it sells quickly. It's big, even if it does need work."

The whole time I was growing up I'd thought our house small and tight. I'd been surprised to discover that it was, in fact, quite spacious. Considerably larger than my own house in Berkeley.

"Silver Creek has changed," Jannine said. "It's not the sleepy little town it was. Heck, we've even got a new movie theater going in on the east side of town, and I guess you know about the K-Mart over where the bowling alley used to be." She paused to scoop up two year old Lily, who had appeared out of nowhere clutching a fistful of crackers in one hand and a mashed strawberry in the other. "This one here," she said, nuzzling Lily's head, "she wasn't even in the hatchery last time I saw you. I can't believe how time flies. So, catch me up on the last, what's it been, five years?"

While I finished my beer, I filled her in on my stint with the D.A.'s office and my subsequent transformation to corporate veteran. It didn't take long. As I'd discovered on previous occasions, the life of a lawyer rarely lends itself to the heady anecdotes people seem to expect.

"How about men?"

"They come, they go. What's new with you?"

Jannine shifted Lily to the other hip. "You know, same old stuff. Right now we're gearing up for a summer of football practice." Eddie, one–time high school hero, was now the high school coach. "Football's big in this town," she said with a sardonic laugh, "that's one thing that hasn't changed."

"Neither has Eddie," I told her.

"Yeah, still the star, cocky as ever."

Before I had a chance to respond, a woman with dark, close–cropped hair sidled up next to me.

"Kali O'Brien. I'm sure glad Jannine warned me you'd be here, or I'd swear I was seeing a ghost."

It took me a moment, but I finally figured out the woman was Nancy Walker who, at seventeen, had had stringy blonde hair and a reputation for cutting more classes than the rest of us combined.

"I thought you were in the East," I said.

"I was, but my husband traded me in for a newer model so I came back here. I teach at the high school. English no less. Dumbest kid in school and now I teach there." She laughed good-naturedly.

"You weren't dumb," Jannine said.

"No, probably not, but I didn't know that then."

"Hey, Jannine!" Eddie's voice rose above the din of

backyard conversation. "Where are the goddamn buns?"

Jannine groaned. "In front of his nose probably. But I'd better go see anyway. Sometimes I envy you gals without a man around to complicate your life." I caught a look on her face, but just for a moment. "Don't you go running off, Kali, not until we've had a good long chance to talk."

Nancy squeezed out of the doorway to let Jannine pass. "Eddie's been a coach so long he's forgotten how to act like a normal human being." She chomped on a carrot stick. "Though he has charm to burn when he wants to. Come on, let's grab another beer, and you can tell me about life in the fast lane."

We made our way out back and found a stash of beer and chips. While Nancy grumbled about overcrowded classrooms and budget cuts, I watched the copper light of early evening gradually fade to darkness. Eddie was flipping burgers, strutting back and forth between the old stone barbecue and the picnic table like a celebrity. There was a lot of back–slapping and buddy–punching with the men, and an equal amount of squeezing and winking with the women. I wondered, as I had before, how Jannine had ever ended up with someone like Eddie. A catch, I suppose, in some people's book, except that he knew it and flaunted it, but definitely not the sort of partner I'd ever pictured for Jannine.

I talked to Nancy for a while longer, and then to one of my sister's old boyfriends. Jannine swooped down on me every so often to introduce me to a new cluster of names and faces, and then marched off to refill the chip bowl or bring out more salad. I heard about Elvira Arujo's hysterectomy, the hail as big as golf balls that had fallen a week earlier, and the Scout Jamboree which was being hosted that summer for the very first time in Silver Creek. There were the usual jabs at San Francisco ("Did you hear they just put heterosexuals on the endangered species list?") and at Berkeley ("Don't you mean *Berserkley?*"), and a sprinkling of lawyer jokes, most of them so dated I'd already forgotten the punch lines. Since I had little to contribute, I listened and for the most part kept my mouth shut.

As the night wore on I moved toward the edge of things, and let the drone of muted conversation roll over me like the gentle summer breeze. The night was warm, the air thick with the sweet scent of prairie grass. It was the kind of evening we rarely got in the Bay Area, where the fog usually rolled in before sunset. I watched Jannine's two middle girls straddle the beam at the top of the play-structure, and wondered what my life would have been if I'd never left Silver Creek. It's a peculiar feeling, finding yourself face to face with your past like that, reconciling what might have been with what is, especially when you find the neat little pictures in your head unexpectedly askew.

I was sitting on the back steps nursing my third can of beer when Eddie dropped down beside me, sloshing his own beer in the process. He'd clearly had many more than three.

"You look like an ad for some high class perfume or something, sitting over here in the moonlight like that." He winked. "Course you always were a classy—looking gal."

I humphed and inched to the left. I can spot a line a mile away, and this one was so blatant it practically blinked in neon.

Eddie, though, seemed to think he was onto something. He leaned toward me so that our shoulders bumped. "God, we had us some good times back in the old days, didn't we?"

We'd had, in fact, only one real "time," and I would hardly have called it good, even then. I seriously doubted that Eddie had found it very satisfying either.

"Real good," Eddie added, listing further in my direction.

I let my eyes meet his. "So good you dropped me like a hot potato right after that night in the shed."

I could see him take a moment to reassemble the past. He poked at the can with his thumb. "Shucks, Kali, a girl like you, it scared me. Shook me up to think I was falling for you."

I laughed. Even at sixteen I hadn't been so much heart-broken as humiliated, although at that age the pain is about equal. "Hang it up, Eddie. I'm not interested."

He looked hurt for a moment, then grinned. "You always were a hard sell."

"You couldn't have done better than Jannine in any case," I told him. "She's one in a million."

He glanced in her direction, and a shadow crossed his face. "Yeah," he said soberly, "I know." Eddie finished his beer, crushed the can with one hand, then turned and asked, "You going to be around town for awhile?"

"Till the end of the week, I think. Why?"

"Maybe we could talk sometime."

My expression must have given me away because he was quick to explain. "No, not like that. I mean professionally. Like, you know, as a lawyer."

"You've got lawyers here in town."

"Yeah, but Silver Creek's a small place. I think I'd feel

better with someone who's not in the thick of it." He had an odd, uncertain look in his eyes I'd never seen before.

"You in trouble, Eddie?"

"Me?" He laughed. "No, I try to stay away from trouble." He stood unsteadily. "I'm serious, Kali, I could use your help. I'll give you a call the first of the week, okay?"

Actually, it wasn't okay. Getting my father's affairs in order was my first priority, and if I felt any hankering for legal work, all I had to do was call my secretary. There was bound to be a thick stack of messages, a good third of them labeled *urgent*. Besides, I didn't want to become embroiled in whatever small town squabble Eddie had somehow fallen into. But I couldn't think how to say any of that without coming across like a total stuffed shirt. "Sure," I told him, "talk to you then."

As Eddie wandered off, I consoled myself with the thought that he would probably never call. Given his glassy-eyed look, I'd have given odds he wouldn't even remember the conversation.

By the time I was ready to leave, the party had moved inside, but was nowhere near winding down. I searched out Jannine to say good-bye.

"Geez, Kali," she said, wrapping me in an affectionate hug, "we never got a chance to really talk. How about coffee some day this next week? Or lunch, if you don't mind bologna and processed cheese."

"It's a date," I said, already looking forward to it. Somehow we'd picked up right where we'd left off, without any of the awkwardness I'd expected.

Early Saturday morning I was awakened by the sound of hammering somewhere in the neighborhood. Not the gentle tap, tap of someone securing a loose board or two, but the steady, head-jarring whack of serious business. I rolled out of bed, ready to run down and deliver a piece of my mind. But by the time I'd dressed, stumbled over Loretta and made it downstairs, I figured *what the heck?* I had intended to start early anyway. I made myself some coffee and dug in, working much more efficiently than I had the day before.

I filled box after box with donations to Goodwill, and an almost equal number of bags with stuff to be junked. None of the furniture was worth keeping, though it pained me to tag my mother's favorite armchair for a donation. I hesitated, if only for a moment. But I liked my life streamlined; there simply wasn't a place in it, or my house, for sentimentality.

By Sunday evening, I had finished going through most of the downstairs and had organized, on paper at least, the remainder of things that needed doing. I hadn't begun going through my father's records or getting the estate in order, but just seeing those steps spelled out on my long things-to-do list was enough to give me a sense of accomplishment.

Feeling pleased with myself and the progress I'd made, I took Loretta for an early morning walk Monday before breakfast. She'd been padding after me for days, her brown eyes following my every movement, oblivious to the fact that I was trying hard to ignore her. It struck me, with a degree of guilt, that she probably missed my father more than anybody.

On the way in I picked up the newspaper and tossed it on the kitchen table while I made myself a cup of coffee, a special decaffeinated grind I'd brought with me from home. Pulling the chair around so that the morning sun hit my back, I took a sip from my mug and opened the paper.

Eddie's face smiled up at me from the center of the front page, right under the bold print headline—POPULAR HIGH SCHOOL COACH SLAIN.

2

I read the accompanying story twice before any of it actually sank in. Even then, the words had a peculiar unreal cast to them. That a man could be drinking beer and laughing one day, and lying dead with bullet through his head the next— it was something I was having a difficult time getting a fix on. It happens, of course; the pages of *The San Francisco Chronicle* attest to the fact daily. But the names are generally not names I recognize, the faces not those whose smiles have touched my own. And that, somehow, changes everything.

The newspaper account, though nearly two columns long, offered maddeningly little in the way of useful information. Eddie's body had been found Sunday afternoon by a backpacker in the woods near the south fork of Silver Creek. Preliminary evidence indicated he'd been shot at close range sometime Saturday. There was no sign of a struggle. His car was found later, parked alongside the road about a half mile away. The remainder of the article was given over to highlights of Eddie's career and testimonials from former friends and colleagues.

My mind played the scene through time after time as I tried to make the words real, to give them the weight that would help me understand. But none of it fit.

Silver Creek runs down from the Sierras in two branches which join about ten miles west of town. The north fork offers spectacular views, picnic areas and, in summer, good swimming. The south fork is smaller, and the terrain around it much more rugged. Eddie's body had been found near the spillway, a couple of miles from the main highway. Although I'd not been there for years, I knew the area well, having spent more Saturday nights than I cared to remember drinking and necking along the same lonely stretch of unimproved county road. I couldn't imagine what Eddie had been doing out there. It isn't a place many people find attractive.

I scanned the article once more, looking for answers that simply weren't there, then I stood and dumped my now lukewarm coffee into the sink. My appetite, as well as my thirst for world news, had deserted me.

I picked up the phone to call Jannine, then thought better of it. She was probably neck deep in condolences already, and the last thing I wanted to do was intrude on her sorrow. But I couldn't simply send a little sympathy note either. I tossed the possibilities around in my head while I showered and finally came up with the idea of stopping by, briefly, with a meal or two. That was the only thing I could remember clearly from the period following my mother's death—the scores of friends and neighbors who passed through, leaving in their wake baskets and pots and Tupperware casseroles filled with nourishment for body and soul. Theirs had all been home-baked, of course, while I would have to rely on the local deli. My skills in the kitchen are pretty much limited to boiling water and opening packages, and I sometimes have trouble with the latter.

I had an appointment at the bank that morning to go over my father's finances, but I could drop by Jannine's on my way home. Maybe, by then, I'd have figured out how you comfort someone when there isn't any comfort to be had.

Mr. Meeder at the bank was very nice, but also painstakingly slow. Although I'd arrived at ten as scheduled, it was past noon when we finished, or, more accurately, when I'd had about as much as I could take. I hadn't been able to find the safe deposit key, so the box would have to be drilled out. The rest of the paperwork could wait as well. I stopped by the deli and loaded up on lasagna, roasted chicken, and an assortment of salads, then threw in a couple of bottles of good wine, figuring Jannine might need that more than food. With the kids in mind, I made another stop at the bakery, and then headed for her place.

It was Nona Greely, Jannine's mother, who opened the door. Her eyes widened instantly. "Kali O'Brien. Gracious me, is that really you?"

I assured her it was, though by then she was hugging me so hard I guessed she'd figured it out on her own. Nona is short and chunky, with an enormous bosom, so that hugging her is something like cuddling a favorite stuffed animal. When I went away to college, her hugs were one of the things I missed most.

"I read about Eddie in the paper this morning," I told her. "I came to see if there's anything I can do."

Her face, which had lit with a smile when she recognized me, darkened again. "Such a terrible, terrible tragedy. How could something like this happen?"

She didn't expect an answer, and I couldn't have begun to give her one. Instead, we held on to each other for a moment longer, muted by visions of lives so suddenly, and unalterably, changed. "How's Jannine doing?" I asked finally.

"Better than I would be in her shoes. But you know Jannine, solid as they come." Nona stood aside and gave me a weak smile. "Why don't you come on in. She's down at the station, but she ought to be back any minute."

"The station?"

Nona ushered me into the kitchen where she was in process of making sandwiches. "The police wanted to get her statement, they said, though they talked to her long enough yesterday. I can't imagine what more they need."

"Probably an affidavit signed in triplicate on official stationary or some such thing," I told her, setting my packages on the counter. "You know how bureaucracy works." I'd expected a flurry of neighbors and friends, but the house was oddly quiet. If it hadn't been for the shrill whoops and screeches of the TV cartoon I'd heard on my way in, I'd have thought we were the only people there. "I brought some stuff for dinners. It was the only halfway helpful thing I could think to do. Shall I just stick it in the fridge?"

"Why, honey, how thoughtful. Yes, just stick it in there anywhere you can find room."

A family refrigerator, I discovered, is not at all like a single woman's. It was so chock-full of milk cartons and plastic-wrapped bits and pieces I couldn't recognize that it was a struggle to find room for more. When I'd shifted and shoved enough to close the door, I stopped for a moment to admire the drawings which papered the front. Most of them were Lily's. Big formless sweeps of purple

and red crayon, her name printed at the bottom in Jannine's neat hand, along with the date. In the very center
was one obviously drawn by an older child—a sketch of a
man I took to be Eddie, standing in a field of flowers, the
words, "I love you Daddy" scrawled across the top. I
could feel the knot in my stomach twist up and grow
tighter.

"How are the kids taking it?"

"Lily doesn't understand, of course. I'm not sure Laurel does either, she's only four. But the two older ones are
pretty shaken."

Nodding silently, I sank down into one of the yellow
rail back chairs. The years fell away, and I was suddenly
back in Nona's big, pleasantly old-fashioned kitchen
where I'd spent so much time wrestling with my own loss.
They'd been my lifeline then, she and Jannine. Sixteen
years, and it seemed like only yesterday.

"How did it happen, exactly? The paper didn't say
much."

Nona had her back to me, spreading mayonnaise on
slabs of bread. "I'm not sure I know much more myself.
Jannine called me yesterday about five to say . . ."

Her words were broken by the sudden, sharp slap of
the back screen door. Jannine dropped her purse in the
corner, and then, without saying a word, slumped wearily
into the chair next to mine. She looked half–dead herself, worn and frayed around the edges like a cast–aside
rag doll.

"Kali brought us some dinner," Nona said, in an
overly cheerful tone.

Jannine looked up at me and smiled, but only for a moment. Then she rested her elbows on the table and stared
woodenly off into space.

"How'd it go, honey?"

Jannine shrugged.

I reached over and covered her hands with my own. "I'm so sorry," I told her. The words sounded hollow, but Jannine nodded numbly.

Then her eyes filled with tears, and her mouth began to tremble. She took short little breaths as though she were gasping for air. "It was awful," she said, pressing her fists hard against her mouth. "Eddie's dead and they don't even care. They kept asking me all these dumb, picky questions, over and over. I'd answer, and they say it back to me like it was the stupidest thing they'd ever heard." Her voice wavered and she swallowed hard. The tears spilled over and streamed down her cheeks. "It's almost like they don't believe me. Like they think *I* killed him."

I gave her a quick, reassuring hug. "That's just their way." I'd dealt with enough cops to know that the brusque manner pretty much came with the uniform, but it didn't always reflect what went on underneath. "They want to make sure they've got it all exactly right," I told her. "Details are important."

"Maybe," Jannine said, but she didn't look convinced. "Do they have any leads yet?"

"Besides me, you mean?" She gave a brittle laugh and wiped her cheeks with the back of her hand. "I don't know, they didn't tell me much. 'We'll be in touch' seemed to be about the extent of it. I'm sorry, Kali, but I've got a splitting headache. I've got to go lie down." She smiled once more, fleetingly. "Thanks for coming by, though, and for bringing food. It was real nice of you."

"Go on and rest, I'll stop by again tomorrow."

Jannine pushed back her chair and stood unsteadily. "Are the kids okay?"

Nona nodded. "I'm making them lunch right now."

Jannine paused by the kitchen door as though she might say something more, but then turned and left without another word.

"Dear God in heaven," Nona whispered, her voice hoarse and trembly. She stood motionless for a moment, staring at the empty doorway, then she took a deep, labored breath and resumed her sandwich-making. "Would you like some lunch?" she asked me over her shoulder. "Or a cup of coffee? It won't take long to make a pot."

I shook my head. "In fact, why don't you let me finish with the lunches. I bet you could use some rest yourself."

"Thanks, honey, but I need to keep busy."

"At least let me help then." I got out glasses and started to pour milk.

Nona turned abruptly and faced me. "You really want to help?"

"Of course."

"Then see if you can find out what's going on."

I must have looked puzzled.

"With the police, I mean."

It took a moment before I understood what she was asking. "You think they might actually believe Jannine killed Eddie?"

Her face closed up tight. It was a look I knew well.

"You can't be serious," I said.

"I know them, Kali. Once they think they've found the killer, they won't look any further."

That was pretty much true everywhere, but I couldn't believe the police, even in a backwoods town like Silver

Creek, would be so slipshod as to ignore the facts. "They can't arrest a person without grounds," I told her.

"Please, Kali, just ask and see what you can learn. Benson was a friend of your father's way back when, maybe he'll talk to you."

"Daryl Benson?"

She nodded. "He's chief of police now."

Benson had been a fishing buddy of my father's years ago, a high-spirited, jowly man who would occasionally show up on Thanksgiving and family holidays. I was never quite sure whether my mother actually expected him, or if somehow he simply found his way to our doorstep at the appropriate time. I'd only seen him in uniform once—on Senior Prom night he'd pulled over a carload of us and delivered a lecture about reckless driving. By that time, however, he'd stopped coming by the house, and mercifully hadn't recognized me.

"I haven't seen him in years," I told her. "I don't think my father had seen much of him lately either."

"Besides," Nona continued, undaunted, "you're a lawyer. That's got to mean something."

"It means they'd close the door in my face faster than ever."

"Please, just try." Nona's knuckles were almost white.

"But why in the world would they suspect Jannine?" I asked. "They can't build a case against her just because she's his wife."

Nona turned and went back to spreading tuna fish. "No," she said thinly, "but it seems it was her gun that killed him."

I didn't think the police would tell me much, and I was right. Daryl Benson wasn't even at the station.

"I'll wait," I told the dour-looking woman at the front desk. Certain clients did this to me on a regular basis. It drove me crazy, but I knew it sometimes worked.

"No point waiting," she barked. "He won't be back until tomorrow."

"Can you tell me who's in charge of the Eddie Marrero homicide?" I smiled pleasantly, but her expression didn't soften in the slightest.

"Doug Southern, but you can't see him either. He's up to his eyeballs in the investigation."

"Is there *anyone* I could talk to then?"

"Not about that, there isn't."

I smiled again. "Do they have any leads yet, any idea who killed him?"

The woman glared at me. She was maybe late forties, early fifties, it was hard to tell. A casting director's dream for sit-com army sergeant. "It's not my place to comment," she said stiffly, turning back to her work and thus missing me with about as much grace as I roll out for the Jehovah's Witnesses who ring my bell first thing Saturday morning.

I might have tried my luck with someone else, but there was no one else around. Wearily, I looked at my watch. Four-thirty. Waiting seemed like an exercise in futility, and I was hungry. I hadn't eaten since breakfast, and then only the half-cup of coffee I'd managed to get down before opening the paper. I'd been about as successful as I'd expected, but that didn't prevent me from feeling discouraged.

I'd have been a whole lot more discouraged, however, if I'd thought there was really anything to worry about. Given what Nona had said about the gun, it didn't surprise me that the police had questioned Jannine. It sounded fairly routine. I was sure the whole thing would be sorted out in no time. Jannine was about as unlikely a killer as they'd find.

Mike's Place, across the street from City Hall, was a combination bar and hamburger joint I remembered from my youth. I'd never been there myself, but it was, at that time anyway, the hot spot for swaggering, cheeky young men armed with fake IDs. The place looked as though it hadn't been touched in the intervening years, but the aroma of fried onions enticed my stomach before my more fastidious side had a chance to protest.

The place was surprisingly crowded for that time of day and, not so surprisingly, very noisy. The pool table at the back seemed to be a major draw; those who weren't playing were busy giving advice. A dart board next to the bar attracted a group that was somewhat smaller, though every bit as vocal.

I considered leaving, but the empty refrigerator at home meant stopping at the store on the way, a mission which required more energy than I had. I ordered a burger with a side of onion rings and a glass of white wine. The man behind the bar snickered ever so slightly and reached for a jug of generic Chablis. It had probably been open for months. "On second thought," I told him, "maybe I'll have a beer instead." A change of heart which only made the snicker more pronounced.

Miraculously, I found an empty table in the corner, away from the bulk of activity. I brushed the crumbs off the chair, sat, and dug into my burger, which was actually pretty tasty. The noise didn't bother me so much now that I'd gotten used to it. I was kind of drifting along, trying not to think about Jannine and her children, and the hundreds of ways, both big and little, that Eddie's death would change their lives. I must have been pretty caught up in it because I didn't notice the woman standing next to me until she set her tray on the table.

"Mind if I join you?" she asked, sliding into the chair next to mine without waiting for an answer.

She caught me with my mouth full, so I gestured an invitation. Not, it seemed, that I had a choice.

The woman smiled tentatively, exhibiting a chipped front tooth. She appeared to be in her early twenties, dusty blonde, with the kind of pale skin that looks washed out and drab rather than creamy. She couldn't have weighed more than a hundred pounds tops, and the decidedly masculine cut of her grey shirt and trousers did little to enhance her appearance.

"I hate coming here this time of day," she said. "The local studs from the construction company leering at me and all. They act like they've never seen a woman before."

I hadn't noticed anyone so much as glance in my direction, much less leer at me, but I guess it's all in how you perceive things.

"Why do you eat here if it makes you uncomfortable?"

"It's convenient." She unloaded her tray—a double burger, fries, milk shake and a piece of apple pie. The meal probably weighed as much as she did. "I work across the street, at the police department. I'm a dispatcher."

I nodded. That explained the drab pants and shirt. Who knows, maybe it explained the hairstyle and lack of make-up, too.

We munched in silence for awhile until my companion looked up and said, "It's an important job, you know. I'm the one took the call about that coach. You read about it in the paper this morning?''

My mind leaped back from the hazy shadows where it had been drifting. "Eddie Marrero? The one who was shot?"

She nodded and took another large bite of burger. "Three times in fact. I guess whoever killed him wasn't taking any chances."

"They have any leads yet?"

She picked at the piece of lettuce stuck on her front tooth. "Not really, except for the wife. Lieutenant Southern, he's the chief investigator on this one, he's betting she did it."

The meat in my mouth suddenly tasted like rubber, and I had to swallow hard to get it down. "What makes him think that?"

"It was her gun. They found it a little ways from the body, under a pile of leaves. And she never reported him missing either. Seems he was shot Saturday, and when he doesn't come home that night she goes to bed as though nothing was the least bit unusual. 'I thought he was with friends,' is what she says, but when they ask her, she can't come up with a single name. No alibi either, at least not one she can substantiate. There's probably some other stuff, too. I don't know the full story, only what I overhear from guys talking. It kinda makes you wonder though, doesn't it?"

It did. I felt a flicker of doubt, then brushed it aside. There had to be another explanation. "Why would she want to kill her husband?" I asked.

The woman shrugged and took a long sip of her milk shake. "Who knows? Cops leave stuff like that to the lawyers."

There was some truth to that statement, but they didn't simply disregard considerations of motive either. "Are they going to arrest her?"

"Not yet. Chief Benson wants to make sure they dot their 'i's and cross their 't's first. He's had some run-ins with the D.A. before. He wants to make sure this one's by the book."

I breathed a silent sigh of relief. Maybe it wasn't as cut and dried as this woman made it sound. "They're still keeping an open mind then?"

"I guess. I mean some witness comes forward, they're not going to throw him out on his nose."

It wasn't a particularly reassuring testimonial. Reluctantly, I admitted to myself that Nona may have been right; the police were looking, but not very hard. It was with even more reluctance that I allowed myself to wonder, fleetingly, if they were on track.

My companion set down her milk shake and threw me a sharp, curious look. "Say, you're not a reporter or anything are you?" It must have finally dawned on her my interest in the case wasn't entirely perfunctory. "I could get in big trouble for talking to you."

"No, nothing like that," I assured her, wishing I could find some way to reassure Nona and Jannine as easily.

3

When Ken finally phoned, early that evening, I was so worn down from worrying about Jannine I didn't even chide him for not calling sooner.

"I've missed you," I told him instead.

"Likewise," he replied.

Ken is one of those Eastern blue bloods with patrician good looks and an equally well-bred sense of decorum. He is definitely not a man to wear his heart on his sleeve.

"How are things coming along?" he asked, moving entirely too quickly from the "missing" part. His tone was tender, however, and I felt that familiar prickly sensation spread across my shoulders, almost as though he'd traced a path there with his fingers.

"Slowly," I said. "There's no way I'm going to get out of here by mid-week. I guess there's a lot more of my past in me than I realized. And now there's this added complication." I told him about Eddie's death and my conversation with the young dispatcher that afternoon. "The idea of Jannine as a killer is preposterous. It would be laughable if it wasn't so frightening."

"It *was* her gun."

"That's hardly conclusive. They're grasping at the first thing that comes along because it's easy."

Ken gave one of those nondescript murmurs he's so good at. "Well, it's not your problem in any case."

"Jannine is my friend."

"She may also be a killer." His tone was gentle still, but the tenderness had given way to the weight of logic. "You haven't seen her in what, five years? You don't have the slightest idea what's been going on in her life." He paused to let the point sink in, then added, with just a hint of reproachfulness, "Remember what happened when you got involved in Mary Ellen's divorce?"

That was something I would rather not have remembered. My young secretary had been emotionally wrung out from dealing with a manipulative husband and a divorce attorney who gave his client about as much compassion as a shark moving in for the kill. I offered a shoulder to cry on and as much moral support as I could muster.

How was I to know that the sweet little thing who so willingly brought me coffee each morning had spent the previous twelve months systematically cleaning out her husband's savings accounts and carrying on a torrid affair with his best friend? One afternoon the husband came looking for her—with a knife. When he discovered she was gone from the office, he went after me instead. Who knows what might have happened if the UPS delivery man, who happened to also be a karate instructor, hadn't happened by just then?

"This is different," I told Ken. "I've known Jannine for my whole life practically. She's the kindest person on earth. She is simply not capable of killing anyone."

He sighed. "Well, there's nothing you can do, so don't waste energy worrying about it."

His attitude irritated me, although he was right about the last part; there wasn't a whole lot I could do. "How was the partners' retreat?" I asked, looking to change the subject.

Ken made a sound, a kind of verbal shrug. "You know how those affairs are, 'work and pleasure' usually translates into all work."

In fact, I knew only by proxy. Associates, even those approaching partnership, were not part of the firm's inner workings. "And?" I asked pointedly, after a moment's silence.

Ken gave a kind of half laugh. "Latham will give you your review when you get back."

"Meaning?"

"Meaning he's your supervising partner, not me."

There was something in his tone which added to my irritation. "I thought you were my partner in other ways," I said. The ways that counted most.

There was a pause, followed by an audible sigh. "Generally the comments were favorable, though a few people expressed concern about the amount of pro bono work and underbilled time you accrue." That was nothing novel, and I knew exactly who those "few people" were. "And then there was that run-in you had with Heritage Development which, I might remind you, is one of our bigger clients."

"But what they were doing was illegal!"

"Shady, maybe."

I let it drop; we'd argued this issue enough already. "So what are you trying to tell me, that I didn't get jumped ahead to partner?" I hadn't really expected it anyway. "That's okay. At least now I'm a level six."

Ken was silent.

My heart skipped a beat. "Aren't I?" More silence. "Are you telling me I'm no longer on track for partner?"

He hesitated. "No one is at the moment."

There'd been an outside chance I'd make partner a year early; I'd been hopeful but not overly optimistic. Instead, I'd been whacked clear out of the picture.

"It's been a tight year," Ken explained. "A tight couple of years in fact. Profits are way down. There's no way we can justify bringing in more partners. Not in the foreseeable future at any rate."

"But I've worked hard, done a good job. I got a commendation last year."

"It's not personal, you know. The partners' draws are way down, too."

As if that was any consolation.

"I knew this would upset you. That's why I didn't want to get into it just now." His voice softened. "I'm sorry, Kal, I know how disappointed you must be."

Disappointed wasn't the half of it.

"Why don't you come on home next weekend, even if you haven't finished things off up there. We'll go out for an evening on the town, anywhere you'd like, get your mind off all this job stuff."

The idea had some appeal, but I was afraid if I went home I might never make it back to Silver Creek. Besides, I was feeling notably slighted by both the firm and Ken—hell, by life itself. And there was no way a nice meal could make up for it.

"I'd better stay here and try to wind things up," I told him.

"Well, it's your call. If you change your mind let me know."

I hung up with a heavy click, but Ken had beaten me to it. My frustration fell on deaf ears.

The Goodwill boxes beckoned, but I was not in the mood. Giving up all pretense of productive activity, I poured myself a glass of wine and turned on the television. Loretta ambled into the room and plopped down at my feet. The leftover hamburger I'd brought home from lunch had won her affections. Not that I was looking. I couldn't understand why my father had decided to get himself a dog in the first place. And I didn't know what in the world I was going to do with her now that he was gone.

Sabrina had been my first thought, but as it turned out, her affection for living creatures was rather closely tied to their pedigrees. I don't care much about pedigrees myself, but I didn't have much use for four-legged creatures either. I figured I'd probably have to run an ad in the paper. Maybe I'd throw her in with the truck or the Skillsaw I had to get rid of as well. Package deal.

I was well into a *Star Trek* re-run when the telephone rang again. I harbored a fleeting hope it was Ken, who had discovered, upon hanging up, how much he actually missed me.

But it was Nona.

I'd put off calling because I couldn't decide what to tell her. The little I'd learned was secondhand information, not much better than gossip. I didn't want to worry her unnecessarily. On the other hand, she'd asked, and maybe she had reason to be worried.

"Did you talk to Benson?" Her voice was hushed, as though she were trying not to be overheard.

"He wasn't in. No one was, in fact."

"So you didn't talk to *anyone*?"

"I spoke to the secretary, briefly. She wouldn't give me the time of day."

Nona let out a sigh. "Then you didn't learn anything at all?"

There it was. "Nothing substantive," I hedged. "I don't think they've reached any conclusions just yet."

Nona's voice was still faint, but it now had an edge to it. "There's something you're not telling me, isn't there? Don't try to keep me in the dark like some addled old lady, Kali. I want to know."

I've never been a good liar, and this hardly seemed the time to hone my skills. I told her about my conversation with the dispatcher. "But that's only rumor. This woman could be completely wacko. For all I know she might not even work for the police department."

Nona wasn't looking for easy assurances. "This is just what I was afraid of. Just what I knew would happen." Her voice trailed off into a thin whisper.

I felt terrible telling her over the phone. I should have gone there that afternoon, in person, where I could soften the impact with hugs and encouragement. I'd taken the easy way out, and Nona was paying.

"Will you help us, Kali? There have be leads the police aren't following."

"I really haven't got . . ."

She interrupted. "Please?"

There was such trepidation in her voice I couldn't refuse. Besides, I owed Nona and Jannine, owed them far more than I would ever be able to repay. They'd been there for me when no one else was. They'd seen me through the tumultuous period of my mother's death, when I'd felt abandoned and unloved and cheated by life itself. They'd been there in the years that followed as well, offering the affection and warmth my father was incapable of. Now it was my turn.

"I doubt there's much I can do," I told her, "but if it will make you feel better, I'll look into it. I can't make any promises though."

"No, of course not." She paused. "But I know you'll turn up something."

"I'd like to talk to Jannine again. Do you think she'd be up to seeing me tomorrow?"

"Oh yes, absolutely." Her anxiety had all but vanished. I wished I could have said the same for my own.

4

The hammering and pounding started again early Tuesday morning, but this time I was already awake, having spent the better part of the night stewing about my prospects with the firm and the mess with Jannine. There wasn't much I could do about the former right then, so I put most of my brooding into figuring out the best way to help Jannine. By morning I'd at least begun to lay out my approach.

One thing law school teaches you is that everything is open to interpretation. What I hoped to do was find some loose ends, raise some additional possibilities. Enough anyway to persuade the police that Jannine wasn't the only potential suspect. The strategy was something like the way the defense approaches a trial; with enough "what ifs" and "supposes" you can turn a case around. In legal terms it's called "reasonable doubt." Not the best defense certainly, but one which is used pretty regularly. It's much easier, however, if you can keep things from reaching that stage in the first place. Easier, and a whole lot less risky.

I had intended to spend a couple hours sorting through my father's things before my meeting with Jannine, but the morning was so glorious and Loretta's expression so hopeful, I left the boxes stacked in the hallway and took her for a walk instead.

Only I told myself the walk was for me, and Loretta was simply free to tag along if she wished. Which she most assuredly did. Then I showered and drove to the bakery, where the gray-haired woman behind the counter looked perplexed when I asked for croissants. Jelly Danish was the closest they came, so I bought half a dozen and headed for Jannine's.

"What are you trying to do?" she asked when I handed her the box. "Make me fatter than I already am?"

"You're not fat, and what I'm trying to do is offer comfort and support." I gave her a quick hug. "It's not very effective, is it?"

Her face took on a sudden solemnness. "Just your being here, Kali, it means a lot." Then she gave me a weak smile and ushered me into the kitchen, where the aroma of freshly brewed coffee greeted me like an old friend. "Cream and sugar?"

"Black."

She laughed self-consciously. "I should have guessed."

Jannine was dressed in a gauzy blue caftan just the color of her eyes. Her hair was freshly washed, and a gloss of pink brightened her lips. The old sparkle was missing, but she looked far less spent than she had the day before. She cut a couple of the pastries into quarters and set them on a plate before joining me at the table.

"Is there going to be a funeral?" I asked, trying to think how best to broach the subject of my visit.

She nodded. "We have to wait for the police to release

the . . . , uh, for the police to finish. They said it shouldn't take long. It's not a complicated autopsy." Her voice was tight, but she finished with a brave smile. "I have to talk to the minister later this morning. Eddie wasn't big on going to church, but I know he'd want a proper burial and all."

I sipped my coffee, seized by a momentary urge to flee. My cowardly streak runs deep.

Jannine cleared her throat and shifted in her chair. "Mom told me what happened, you know, down at the police station. And why you're here."

"The spouse is always the first person they look at," I said. "What's happened so far doesn't necessarily mean anything."

"That's what I tried to tell Mom, but you know how she is." Jannine reached for a square of Danish and absently picked at it until the table in front of her was covered with a layer of tiny crumbs. Then she brushed them into a pile with her fingers. Finally, she took a deep breath and looked me in the eye. "So, tell me what you want to know."

I took a deep breath, too. "Let's start with the gun. The police are certain it was your gun that killed Eddie?"

"Oh yes. They found it right away, and the bullets match up. I could tell it was mine because it has this scratch in the barrel where I dropped it once on a rock."

I choked, though I tried hard not to let it show. "You voluntarily identified the gun as your own?"

"Well, it's registered in my name anyway, but sure, I tried to help out."

At some point we'd have to have a little discussion about dealing with the authorities. "Was the gun ever stolen?"

"No." A pause. "I mean, I guess it must have been."

"When did you see it last?"

"A month or so ago when I was looking for a pair of stockings. That's where I kept it, under the lingerie case in my top dresser drawer. I didn't even know it was missing until the police showed it to me Sunday evening." She smiled halfheartedly. "I don't wear stockings very often."

"Could Eddie have taken it?"

"He could have, I suppose. I don't know why he would, though. He has a couple of his own."

That was an aspect of small town life I'd forgotten about. While some of my urban friends owned guns (though they were loathe to admit it), most did not. But in places like Silver Creek, where the Old West was family history, guns were as common as back fence gossip.

"Well, somebody took it," I reasoned. "Any ideas?"

"I told you, I didn't even know it was missing."

"Think about who might have known where you kept it, or had access to your bedroom recently—workmen, house guests, cleaning lady . . ."

"Cleaning lady? My God, Kali, what do you think I am?" She threw me a sharp look, then slouched lower in the chair. "Anyway, I haven't a clue who could have taken it."

I put the question of the gun aside for the moment. It had somehow made its way from Jannine's dresser drawer to the woods outside of town, killing Eddie along the way. Figuring out how that had happened seemed pretty important to me, but it was clear I wasn't going to get any answers going about it the way I was.

"Tell me about Saturday," I said, switching course. "What was Eddie doing out by the South Fork anyway?"

Jannine studied her coffee for a moment. "I don't know. He left here that morning about eleven. Said he had some errands to run and might spend the afternoon at The Mind Shaft. That's a tavern his uncle owns over in Crystal Falls. Eddie helps out there sometimes, especially on weekends."

"That was the last time you saw him?"

She nodded, biting hard on her lower lip.

"Weren't you worried when he didn't come home that night?"

Her breath caught and she looked away. I could see the tears threatening. "I thought maybe he'd decided to stay in Crystal Falls," she said.

"Spend the night there?"

She nodded, picking at a patch of chipped formica near the table's edge. "He does that sometimes when he's there late. Apparently there's a vacant office above the tavern, kind of like a studio apartment or something."

"But wouldn't he have called?"

"Not necessarily, especially if it was a last minute decision."

Jannine looked none too happy about the arrangement, but I could imagine Eddie having his way, regardless.

"Okay, so Eddie leaves here a little before noon. What did you do the rest of the day?"

She brushed away a tear. "It's so hard to think about all this."

"I know. But I need to understand what happened."

Jannine nodded, and I waited. She got up and poured us each a second cup of coffee, then took her time adding NutraSweet and creamer. By the time she sat down again, she'd regained an element of composure.

"After Eddie left, I helped Erin with her book report. Then after lunch, I took the kids to my mother's and went shopping down at the mall." She paused. "I didn't buy anything, so I can't prove I was there. The police seem to think that's highly irregular. Maybe their paychecks are fat enough they don't have to count pennies the way we do. Anyway, I got back to Mom's a little before six. We had dinner there and didn't get back here till almost nine."

"What about Eddie? At that point you were expecting him to come home, weren't you?"

Silence.

"Didn't you worry he'd wonder where you were?"

"He'd have known where to find me," she said evenly. There was a long pause, then a heavy sigh. She looked over at me out of the corner of her eye. "We had a bit of spat that morning, okay? Nothing big, but I figured it might serve him right if he came home to an empty house."

"And when he didn't come home at all, you thought maybe he was pulling the same thing on you?" It was the old let-'em-stew-in-their-own-juice maneuver. I'd used it myself once or twice.

Jannine raised her head, her expression slightly off balance. "Yeah, I guess I did."

I backtracked and began questioning her in more detail about the shopping trip. An airtight alibi is always a good defense. Unfortunately, we weren't even close. "I'll check it through, just in case," I told her. "Maybe I can find someone who remembers seeing you that afternoon."

She nodded mutely, as though her mind were a hundred miles away. I wondered which was worse, losing a husband or being accused of his murder.

"Did Eddie seem worried about anything the last couple weeks? Distracted, upset, anything at all unusual?"

She thought a moment. "Not really. Eddie's always going a couple of different directions at once. It's just his way."

"Friday night at the party he mentioned something to me about needing a lawyer. Do you have any idea what it was about?"

Jannine thought some more, twisting her wedding band with her right hand. "Not unless it was about The Mine Shaft. Eddie and his sister inherited an interest in the place when their father died. Their uncle wanted to buy them out; Eddie didn't want to sell. It got real ugly there for awhile, but I think everything was pretty much settled. You'd have to ask Susie about the details though. Eddie didn't talk business with me."

I'd about run out of questions, and I sensed Jannine had about run out of energy. There were a couple more things I needed though. "Does Eddie have a desk or someplace where he keeps phone numbers, business records, that sort of thing?"

"Just this sort of table and file cabinet off the bedroom. You want to see it?"

I nodded.

The table was old—scratched and nicked and a little wobbly, but everything on it was neatly arranged in canisters and plastic bins. The file cabinet was the same. There were folders for tax records, insurance, car maintenance, and such—every one of them carefully labeled.

"I'm the messy one," Jannine said. "My drawers look

like the aftermath of a hurricane; Eddie's are neat as a pin. You should see the way he folds his socks." A shadow crossed her face. "Folded them, I mean."

"I know it's going to be hard, but I'd like you to go through Eddie's papers—checks, receipts, phone records, that kind of thing. There might be something there that would help us. I'll come back later and work with you, if you'd like."

"That's okay. I think I can do it." Her voice was flat and quiet. "I'm going to have to go through everything sooner or later anyway."

The phone rang just then, and while Jannine went to answer it, I made a few quick notes to myself.

"That was Jack Peterson," she said when she returned. "Remember him? Only it was *Mr.* Peterson in those days. He's principal now and kind of like Eddie's mentor. I tried to make it quick, but he's been so good to us I couldn't very well hang up on him."

Mr. Peterson had been hired in the middle of our sophomore year when Miss Locke, the typing teacher, ran off with the father of one of her students. I'd never had him as a teacher myself, having been labeled somewhere in the early grades as one of those students better suited to Latin and chemistry than business courses, but I had a vague recollection of a thin, pale young man who sported bow ties in a town where most of the teachers wore jeans.

"He's moved around quite a bit," Jannine continued, "only came back here about three years ago. He's in line to run for state assembly in the next election."

"He's done quite well by himself, hasn't he?"

She nodded. "Of course, he did it the easy way. His wife has money and a long history of political connections. She was one of those dutiful daughters who never left home until her parents died. That was only a couple of years ago. Jack Peterson's star has risen rapidly since the marriage."

"Does he still wear those silly bow ties?"

She smiled. "And stiffly starched shirts. He and Marlene would have been at the party Friday except that Jack had the flu. Marlene dropped by briefly to bring some brownies she'd baked, but I don't think you met her."

As we wandered back toward the kitchen, I got her to give me a list of Eddie's friends and co-workers, and a promise to go over everything once again in her own mind. "What we want to do is point the police in a different direction," I told her. "Get them started thinking about someone besides you."

"But they have to prove I did it, don't they? Even if they can't find anyone else."

"Proof comes later. At this point, it's more a question of coming up with the most likely scenario."

And that didn't bode well for Jannine who, based on what she'd told me, fit the scenario to a tee. That fact must have dawned on her too, because she seemed considerably gloomier than she had an hour and a half earlier.

"It doesn't look good, does it?" she asked softly.

I had to admit it didn't.

"You know though," she said, as she walked me to the door, "if I was going to kill somebody, why would I leave my gun sitting right there practically in plain view?"

If I were a prosecutor, I could think of several reasons, but I wasn't, so I kept my mouth shut.

5

Outside, the day was still grand—the air fragrant with the scent of mountain lilac and freshly turned soil, the sky a clear, deep blue the likes of which we never see in the Bay Area. My spirits, however, were considerably less bright.

With almost no effort at all, I could see the State's case taking shape, and it wasn't a comforting sight. They would see motive in the fight Jannine and Eddie had that morning, play up the fact that she hadn't seemed surprised when he didn't come home at night—might in fact find therein the cause of her anger. They would argue that she'd taken the children to her mother's, then tracked or lured Eddie to a remote spot and killed him, using a gun to which she clearly had access.

It was a tidy picture. I wondered, bleakly, if there was any truth to it.

I stood by the car for a moment, enjoying the sun's warmth on my back while I tried to organize my thoughts. The story in that morning's paper had been largely a rehash of yesterday's news. The police were continuing their investigation, and while there were several leads, no arrests were imminent. I would have found the report heartening, particularly the part about "several leads," except I thought there was a good chance it wasn't entirely accurate. When the law enforcement folks aren't forthcoming with details, reporters are forced to make do with an assortment of stock phrases. I had a feeling today's column was nothing but generic news-speak. It made the next step pretty obvious, however.

I'm no fonder of tilting at windmills than the next person, but I thought I should give Benson another shot. The cops undoubtedly had information I would find useful. I was willing to risk being thrown out on my rear for the chance to learn some of it.

The desk sergeant was once again intent on poking at the computer terminal in front of her when I arrived. She didn't even bother to look up.

"Benson's out," she barked.

"Still?"

"Again."

I noticed a nameplate I'd missed the day before. A. Helga Smelski. I wondered what the "A" could possibly stand for that she would choose to go by Helga instead. Some pretty awful possibilities came to mind. Or maybe she just liked the name Helga. It suited her, anyway.

"I thought you said he was going to be back today," I said.

Helga poked a few more keys, then hit a switch to her right. The computer made a whirring sound, then began to print out a list of some sort. Finally, she looked up. "He *was* back. Now he's gone again."

"Can I leave him a message?"

Helga squinted one disapproving eye at me, as though I'd trampled her prize rosebush, but she handed me a piece of paper and a pen. I wrote a quick note, then asked for an envelope.

"You going to mail it?"

I'll say one thing for the woman, she was an effective gatekeeper. I handed her the note, *sans* envelope, and left to try my luck elsewhere.

At the corner gas station, I stopped to phone the school and inquire about Nancy Walker's schedule. Not only was Nancy familiar with the town, she knew Eddie—knew him better than I did at any rate. I was hoping she would be able to give me a quick run down of the "who's who" variety, and save me some time.

I was planning to swing by and catch her at the close of school. As it turned out, she had a prep period coming up in twenty minutes. I hopped in my car and took off. The timing would be just about right.

The high school is out on El Camino Road at the eastern edge of town. When I was growing up, there wasn't much out that way but open grassland where cows, and occasionally a truant student or two, vied for shade under the smattering of twisted oaks. Things had changed though. Rows of flat, box-like houses had sprung up along the sloping terrain on both sides of the road, and at the intersection of El Camino and Marsh, a three–way light provided easy entrance to a fancy new 7-Eleven. There wasn't a cow, or an oak, in sight.

The school itself hadn't changed at all, however, at least not from the outside. The big brick building with its wide steps and carefully trimmed oval of lawn looked just as somber as I remembered.

I got out of the car and locked it, taking care to set the

alarm. Interest in cars has always run high among Silver Creek youth, and I figured a shiny silver BMW might just push their infatuation to new heights. I'd worked long and hard for that car, and I wasn't about to take any chances.

The school hadn't changed much on the inside, either. The hallways were still a dingy greenish-brown, a good half the lockers still bent and broken, the linoleum on the floor cracked in exactly the same spots. The smell of the place had an unpleasant familiarity as well. How many years of sweaty bodies, cleaning solvents, and God knows what else hung there in the air? I found myself taking short, shallow breaths, as if that made any difference.

The main office, directly to the right of the stairs, was staffed with a student assistant, just as it had been in my day. Usually timid and quiet kids, almost always female, they helped out by sorting attendance records, carrying messages to teachers, and filling in for the secretary when she was away from the front desk, which was the case when I arrived.

"I'm here to see Mrs. Walker," I told the girl who greeted me. She had to have been at least fourteen, seeing as how she was in high school, but she didn't look a day over ten. Her blonde hair was baby fine and hung in her eyes so that she had to brush it away to see me clearly. "I called about fifteen minutes ago and left a message."

"Oh, gee." Obviously flustered, she looked at her hands, then toward the door. "I don't usually work in this office; I'm in attendance, across the hall. But the girl who's supposed to be here, she's out today and Mrs. Green had to, um, use the rest room, so she asked me to cover for her." The girl finally managed a weak smile. "She should be back any minute."

Just then, Nancy herself popped in. "Got your message just a minute ago." She retrieved a stack of papers from her mailbox and leafed through them quickly, tossing a considerable portion into the trash. "Let's go upstairs to the teachers' lounge. It should be pretty quiet this time of day." Here she half–covered her mouth with a hand and whispered, "And I'm dying for a smoke."

The whole four years I'd been a student at Silver Creek Senior High I'd speculated about what lay behind that dark oak door which led to the teachers' lounge. The notion of grim Mr. Bayles or straitlaced Miss Johnson eating and drinking, or joking with another teacher—it was a concept so tantalizing I'd once offered Jannine my entire collection of Kenny Rogers tapes if she would just knock on the door, while I stood behind her, ready to gape. She had refused, and the room had remained a mystery.

I don't know quite what I'd imagined, but certainly nothing like the dark little room Nancy ushered me into. It looked more like the janitor's office at the back of the cafeteria than a den of intrigue. Along one wall were a couch and a couple of chairs, along the other a wobbly bookcase. At the far end, with a door which opened smack onto a table set with hot plate and toaster oven, was a single commode bathroom. The last occupant had left the light on and the seat up. The place was littered with half-filled coffee cups, and smelled strongly of stale smoke and tuna fish, a most unappetizing combination.

The effect was lost on Nancy, however. She settled easily into one of the worn gray couches and lit a cigarette. "Now, what's this all about?"

"I wanted to talk to you about Eddie Marrero."

"God, wasn't that something? Kind of brings you up short, doesn't it?" She rolled her eyes to the heavens while inhaling deeply on her cigarette. When she finally exhaled she had the graciousness to blow the smoke in the other direction.

"The police seem to think Jannine might have had something to do with it."

"Not seriously!"

"I don't know how seriously actually, that's part of what I'm trying to find out." I explained, briefly, what I'd learned so far and why Jannine was worried.

"I don't know what I can tell you really. I didn't know him all that well. English and football aren't the most compatible disciplines."

"Just tell me what he was like, help me get some kind of impression of the man. Except for that party Friday night, I hadn't seen him in years."

Nancy kicked off her shoes and tucked her feet under her while she considered the question. "I guess you'd say he was somewhere between your all around guy and your typical jack-ass jock. He had a puffed up idea of his own importance, but you never could hold it against him for long. He was one of those people you like, even when you know you probably shouldn't. And he was good with kids. They all liked him, even the ones who weren't super athletes. Of course the parents, or some of them anyway, are another story. They think the sun rises and falls on their kid, and when he's not *numero uno,* they're only too happy to blame the teacher. I think coaches probably get it worse than anybody."

"What about the other teachers? Did Eddie get along with them?"

She ran her fingers through her hair, brushing it back from her face, then shrugged. "He seemed to. Of course anybody who sees himself as bigger than life is bound to alienate a few people. Some of the teachers here thought he got away with murder . . ." Horrified, she slapped her hand over her mouth. "Jeez, I didn't mean that the way it sounded. It's just he was real tight with Peterson and a lot of people resented that."

Office politics—I understood it all too well.

"Still," she said, "I can't imagine any of them killing him because of it."

"What about vices? Drugs, booze, gambling, sex."

"Are you kidding? Eddie was Mr. Clean himself. Drove most of us crazy with his moralizing. I sometimes wondered how Jannine put up with the man, but then again, he was never my type. Whatever *that* is. I've never been able to figure it out exactly, but I'm working on it. Process of elimination, you know?"

I knew. I'd eliminated quite a few myself over the years.

She opened her purse and applied fresh lipstick, then spritzed her mouth with Binaca. "Not that this stuff helps any. I've promised myself I'm going to stop smoking just as soon as school's out."

"I've heard it's tough."

"Yeah, this'll be the fifth time I've quit." She laughed self-consciously, then slipped on her shoes and stood. "I hate to cut this short, but I've got to run off a test before next period."

"One more thing," I said, as Nancy began gathering her papers. "Last Friday night Eddie said something to me about needing a lawyer. Do you have any idea what that might have been about?"

She shook her head. "Sorry." With the ease of routine, she hooked her purse over her shoulder and scooped up her belongings. Then she paused, brows furrowed. "You know, now that I think of it, he said something last week about law or legal proceedings, or some such phrase. I can't recall what it was exactly, but I got the impression he was involved in something unpleasant."

"Did he seem worried?"

"No, it was more like he was wishing things were different. It wasn't much of a conversation really. As I said, I didn't know Eddie all that well, but we had cafeteria duty together last week." She made a sour face before continuing. "It's a thankless assignment. You've *got* to talk to each other just to keep from going completely loony."

I saw Nancy glance at her watch. I stood. "Thanks for the briefing," I told her.

"I hope it helped. Anybody who knows Jannine knows she's not a killer."

Nancy raced off to prepare for her next class, and I used the rest room, newly appreciative of the law firm's spacious, well-appointed women's lounge. As I opened the door to leave, I bumped against a lank-looking man who was pouring himself a cup of coffee from the hot plate in the corner. A stream of brown liquid dribbled from the cup and formed a puddle on the counter top.

"I'm sorry," I said, reaching for the roll of paper towels.

"No harm, it missed my clothes, and it's not nearly hot enough to burn my hand."

I'm not sure I would have recognized him if I'd run into him on the streets of San Francisco, but here on his own turf I placed Jack Peterson immediately. His hair remained blond, with only a touch of gray at the temples, and although he'd filled out some, he still had the angular boniness of a wolfhound. Somewhere along the line, though, he'd acquired a winning smile which softened the edges considerably.

"I'm Kali O'Brien," I said, when I'd finished mopping up the mess. "I graduated from here years ago. You were the new business teacher my sophomore year."

"Ah, that *was* a while ago." Peterson ventured a second cup of coffee.

"I'm also a friend of Jannine Marrero. And I went to school with Eddie."

Peterson cleared his throat. "You've heard then, about his death?"

I nodded.

"Such a tragedy. The news has really hit us very hard, staff and students."

He began moving toward the door, and I followed after him. "I'm helping Jannine with some of the, um, legal aspects of Eddie's death. Any chance I could look through his office while I'm here? It would be a big relief for Jannine not to have to do it herself."

Peterson stopped long enough to offer me an apologetic smile. "I'm sorry, I can't allow anyone in there. Not until I've checked with the police."

"They haven't been here?"

Peterson glanced at his watch and frowned. "Not yet. There's nothing urgent about this, is there?"

There was, but I'd have a rough time explaining. I shook my head.

"Well, it was nice meeting you, Miss O'Brien, now if you'll excuse me . . ."

If he finished the sentence I never heard, because he was already out the door. I poked my head out after him. When he went to the left, I went to the right, and then continued out the south wing to the gym.

The physical education staff had a row of tiny offices behind the gymnasium. I checked the nameplates on the doors and saw that the female teachers shared offices, as they had in my day; each of the male teachers had space of his own. Eddie's office was one of the bigger ones, at the end. I tried the door, which was locked, and then peered through the glass into the dark interior. Metal desk, file cabinet, a couple of chairs and a floor–to–ceiling bookshelf—it was hardly elegant, but in the hierarchy of faculty entitlements, it was probably a coveted prize.

My nose was still pressed to the glass when I heard footsteps behind me.

"He's gone," said the young man who tossed his clipboard into the next office. He drew a finger across his throat in vaudeville emulation of death. "About as gone as you can get."

I nodded. "I know, I'm a friend of his wife's."

The man looked suddenly stricken. "I'm sorry, I shouldn't have been so flip. It's just that . . . I mean, oh gosh." His face had turned a deep crimson. "Peterson's been going on like Eddie was the heart and soul of this place. I've had about as much of it as I can stomach."

"You a coach, too?"

"Assistant coach. Football. I run the frosh team as well." He rubbed his cheek. "I know what I said sounded pretty bad, but I didn't mean any disrespect. I guess I'm a little shook up by the whole thing, to tell you the truth."

I nodded silently.

"Look, what was it you needed? Maybe I can help."

"I'm trying to help Eddie's wife get his things in order. I thought I'd go through his office, save her the trouble. You wouldn't happen to have a key, would you?"

He shook his head. "Every door is different. There's a master key though, you could check with Mr. Peterson, the principal." He walked over and tried the door while he spoke. "That's funny."

"What is?"

"Nothing really. It's just that Eddie always left the chairs lined up just so, square with his desk." The man looked embarrassed again. "It was kind of something we used to laugh at, when he wasn't around. I guess he was in a bit of a rush last time he left."

That was one explanation certainly. But I could think of at least one other.

6

Betty's Cafe on West Main had been remodeled when I was in junior high, and from the looks of it, not touched since. The exterior paint was peeling, the red and white checkered curtains frayed, and the overhead sign so faded you almost had to know what it said in order to make out the letters. I was pretty sure the food would be as bleak, but all in all, the place looked more appealing than the Jack in the Box I'd passed leaving school.

I ordered a turkey sandwich on rye and a Diet Coke, forcing myself to ignore the big piece of lemon meringue pie calling to me from the glass case. While the woman behind the counter was spreading the bread with thick globs of mayonnaise, I used the pay phone at the back of the restaurant to call Eddie's sister.

The gravelly male voice on the other end was accommodating, but just barely. "Susie's at work, won't be back 'til six."

I didn't want to wait until six. I wasn't any too excited about talking to Susie with this fellow lurking in the background either. "Maybe I could reach her at work," I suggested.

"Cozy Corner Books, over on Jackson," he grunted, and hung up.

Since Jackson ran clear across town and over to Hadley, I had to take out the phone book again and look up the address. By the time I'd finished jotting it down, my lunch was ready. I slid into an empty booth and dug in. The sandwich was surprisingly good, and the lump of limp cabbage I'd expected to find on the side turned out to be a crisp vegetable salad instead. What Betty saved on maintenance, she obviously plowed into fresh ingredients. For a moment there, I was tempted to see if the lemons in that pie were as fresh.

When I'd finished eating, I stopped by the rest room to check my teeth for stray bits of lettuce, and then headed for the street. The day had warmed up considerably. By the time I got to my car, I could feel dots of perspiration forming across my nose and along the back of my neck. I was opening the car door and bracing myself for the inevitable flood of hot air, when two men approached the vehicle next to me.

"Hey, Red," one of them called. "That really you?"

The only person besides my brother who ever called me Red was his friend Tom, who had been John's companion in teasing me all through grade school and junior high. I'd been thrilled that they were both off to college by the time I got to high school.

I turned and looked hard to see if I could recognize any of the devilish boy I remembered in the tall, sandy-haired man before me.

"Looking good, Red. Looking real good." He thrust

his hands into his pockets and rocked back on his heels, an amused smile playing at the corners of his mouth.

The smile was what finally convinced me. It was the same cocky half-smile that had made me want to punch him in the nose on more than one occasion. Fortunately, I'd attempted it only once.

"I thought you were living in Los Angeles," I said.

"I was. But I'm here now."

"Still a journalist?"

"More or less. How about you? Last I heard, you were in law school."

I smiled mildly. "Right, only I graduated."

Tom smiled back. "I figured." His companion tooted the horn, and Tom motioned that he was coming. "You living in the Bay Area still?"

I nodded and slid into the car. It was like stepping into an oven.

Tom leaned on the door as I buckled my seat belt, then whistled low under his breath. "Fancy new car, BMW no less. I guess they treat you lady lawyers all right down in the big city."

Until they give you the shaft anyway, I thought to myself. "I work hard for every cent," I told him tartly. "And I'm a lawyer, not a *lady* lawyer."

"You may be a lawyer, but there's no denying the other part either." He winked, closed the door for me and then meandered over to the driver's side of a dirty blue pickup.

As I backed out of the parking space, he honked rowdily and waved. Twenty years had added a few pounds to his frame and etched character into his face, but I had the feeling it hadn't touched his basic disposition.

Cozy Corner Books was one of those homey, old-fashioned bookstores that's close to becoming extinct. Hardwood floors, a couple of chairs, classical music playing softly in the background, even the obligatory cat curled peacefully in the window. It wasn't as big or plush as some of the newer chains, but when it came to atmosphere, the place was a hands-down winner. On days when the practice of law wears me down, I fantasize about running away to a quiet valley somewhere and opening a shop just like it.

I had only a vague recollection of Susie Marrero. She'd been fourteen to my seventeen the last time I'd seen her, a skinny thing with a mouth full of metal and shoulder–length curls. Nonetheless I was pretty sure the woman at the register was Susie. The curls had been cut short and were now several shades lighter, but she had the same wide mouth and dark eyes as her brother. And the same easy manner.

I waited until she had finished with a customer, then introduced myself and apologized for bothering her so soon after her brother's death.

"It's still such a shock." She drew in a breath and was still for a moment. Then she held out her hand, her expression determinedly cheerful. "Jannine called a little while ago. She told me you might be in touch. Something about the tavern, right?"

I nodded.

Susie gestured to a tall chair behind the counter, next to her own. "Have a seat. I don't know how much time we'll have before the next customer, but I'm happy to help if I can."

"When I was talking with Eddie last week, he mentioned needing a lawyer. Jannine thought it might have had something to do with your uncle's business.''

"I doubt it. That's pretty much wrapped up. Eddie had the documents all prepared and everything.''

"You'd worked something out with your uncle then?''

"I guess.'' Susie crossed her legs and contemplated the toe of her left shoe. "The whole thing was a real mess, actually. My uncle was furious at both of us, and for awhile there, Eddie and I weren't speaking to each other either. I'm sure glad we got things resolved before he died.''

"What was the trouble?''

"Money.'' She sighed. "Dad and my Uncle George owned this place called The Mine Shaft. They both worked there until Dad's heart attack a couple of years ago. After that, my dad got a percentage of the profits, but it was my uncle who actually ran the place. The arrangement suited everybody just fine. Dad didn't get much, but he didn't need much to live on either. He was content to fish and putter in the garden. And for his part, George was just as happy to have Dad out of his hair. My uncle is the kind of guy who wants to do things his own way, at his own pace. He doesn't take kindly to anyone who interferes. Before Dad retired, George was always fuming at him about something.''

I nodded to let her know I understood.

"When Dad died last year, he left his share of the business to Eddie and me. That's where the problem started. George wanted to buy us out, fifteen thousand each. I was all for the idea. Al and I are sort of strapped for cash at the moment.''

"Al's your husband?'' I figured he must also be the Mr. Personality I'd spoken to on the phone.

She nodded and began folding the stack of advertising flyers on the counter. "He's disabled. Hurt his back about a year and a half ago. We still haven't paid off all the medical bills." Susie stopped folding for a moment. "This is a great place." She gestured to the walls lined with books. "But the owner can only use me part-time, and the job doesn't pay much anyway. So when my uncle offered us cash, well, it seemed like the answer to all our problems." She laughed halfheartedly. "Well, some of them anyway."

"But Eddie didn't want to sell?"

"No. In fact, he wanted to take an active role in running the place. Claimed George was a great bartender, but a lousy businessman. He lacked vision, was what Eddie said. The bar is kind of a good old boys hang-out now, but Eddie had plans to expand. He wanted to serve light meals, bring in live bands on weekends, that sort of thing. Said we'd all come out money ahead."

I picked up a stack of mailers myself and began folding with her. There was an odd appeal to the steady routine of lining up edges and setting a crease with your thumb. "Couldn't you have sold your share," I asked, "and let Eddie keep his?"

She shook her head. "It didn't work that way. Once George got a majority interest, he could buy the remaining share at a price he and my dad fixed years ago. George actually offered more than he had to."

"No wonder you and Eddie almost stopped speaking."

"I really didn't want to stand in Eddie's way. Even though we've never been close, he was all I had left in the way of family. On the other hand, it didn't seem right that I should have to go along with something just because it suited *him*." There was a sharpness to her voice

that hadn't been there earlier. "Eddie's always had
easy. Things have a way of working out for him in a
they never do for me."

Except that, ultimately, things hadn't worked out so
well for Eddie after all.

"You finally got it resolved though?"

Susie nodded. "Well, almost. Last week Eddie came up
with a compromise. He'd give me ten thousand right now
for my share of the business, and a percentage of the
profits for the next five years. The cash wasn't quite what
Uncle George was offering, but Eddie convinced me I'd
come out ahead in the long run. He'd get what he
wanted, and Al and I would have the money we needed."

It was a good plan; everybody got something, except
maybe Uncle George. "How did your uncle react?"

"He increased his offer, a couple of thousand each."

I'd already folded the flyer in front of me, but I ran my
finger down the crease again. "You weren't tempted to
take him up on it?"

Susie sighed. "No, I finally agreed to go along with
Eddie. He was going to bring the papers over for me to
sign this week. He said he'd try to come up with an extra
thousand, but I would have signed even if he didn't."
The gray cat ambled out of his spot in the front window
and jumped up onto the counter, taking an obviously familiar route over a stack of boxes. Susie pulled him into
her lap and began scratching his ears. "Al thought it was
stupid not to take my uncle's offer, but Eddie *was* my
brother after all. A pain in the ass sometimes, but that's
part of being an older brother I guess, isn't it?"

My own brother John had definitely been a pain when I
was growing up, but I've since realized there was a bond
there, too. I knew what she meant.

"Your uncle must not have been any too happy. It sounds like he was pretty intent on keeping the business to himself."

"Yeah, he was. He claimed there wasn't enough money in the place to warrant more than one owner, but I think money was just an excuse. If you ask me, it was a case of there not being room for more than one ego. Especially where George and Eddie were concerned. They're both as bullheaded as they come."

We lapsed into silence, folding our flyers almost in unison. "I suppose Jannine will be as eager to sell as you are," I remarked absently. "It's going to be a struggle for her financially with four kids to support."

Susie stopped her folding. "Jannine won't get anything. Eddie's share reverts to me."

I looked up. "So you'll get the whole thirty thousand plus?" I tried to keep my voice neutral, but I didn't succeed.

Susie's eyes met mine, briefly. Then she turned her attention back the stack of flyers. "I doubt George will follow through with his offer of the extra money, now that he doesn't have to."

"Still, you'll end up with more than you would have."

This time her eyes met mine and held. "Yes, I suppose I will. But I didn't kill Eddie."

"I didn't say you did."

She smiled. "No, but you were thinking it."

Not *thinking* it exactly, but close enough. And the smile didn't entirely convince me otherwise.

"Where was Eddie going to get the ten thousand to buy your share?"

"I have no idea. He and Jannine were always short of money. Eddie was taking some business classes at the university, and they gave up going out to the movies just so he could afford the tuition. That's why I was surprised, and a little suspicious I admit, when he called with his proposal. But I figured if he came up with the money, it was really none of my business where he got it."

I added that to the list of things I wanted to run by Jannine. She'd seemed fuzzy on the details of Eddie's deal with his sister, yet if they'd had to borrow money or dig into their bank account, Jannine would have known about it.

"Seems like Eddie was setting himself up for misery," I commented, "forcing himself into a situation where he wasn't wanted."

Susie smiled. "That's what I told him, too. But he said not to worry, he could handle 'old George.' " Just then the door chime jangled, and a group of sprightly, gray-haired women entered the shop. "Here comes the Tuesday group," Susie said, with a twinkle in her eye. "We spend an hour and a half discussing new books, and they leave with one paperback among them, which they share."

"At that rate it's a wonder the store makes any money at all."

"Money isn't everything," she said, laughing. "Which is a darn good thing for those of us who have none."

I didn't point out that she had considerably more now than she'd had a week ago.

7

Susie wasn't the only one better off though. For whatever reason, George Marrero had wanted to keep the tavern to himself. With Eddie dead, he would be able to.

I figured it would be easier to meet with George now rather than waiting until later in the evening when the tavern was busy. I was halfway there anyway, and I could loop back home by way of Route 3, which would bring me in near Jannine's place.

The drive over to Crystal Falls took me through apple orchards, open pasture land, and a cluster of newly constructed ranchettes, a fancy developer term for modest, unimaginative houses set on oversized lots. As I approached town, the ranchettes gave way to a tightly packed development of equally bland town houses. I was used to such signs of suburban blight around the Bay Area, but it brought me up short to find the same signs of frenzied progress in what I'd always referred to as "the middle of nowhere."

I found The Mine Shaft on the north edge of town, set

back under a couple of gigantic oaks. It looked like something straight out of an old *Gunsmoke* set—pitched roof, wooden plank porch, weathered hitching post, and by the front door, a brightly painted, life-sized carving of an Indian. The large screen television inside didn't do much to sustain the atmosphere, but I suspected the sour smell of beer and stale cigarettes was pretty authentic.

There were only a few customers in the place that time of day, an old guy propped against the far end of the bar, and a middle-aged couple engaged in the sort of public display of affection Ken calls disgusting.

The bartender, who looked barely old enough to drink, had the blond, bronzed good-looks of a California surfer. Since we'd only just left winter and were miles from the ocean, I figured his came from a tanning lamp and a bottle of bleach. It was clear he wasn't Uncle George. I took a seat at the bar anyway, and did my best not to blush when he flashed me a big, lady killer grin.

"What are you drinking, darlin'?"

"I'm not. I'm here to see George Marrero."

"He's not here." A wink. "Guess you'll have to make due with me." The grin stayed right there, plastered on his face like it was cut out of cardboard and glued tight. "The name's Seth."

"When *will* he be here?" I asked, ignoring the come-on. I could probably track George down at home if necessary.

"He won't be back till Thursday."

"Back? You mean he's gone somewhere?"

"Tucson. His wife's relatives are having some big shindig at the family ranch."

"When did he leave?"

Seth shrugged. A shank of straight blond hair fell

across his eyes, and he brushed it back with a practiced gesture. "Last Saturday."

"Morning or evening?"

Seth gave me a curious look. His eyes were a bright, almost startling blue. Tinted contacts, I was willing to bet. "Morning, I think. What is this, he stand you up or something?"

"I wanted to talk to him about his nephew, Eddie Marrero."

"Awful, wasn't it?" The grin faded, but only slightly and only for a moment. "You another cop?"

Another. That was good news. At least Benson's men had been talking to someone besides Jannine "No, I'm a ..."

"Wait, I know." Seth tossed the dishrag he'd been using into the sink, basketball style. "You're a reporter, right?"

What the heck, it was as good a story as any. I nodded.

"Thought so." He rested his arms on the counter and leaned close. "You got too many curves to be a cop."

I smiled blandly and inched backwards on the bar stool. "Have you been working for George Marrero long?"

"About six months. I'm a drummer mostly, but things are kind of slow right now." He gave me a pantomime demonstration, followed by another grin.

"What's George like to work for?"

"Decent enough, as long as you do your work and stay out of his hair."

"Eddie worked here occasionally, too, didn't he?"

"Oh, he nosed around some, but I wouldn't say he ever *worked* exactly. The way I understand it, he got some small part of the business when his old man passed away last fall. Now suddenly he's an expert on running the place. He was always asking questions, going over invoices, nit-picking everything till we all wanted to strangle him. Only saving grace was he never stayed long."

That didn't fit with what Jannine had told me. "I thought he spent quite a few Saturdays here."

"I don't know where you got that. George didn't want him hanging around at all. Finally got so fed up he wouldn't let any of us even talk to the guy."

"Then why did he let Eddie stay nights in the office upstairs?"

"Upstairs?"

"Isn't there a studio upstairs that doubles as an office?"

"The office is in back, about three feet by three feet. There's an apartment upstairs, but Eddie never stayed there."

"You certain about that?"

"As certain as I can be." Seth winked at me. "It's mine, darlin', and I'm real particular about who I bring home." His elbows were resting on the bar top, and he took the opportunity to brush his hand lightly against mine. "You, though, I'd be only too glad to take in. Want to have a look a bit later?"

I shook my head and made a show of moving my hand.

"What's the matter, you got a boyfriend or something?"

"Yeah, and he's a two hundred pound black belt with a quick temper."

"Hey, I like women with a sense of humor."

"Seth, you're a sweetheart, but I'm old enough to be your mother." That was stretching it, but I had to have had a good ten years on him.

Seth cocked his head and set his big blue eyes on me. "That right? Then I bet you've never had the kind of good time I can show you."

Maybe, but it would remain my loss. I slipped off the bar stool and out the door before he had a chance for another wink.

No upstairs apartment. No Saturday nights at the tavern. I tried to tuck those details away because I didn't want to think about what they meant. My mind has a will of its own though, and all the way over to Jannine's I did nothing but dwell on the reasons why Eddie might have told his wife he spent Saturday nights someplace he didn't. I came up with only one, and it left a pretty sour taste in my mouth.

By the time I got to Jannine's the sour feeling had made it all the way down to my stomach. I almost turned around and drove home—my cowardly streak again. But it turns out I also have a strong sense of duty. Sometimes that's good, sometimes it's not.

I could hear the kids hollering even before I got out of the car.

"I did not."

"You did, too."

"Liar."

It reminded me of the fights Sabrina and I used to have, fights that often escalated to the point where we were both shaking with rage and imagined injustice. And then I caught a quick, fleeting image of my mother, her soft eyes unusually grave as she tried reasoning us out of our anger. It was summer, and my parents were getting ready to go out for the evening. My mother was wearing a yellow dress with a full skirt and a scalloped lace collar. Her hair was tied at her neck with a yellow velvet ribbon, and she smelled of floral cologne. I can't remember what we were fighting about that time, or how it ended. But the image of my mother was so real my breath caught in my chest.

It happened like that sometimes, out of the blue. I could see her plain as day, hear her as clearly as though she were sitting next to me—and then, just as suddenly, it would be gone. Whenever I shut my eyes and actually tried to picture her though, I could conjure up nothing but gray shadows.

I clung to the memory for as long as I could, then got out of the car and made my way to the door. Melissa yanked it open with a frown. Before I had a chance to speak, Laurel snuck up from behind and shot her with a rubber band, which sent Melissa shrieking off after her sister. Finally, Erin appeared at the door grasping Lily tightly by the wrist. Lily's face and hair were thick with a gooey substance I finally identified as grape jam. (At least I hoped it was jam, and not blood.)

"Hi," I said. "Is your mom here?"

"She's resting."

"How about your grandmother?"

"She's gone."

"So who's in charge?"

A moment of steely silence. "I am."

"Oh." I smiled brightly, which was totally inappropriate under the circumstances. I couldn't think what else to do. I've never been good at talking to children, and Erin wasn't helping me out at all.

"Do you think your mom will be up soon?"

Lily started to reach for the door handle. Erin yanked

her up short. Then she turned to glare at me as though Lily and I had conspired to give her a hard time.

I backed off. "Tell your mother I stopped by and that I'll be back later, okay?"

She got in about half a nod before a series of shrieks from the back of the house sent us both running. By the time we got to the kitchen, a thick gray cloud hung in the air and flames licked at the corners of the oven. Melissa hopped from foot to foot, pointing, while Laurel continued to scream. Erin let go of Lily's wrist and reached to turn off the burner. I grabbed a pot holder and dumped the charred remains of Erin's culinary efforts into the sink. Then I opened the windows and started fanning the air with my arms.

"Shit," Erin muttered.

"Oh-oh, you're gonna get it. You know what Mom said." Melissa and Laurel stood in the doorway shaking their heads in unison. Their earlier argument had apparently given way to the excitement of the moment.

"Oh, just shut up," Erin said. "If you two hadn't been fighting I would have remembered before it burned."

"We weren't fighting," Laurel sniffed, "we were playing."

I surveyed the kitchen, which looked something like the "before" scene from an Extra-Strength Tylenol ad. "There's no damage done," I said, with more conviction than I felt. I'd have personally shot anyone who treated *my* kitchen as badly. "Look, why don't you all take a rest while I clean up, and then I'll make some dinner. How does that sound?"

"Sounds stupid," Laurel said. "That's Erin's job."

"Yeah," Melissa echoed, before they stomped off, letting the screen door slam behind them.

Erin looked at me soberly. "You want help?" she asked.

I shook my head. "You deserve a break. I work better by myself anyway."

She rolled her eyes at me, and left without a word.

Lily crawled under the table and began to spoon-feed jam to the cat, taking alternate bites for herself. I left her there while I began tossing dishes into the sink. The cat couldn't have many more germs than Lily, and the jar was almost empty anyway.

As it turned out, the mess was mostly superficial. By the time I'd washed the dishes, wiped the counters and swept the floor, the place was much improved. Cleaning up Lily was a bit more of an undertaking, and something of an education. Two year olds do not scrub up anywhere near as obligingly as a greasy pot.

When I'd finished dressing her, having learned in the process why so many mothers allow their children to wear mismatched clothing, I whipped up a bacon and cheese omelet, microwaved some frozen French fries, and poured four glasses of chocolate milk.

Laurel didn't like bacon, Melissa wouldn't eat French fries without catsup, which was nowhere to be found, and Erin was allergic to chocolate. Nonetheless, the prospect of food engendered enough of a cooperative spirit that I was able to leave them alone and check on Jannine.

8

The bedroom door was shut. I knocked softly, taking the murmured response as an invitation to enter. The drapes were pulled, the lights off. The air was hot and heavy with the flat, slightly rank smell of unbound sorrow. Jannine lay sprawled on the bed hugging a pillow to her chest and staring blankly at the far wall.

"Jannine?" I hesitated by the door. When she didn't answer, I moved closer. "Are you okay?"

She hugged the pillow tighter and moaned softly.

I sat on the edge of the bed and stroked her head. I couldn't think of anything to say that didn't sound hollow. Finally, Jannine rolled onto her back and shoved the front page of *The Hadley Times* in my direction.

"Have you seen the afternoon paper?" she asked. Her voice was thin and barely audible.

For the second time in two days, the face of a Marrero stared back at me in black and white. This time the face was Jannine's. Above it, the headline, "Wife Questioned in Coach's Death."

I read through the story quickly. Not a direct quote or named source in the whole piece. "There's nothing concrete here," I told her. *"The Hadley Times* has always been a sensationalist paper. I'm sure there's nothing more to it than what we already know."

Jannine propped herself against the pillows. She took a deep breath and swallowed hard, but her face crumpled anyway. "Oh God, Kali, how did this happen?" The tears welled up, and then, suddenly, she was crying for real—deep, racking sobs that went on and on. Occasionally she'd sputter a few incoherent words, as though she were trying to drag herself from the edge of the abyss, but the effort seemed to throw her back once again into primitive, all encompassing despair.

I wrapped my arms around her, holding her against my chest as though she were a child. Finally the flood of tears subsided. She released her grip on my shoulders and sighed, a ragged, weary breath that seemed to consume her entire body.

"Shit, shit and double shit," she said.

I seconded the notion.

"You know what's funny?" Jannine said, drawing in another deep breath. "I'm scared out of my mind, and the person I want to run to for comfort is the very same person they're accusing me of killing."

"No one's accused you yet," I reminded her.

"Maybe not officially. That hardly matters though."

It mattered a great deal, but I didn't think it was worth arguing the point right then.

Jannine pulled the pillow into her lap and began smoothing it with her hand. "Eddie could be such a pain when he put his mind to it," she said wistfully, "but, my God, I loved him. So much it scared me sometimes."

I nodded. There was nothing I could say.

"I'll listen for him, or look for him, or think about something I want to tell him, and it takes a second or two before I realize he's not here anymore, that he's never going to be here again." Jannine was swallowing hard and talking in short, shallow-breathed spurts. "I never imagined such emptiness."

I nodded again, and we sat silently while Jannine pulled herself together.

"I heard all the commotion down in the kitchen," she said, after awhile. Her voice was thin still, but her face had taken on an element of composure. "Thanks for stepping in. I just didn't have the strength to cope any more."

"Where's Nona?"

"She was getting one of her migraines, so I told her to go home. She's been here since Sunday. It hasn't been easy on her either."

"You want something to eat?" I asked.

Jannine shook her head.

"How about something to drink then?"

"You don't need to wait on me, Kali. I'm fine, really."

"Well, I'm not so sure *I* am," I said. "Why don't you freshen up while I pour us some wine."

When Jannine came downstairs half an hour later, she wasn't exactly the picture of cheer, but she did look much better. Though her eyes were puffy, she'd brushed her hair, made a stab at putting on some make-up, and fixed a brave smile on her face.

I handed her a glass of wine and directed her to a clear spot at the kitchen table. "The kids are watching television, and I'm boiling water for noodles. You want a bite of cheese or something while you wait?"

She shook her head. "Won't it be ironic if I lose weight now. Eddie always thought I got fat just to spite him."

"You're not fat."

"Not thin either," she said. "Last fall I even joined Weight Watchers. I measured and weighed and charted everything I ate for a whole bloody month, and I *gained* five pounds." She sighed and ran a finger around the rim of her wine glass. Without looking up, she said, "You never knew I had a crush on Eddie in high school, did you?"

I shook my head.

"Ever since ninth grade. When you started dating him I was so jealous. Well, not actually jealous, I guess, because I would rather it was you than anybody else. That way I got to hear everything at least. It was actually harder when you two broke up and you started talking about what a jerk he was. I wanted to stand up for him, but I didn't want you to be angry with me either."

I stopped dicing garlic and looked at Jannine with astonishment. "You should have said something."

"It was so embarrassing," Jannine said. "Plain old me and gorgeous Eddie. If anybody had gotten wind of that, I'd have been the laughing stock of the entire school."

"I wouldn't have laughed."

She half shrugged.

"And what do you mean, 'plain, old me?' You had the most beautiful skin I've ever seen, not a blemish or freckle on it."

"But I was a real nobody, you know that. All through school. All my life I guess. Then that summer when Eddie came home from college with both arms in a cast, and his mother hired me to help out . . ." Jannine paused for a moment, her expression suddenly dreamy. "He made me feel I was somebody special. It was the first time I'd ever felt that way in my entire life.''

While I was figuring out the best way to tell her she had always been someone special, Lily came into the kitchen and crawled into her mother's lap. Jannine gave her a noisy kiss on each cheek, then rubbed noses with her Eskimo fashion.

"And now I have his daughters. The four most wonderful kids in the whole world. Who'd have ever imagined that?"

We lapsed into silence while I toasted some bread and sprinkled cheese on our noodles. Then I joined her at the table. Neither of us ate much, but I polished off a second glass of wine and watched Lily tear her mother's toast into tiny pieces, then toss it in the air like confetti. For her part, Jannine seemed content to stroke Lily's hair and stare off into space.

"Were you able to talk to Susie today?" she asked after a moment.

While I rinsed our plates, I filled her in on my day's activities, leaving out the part about the Saturday nights Eddie never spent at the tavern. At some point I would probably have to tell her, but there was no way I could bring myself to do it right then.

"I don't think this business with the tavern was what Eddie wanted to talk to me about," I told her. "The papers were apparently all drawn up and ready to be signed."

"Susie had agreed to hold onto it then?"

"Not quite. Eddie was going to buy her share, for ten thousand plus a portion of future profits. That way she would get almost as much as your uncle was offering, and Eddie would get to keep a piece of the business."

"Ten thousand!" The words squeaked out like a hiccup. "Are you kidding? Where would he get that kind of money?"

"I was hoping maybe you could tell me."

Jannine shook her head in bewilderment. "We live from paycheck to paycheck, and just barely that. Mom had to lend us money for Erin's orthodontia. Susie must have misunderstood."

"She said the papers were ready to be signed."

"Ten thousand . . . Holy cow, Kali, that's a hunk of money."

"Why don't you call the bank tomorrow? See if they can tell you anything."

She looked skeptical, but agreed to put in a call.

"I don't suppose you've had a chance to sort through Eddie's papers?"

"I can't even go into the room without breaking down."

"It could be important."

"After the funeral, okay?"

"It would be better if you could do it sooner."

Jannine looked at me, then nodded mutely, like a child chastised. I felt like a heel.

"You want me to help?"

"No, you're doing enough already. I'll get to it. I promise."

"I thought I'd head out to the mall tomorrow," I told her. "See if I can find somebody who remembers seeing you there last Saturday."

"Nobody's going to remember me. I just wandered."

"You never know."

Jannine twisted her napkin around her fingers. She looked at me, started to say something, then shrugged and turned away. "I just hate to have to waste your time is all."

"We won't know whether it's a waste or not, until I do it. I thought I'd also check through Eddie's office at school. I stopped by there this afternoon, but it was locked. Do you think there's a key around here?"

"I don't know. He kept one on his key ring. The police haven't returned any of his personal belongings yet, but there might be a spare in the desk." She went to check and returned a few minutes later with a handful of assorted keys. "It might be one of these. You can take them all."

I pocketed the keys and checked the kitchen. It wasn't sparkling clean, but it looked a whole lot better than it had when I arrived. I was gathering up my own keys and my purse when Jannine sat up straight.

"You know, I just remembered Eddie got a phone call last Saturday, about half an hour before he left. It may be completely unrelated, but right after that he came in and told me he'd be going out for a bit."

"You know who it was?"

"No, I was in the other room. It wasn't a long conversation though."

"Did you hear *anything*? Even a word or two?"

She shook her head. "Not a thing."

Just then the doorbell rang. Jannine answered it and returned with Jack Peterson and a tall, angular woman who she introduced as his wife, Marlene.

"I made up some muffins and banana bread," Marlene said. "I thought the kids might like a treat."

Jannine took the several paper sacks Jack handed her. "How thoughtful. Come sit down and I'll put water on for coffee."

"Thank you, dear, but we can't stay. We're off to a Republican Coalition dinner. Jack is giving a talk there."

Looking embarrassed, Jack thrust his hands into his pockets. "Marlene wanted to check and make sure everything was in order for the, uh, for Thursday."

It took a moment before I remembered; Thursday was Eddie's funeral.

"There's going to be an announcement in tomorrow's paper," Marlene said. "I double checked this afternoon to make sure they had the time right. Mrs. Langley and I are taking care of refreshments for afterwards, so don't you worry about that. She's volunteered her home, too. It's just lovely, and there is plenty of room. I imagine there might be a good sized turn-out, don't you?"

Jannine nodded. A strained smile pulled at her mouth. "Thank you, for everything. You've both been so kind."

Marlene gave her hand a quick little pat. "Our faith and our friends the nourishment that sustains us in times of need. Jack and I are grateful we can be of help."

"If there's anything you need," Jack added, "you just let us know."

When they'd left, Jannine turned to me with an odd little laugh. "That woman used to drive Eddie nuts, and now she's orchestrating the finer points of his funeral. I should feel guilty, but the truth is, I'm not up to it myself."

"I wouldn't feel guilty," I said, in my most reassuring tone. "I'm sure Eddie would understand."

Her soft brown eyes blinked at me. "Maybe," she said softly, "maybe not."

9

When I left Jannine's, I headed for the high school. Dusk had turned the air chilly and dimmed the afternoon's rich glow to a flat, drab gray. The buildings were dark too, which suited me just fine. The last thing I wanted was to have to explain myself to some guardian of the public welfare. Even with a key and Jannine's permission, I thought I was probably on somewhat shaky ground.

I parked my car in the lot and locked it, cursing under my breath as the high-pitched chirp of the BMW's alarm cut through the evening's stillness. I checked to make sure no one was around, then headed right, past the athletic fields, and up to the physical education wing.

One dimly lit bulb flickered at the end of the corridor. The light closer to Eddie's office was burned out completely. There was just enough illumination to cast a shadow, and as I fumbled around in my purse, I watched my silhouette against the pavement, oddly elongated and jerky. Finally, I pulled out the handful of keys Jannine had given me and tried them all. Although one fit obligingly into the lock, none worked.

Cursing again, I pocketed the keys and peered into the dark interior. That's when I noticed the rear window had been left open a couple of inches. The good little girl inside me was stamping her feet with disapproval, but I went around back anyway. By standing on my tiptoes, I was able to reach my hand through the window with enough leverage to open it farther. But there was no way I could pull myself up and through like some young Hollywood hulk.

So I did what women (and probably most men) have done for ages—I found something to stand on. A sturdy metal garbage can facilitated my climb, and although it was still a struggle, I was finally able to get a leg up and over the sill. The rest was easy, though decidedly unladylike. Before I knew it, I was inside Eddie's office. I didn't even try to wipe the self-satisfied grin from my face.

Pulling a flashlight from my purse, I began poking around, and discovered almost immediately the difficulty of conducting a one-handed search. I took a deep breath and flipped on the overhead light.

While my eyes adjusted to the brightness, I took a moment to survey the room. The wall to my left was lined with award plaques and banners, the wall to my right with a nicked gray filing cabinet and a tottering bookshelf. The center of the room was taken up with a large metal desk and a couple of chairs, neither of which was pushed square with much of anything. Still, I wouldn't have noticed if the assistant coach hadn't mentioned it that afternoon. If Eddie's office had been searched, it was hard to tell.

Of course, if Eddie's office had been searched then I

was already too late. On top of that, I wasn't even sure what I was looking for. But Eddie had told me Friday night that he needed a lawyer, implied that the issue was sensitive. And he'd somehow come up with ten thousand dollars his wife didn't know about. The office seemed a likely hiding place for anything he might have wanted to keep from her.

I started with the desk. The drawers were filled with the kind of everyday junk you'd expect, pens, rubber bands, paper clips, a couple of opened Lifesaver rolls and a grade book—all neatly arranged with plastic dividers. In the bottom drawer I found a ratty–looking Stephen King novel and a can of Desenex, each in its own partitioned space. The bookshelf held an array of jock books, a sweat shirt (tidily folded) and a couple pairs of shoes. There wasn't a cryptic message or incriminating clue to be had anywhere.

By the time I got to the file cabinet though, I'd have been willing to bet that someone besides Eddie had been in the office. In typical Eddie fashion, the file drawers had been organized with color coded dividers. But the manila folders inside were twisted, and jammed in at odd angles, the papers spilling over and already dogeared. I couldn't imagine any coach, especially Eddie, treating his team photos or player stats so poorly.

I went through the files anyway, hoping I might find some hint of what had been taken. So intent was I at this business of snooping, that I didn't hear anyone approach until the office door creaked and a cool draft blew across my neck.

By then it was too late.

Before I could turn my head, a powerful hand grabbed my shoulder and shoved me roughly against the wall.

"Stay where you are and don't move." The voice was low and guttural. And tough enough that I had no intention of disobeying.

Swallowing hard, I braced myself for a bash on the head or the terror of a knife at my throat. The moment seemed to go on forever. Finally there was a shuffling sound, and then my attacker coughed—protracted, hacking cough that sounded like Doc Holiday caught up in a fit of consumption. "Okay, lady, you can turn around now, just make it real slow. I gotta gun here, and you wouldn't be first person I've used it on."

I did what the man said, although I would have preferred not to. There is some small comfort in never having to actually set eyes on the creature who is preparing to do you in.

The reality wasn't nearly as bad as I expected. The man I faced was gaunt and wiry, with thinning blond hair that hung limply to his shoulders. A large tatoo covered his right forearm; a smaller one was on his left. His eyes were bloodshot, his face colorless and creased, like a piece of crumpled tissue paper. But to be honest he didn't look anymore menacing than half the people I passed each morning on my way to the Berkeley BART station. Except of course for the gun.

The man sniffled, then glowered at me. He had the quick, jerky motions of someone with a nervous disorder or a history of drug abuse. "You want to tell me who you are and what the fuck you're doing in this office?"

It was then that I noticed the little patch on the sleeve of his shirt—*S.C. SECURITY*. I let out the breath I'd been holding. I was probably in big trouble, but not in any imminent danger of bodily harm.

"My name is Kali O'Brien," I said, surreptitiously

double—checking to make sure I'd remembered to close the window. "Eddie Marrero's wife gave me a key." I held out the key that had fit but not turned, praying he wouldn't give it a try himself.

The man started to say something and then another coughing fit took hold. The hand with the gun shook unsteadily. I know zilch about guns, but I'd heard the words "hair trigger" often enough that the coughing spasms made me nervous.

"If you don't believe me," I said, "why don't you call his wife and ask her."

"Even if you got a key, it don't make sense your snooping 'round here in the black of night. That's why they hired me, you know. Been having all sorts of trouble. Vandalism, theft, that sort of thing. I'm s'ppose to keep an eye on the place."

"Obviously there's been a little mix-up," I said, with a calmness I thought remarkable. "I was just trying to help out. I certainly don't want to cause you any trouble."

"I can't afford to screw up. Done that too many times in my life already."

"But finding trouble where none was intended, that isn't so smart either." I did my best to come up with a reassuring, down-home kind of smile. "I'm a family friend from way back. Eddie and I went to school together in fact. Right here in Silver Creek."

"You went to school here?"

I nodded.

"O'Brien," he said, fixing the watery eyes on my face. "Yeah, thought you looked familiar. Yours was the old lady who killed herself, right?"

I flinched. "Right."

"Weren't you some hotshot cheerleader?"

Wrong. "You must be thinking of my sister, Sabrina."

"Yeah, Sabrina, that's it." The gun danced in his hand while his mind delved into the past. "Blonde, blue–eyed, stacked. I remember her. So how's she doing these days?"

I forced another smile. "Oh, just fine. She's got three little kids now, all cute as can be."

"Must be nice," he said, looking off through the window into the growing darkness. "I got me a kid somewhere, too. Don't even know if it's a boy or a girl." He paused a moment, then said, "That still don't explain what you're doing here."

The man was sharper than I'd given him credit for. "Eddie's wife isn't up to this, so she asked me to go through her husband's things for her." It sounded lame so I tried again. "She especially wanted me to check for Eddie's watch. Seems he left it here Friday by mistake. It isn't worth much, but it has sentimental value. She was worried it might get misplaced when the school starts cleaning things out."

My companion scratched his nose. "You find it yet?"

"No, not yet."

"You say Eddie left it here on Friday?"

I nodded. God help me, Eddie *did* wear a watch, didn't he?

"I bet he picked it up when he stopped by Saturday morning. You tell the missus the police probably have it with all his other things."

"Eddie was here Saturday morning?"

"Yeah. Saw him a little before noon when I was making my rounds."

"Was he alone?" I tried not to sound too eager.

"Near as I could make out. Might have been someone

with him later. I thought I heard voices when I passed by on the other side, but he might have been on the telephone, too."

"Was there anybody else around?"

"Couple of kids, that's about it. It's pretty quiet around here on weekends. Why?"

"Just curious, I guess."

"Look, you really shouldn't be here, but seeing as how you've got a key and you're helping out the missus, I'll let you stay while I finish with this wing. Then you gotta leave and let me lock up, okay?"

There was nothing forced about my smile this time. "Thanks," I said, with genuine heartiness.

"The coach, he was always real nice to me. You tell his wife I hope she finds that watch."

Alone again, I sank into the chair, letting the what-ifs roll over me. What if the guard hadn't believed me? What if the gun had gone off? What if it had been Eddie's killer who'd come through that door?

Then I pulled myself together. I had maybe five minutes to finish my search; the shakes would have to wait. Leaning forward, I rested my arms on the desk and tried to think. I'd hoped to find some loose thread that might tie in with Eddie's murder. Now there was a new twist. A couple of them in fact. Eddie's office may have been searched. I wanted to know why and by whom. And I wanted to know why Eddie had come to the school Saturday morning when he'd told Jannine he was going to the tavern.

While my mind tried to sort through the possibilities, my fingers played with the smooth leather of Eddie's desk set. It was a deep mahogany color, with matching picture frame and calendar. The sort of practical, but elegant thing that had "family gift" written all over it. The calendar was turned to Sunday. Absently, I flipped it back to Saturday.

Except that Saturday was missing.

I sat up straight and looked again. Sure enough, Friday gave way to Sunday. When I looked closer I could see the paper shreds where the page had been ripped out. Then I noticed on Sunday's page, the indentations of a hastily scrawled message. I ripped the page out and stuck it carefully into my purse. I made a quick inspection of the remaining file drawer, then turned out the lights and left, taking care to move the trash can from under the window before heading for my car.

Back home, I pulled the page from my purse and poured myself a glass of wine. Then, before I'd had a chance to take a sip, I set the wine glass back down on the counter. Loretta really knew how to lay on the guilt. "All right," I grumbled, "a quick one." But she had something more leisurely in mind than a short spin down the road. It was almost half an hour before I was able to retrieve my glass of wine and finally examine the page from Eddie's calendar.

As near as I could make out, there were the initials CN and a phone number. I couldn't tell if the last digit was an 8 or a 6 so I tried it both ways. The first time I got a recording telling me to hang up and try again. Which I did, this time using the number 6 instead. The phone rang four times before the answering machine clicked in.

The voice was throaty and female. I had reached the Newcomb residence.

10

There were three Newcombs listed in the phone book—a Bill, a Carla and a J.P. Carla's number matched the one I'd dialed, but it was one of those listings with no address. I'd taken a step forward, only to run smack into a brick wall. I cursed my luck, doubled checked the phone number, and tried to figure out what ploy I could use to convince Carla to give me her address. Then I thought of Nick Logan, a friend from law school whose specialty is brick walls.

Early on, Nick spent a couple of years with a major downtown law firm, then jumped ship to follow his first love, computers. He still maintains a small legal practice, heavily weighted with *pro bono* cases, but he derives most of his income (and his pleasure) from his work as an information broker. I've always been impressed with the term, but Nick tells me it's just a fancy name for computer snoop. Of course, I find that impressive, too.

Nick answered the phone on the first ring. "Hey, babe," he said, "don't tell me you've got your nose to the grindstone at this hour."

"I'm not at the office, not even in San Francisco." I explained about my father's death and my trip home to sort things out. "But it wouldn't be unusual to find the firm's associates still toiling away at this hour."

"Not anymore. From what I hear things have really gone to hell in a hand basket over there."

"They've put off taking on any new partners, if that's what you mean."

"Yeah, and they've also put off giving raises and bonuses."

"Where'd you hear that?" Bonuses had always been a significant part of our compensation.

"I had lunch with Sara. She says everybody's pretty bummed out."

Sara Stewart is an associate a couple of years behind me. She's also an on-again-off-again girl friend of Nick's. I'd introduced them years back. I've tried to stay out of their way since, so I didn't pursue the lunch angle, but it was the only heartening sliver of news he'd handed me.

"Terrific," I said gloomily. "I can't wait to go back."

"So don't." Nick's been telling me for years I'm making myself old for nothing.

"At the moment, I don't have much choice."

"There's always a choice, babe. But you didn't call me for spiritual advice, did you?"

"Actually, I was hoping you might be able to get an address for me."

He chuckled. "I figured it was something like that."

I gave him Carla's name and number, and he promised to get back to me as soon as he could. Then I sat and stared at the blank page I'd pilfered from Eddie's office. Was this Carla the "other woman," his companion on those nights he'd claimed to be staying at the tavern? Was she somehow tied in with the ten thousand? There weren't many women who would lend that kind of money to a married lover. Not willingly anyway, and not without some pretty steep assurances. And what about the tavern buy-out and Eddie's self-proclaimed need for legal advice? Was any of it connected or was I simply chasing my tail?

I had questions. Lots of them. But I was short on answers, and there wasn't a whole lot more I could do about it right then. I didn't want to sit and brood about my future at Goldman & Latham either, so I decided to tackle my father's desk, a chore I'd been putting off all week.

My father believed in the open drawer system of record keeping. His desk was an old fashioned oak roll-top, and every nook, cranny, cubbyhole and drawer was stuffed to overflowing. Bills, announcements, coupons, credit card receipts, empty match boxes—they were all jumbled in there together. There was absolutely no central record of what he owed or owned. He'd gotten along just fine that way, but the probate process requires hard data, exact figures, and inordinate attention to detail. All three were in short supply. In order to come up with a schedule of assets and debts, I was going to have to piece things together myself, starting with the bits and scraps in his desk.

I found an old folding table in the back room, dragged it over next to the desk and began methodically sorting the pertinent from the dispensable. First I emptied all the cubbyholes, tossing what I didn't need into the metal trash can I'd dragged in from the kitchen. Then I arranged what was left into piles, and started taking notes. When I finished with the cubbies, I started on the drawers. I was more than halfway through when the phone rang. For a moment I held on to the hope it might be Ken.

"Hi, babe," Nick said. "I got that address you wanted. Thirty-four Ponderosa, right there in Silver Creek."

I grabbed a pen and wrote it down.

"Your gal's a thirty-six year old registered Republican with a good driving record. Five–foot–five, a hundred and twenty–four pounds, and single, at least at the moment."

"Nick, you're amazing."

"It's the database. This kind of stuff is easy. You want more?"

"Not at the moment, but thanks. As a token of my gratitude, I'll buy you dinner when I get back to town."

"I'll let you, so long as you don't go getting fancy on me."

"Not a prayer," I told him.

It was too late to go calling on a woman I'd never met, so I tucked the address into my purse and turned my attention back to the desk. Half an hour and another glass of wine later, I made it to the bottom drawer, where I found last month's utility bill and a take-out menu for China Gardens on East Main.

I also found three shoe boxes filled with letters and cards, one box for each of us kids. Mine seemed to hold just about every letter I'd written since leaving home. Most were from my college days, when I still considered a long distance call an extravagance.

Pouring still another glass of wine, I settled onto the sofa and began to re-read some of the letters. They were pathetic. Filled with empty, impersonal chatter about class assignments, sporting events, even the weather, for God's sake. And they were short, most of them barely a page. The birthday and Christmas cards I'd sent more recently were just as bad. Sometimes I'd penned a "Have a good day," at the bottom, but usually I'd simply signed my name.

And yet he'd kept them all. Every single one.

My throat grew tight, and my stomach knotted over on itself. It was little consolation that my own box was fuller than either John's or Sabrina's.

I finished off the bottle of wine, which had been two-thirds full when the evening began, then tumbled into bed, where I dreamed of my father. I saw him building the back yard tree house, a special hideaway we all three used right through high school. I saw him helping my mother stuff the turkey on Thanksgiving, humming under his breath. I curled next to him in the backyard hammock, snug and safe as a kitten, listening to the even flow of words as he read aloud.

A little after one, I awoke, soaked in sadness. As the night crept forward, I huddled under the covers and tried to clear my mind. I saw nothing, though, but the pictures I tried not to.

I finally fell back to sleep sometime after five, only to be awakened, what seemed like minutes later, by the screech of an electric saw. I checked the bedside clock—6:45. My head was pounding, the fallout from too much wine and too little sleep, and my spirits weren't so good either. But there was no getting back to sleep, not with that racket, so I stumbled out of bed and into my slightly rank sweats. I put a kettle of water on to boil, then remembered I'd run out of the special grind decaf I'd brought from home. The only thing in the cupboard was a jar of generic instant, but I was desperate. I made myself a cup, tasted it, then poured the rest down the drain. Maybe I wasn't so desperate after all.

The saw continued to screech, my head continued to pound, and my mouth felt like the bottom of a bird cage. I took two aspirin, called to Loretta, whose spirits were as high as mine were low, and stomped angrily out of the house.

The racket seemed to be coming from the old Gallagher place down the road. I didn't know who lived there now, although I was pretty sure it was no longer any of the Gallaghers. They wouldn't have been hammering and sawing first thing in the morning. Or any other time for that matter. Two of the upstairs windows had been missing the whole time I was growing up, and when a falling tree had knocked a hole in the front door the winter I was twelve, Mr. Gallagher simply nailed a sheet of plywood across the whole thing. From then on, the family used the back door.

I walked up the rutted driveway, past the old orchard, and knocked. The front door had been replaced. It was a beautifully crafted, eight panel door with shiny brass trim. A real improvement over plywood.

After a moment, I knocked again. Up close like that, the rasp of the saw was piercing. There was no way a gentle knock would be heard, so I started pounding and kicking and hollering with a vengeance. The sawing stopped; my banging and kicking continued for a moment longer a window-rattling ruckus almost as unpleasant as the sawing. Then the door opened, and I stood nose to nose with my brother's friend Tom.

"You?" My voice was about as pleasant as everything else that morning. "What are you doing here?"

"Good morning to you, too," Tom said, lifting the pair of protective goggles to his forehead. "I live here."

"What happened to the Gallaghers?"

"Mr. Gallagher died. Mrs. Gallagher went to live with her daughter in Florida. Is that who you're looking for? I've probably got her address somewhere."

I pulled myself to my full five–foot–five and scowled. "Do you realize that it's seven o'clock in the morning?"

"Seven–fifteen actually. And a truly lovely morning, too. You want to come in? I'll make up some coffee." Tom pulled the goggles all the way off, then brushed the sawdust from his bare arms. "It'll take me just a minute to wash up."

He turned and headed inside without waiting for an answer. I wasn't about to be left talking to an empty door, so I followed. "No coffee," I said tersely. "Caffeine makes me jittery."

"I'll make decaf then. Or herb tea. Jesus, are you always so surly?"

"Do you always wake the neighborhood with your God-awful hammering and sawing?"

"Ah," he said, stopping midway through a room stacked with plywood and sheetrock. "This isn't a social call."

I gave him one of those icy glares that's intended to convey more than words. "Quite a job you've taken on here," I said, surveying the gutted interior. The nasty tone I'd tried for was muted somewhat by grudging respect. Anyone who would tackle a job like that with the confidence it would end up whole again deserved credit.

"Yeah, it is quite a job, taken on more by necessity than choice. I'm sorry about the noise. Your dad never minded, and I guess I didn't think that with you here it might be different. I have to fit this construction stuff into the hours I'm not at work so I don't have a lot of leeway."

"What about Sunday?" I smirked. "That your day for golf?"

He looked puzzled.

"You didn't work Sunday. It was quiet all morning."

The puzzled expression gave way to a grin. "It was my weekend with my kids." He tossed his goggles onto a make-shift workbench. "Cappuccino okay? Strictly decaf, I promise."

We passed through the re-hab zone and into a kitchen straight out of *House Beautiful.* A large, open space with hardwood flooring, granite counter tops, gleaming new appliances, and a profusion of sunlight. "This is beautiful," I said, genuinely impressed. "You did it yourself?"

"Not the finish work. I'm merely the grunt labor and gofer. It cuts costs considerably. It did turn out nicely though, didn't it?" He filled the cappuccino machine with water, flipped on the switch, then poured milk into a small metal pitcher.

"Your weekend with the kids," I said. "You're divorced?"

"Just about." The machine began to gurgle. Tom pressed water through the coffee grounds, then frothed the milk and ladled white foam into the cups. "Lynn and I moved back here because we hated the phoniness and self-indulgent atmosphere of L.A. We wanted a good, wholesome place to raise a family." He offered me a cup and a crooked smile. "Eight months later she ran off with the contractor. A double whammy. I lost both a wife and a contractor. How about you, happily married?"

I shook my head. "Never married."

"Never?" He seemed to find the idea amusing. "You one of those ambitious, hard-nosed career women we read about? Somehow I never pictured you in that role."

"Well, that's me," I told him. Though in truth, I'd never thought of myself in quite those terms.

"Relationships though. I bet you've had your share of those."

"A few."

"You got a boyfriend now?"

"I guess you could call him that." I wasn't so sure Ken would agree.

Tom sipped his coffee, watching me over the rim of his cup. He rocked back in his chair, started to say something more, then apparently thought better of it.

"What do you do when you're not hammering and sawing?" I asked.

"I'm with *The Mountain Journal.*"

"Must have been quite an adjustment, coming from *The LA Times.*" And a big step down, I thought.

He shrugged. "All depends on what's important I guess."

We were sitting in an alcove at the end of the kitchen. Sunlight filtered through the pines and cast the room in a soft golden glow. I licked at the foam in my cup and felt the sharp edge of tension that had been with me since last night begin to slacken.

"I'm sorry I came banging on your door like a banshee," I said. "I'd had a rough night."

"I've had a few of those myself. From now on I'll try to keep the noise down in the morning."

"That's all right. I won't be staying here much longer."

"Which one are you in a hurry to get back to, career or boyfriend?" Tom grinned and I glowered. "Both?"

At that moment, neither, but that wasn't the issue.

"You could stick around awhile. You know, take some time to smell the daisies."

It had been my experience that people who took time to smell the daisies rarely made it out of the pasture. "If I wanted to smell daisies," I told him, "I could pick up a bunch at the flower stand."

Tom grinned. "I'll let you in on a secret, Red. It's not the same."

Back home, I fixed myself a piece of toast and munched it on my way to the shower. I tossed my sweats into the laundry, which was something I should have done several days earlier, and promised myself I would never again leave the house without make-up, even in a fit of anger. The hot water finished what the aspirin and coffee had begun, and by the time I dried my hair and added a little color to my face, I felt like a new woman. I'd just stepped into my underwear when the phone rang.

"Daryl Benson here. I hope I didn't wake you."

"I've been up for hours."

"Good. I tried you yesterday, but you were out. I didn't want to take a chance on missing you again today. Your note said you wanted to see me about the Marrero case."

"Right."

"You know something?"

"Not exactly." Not the kind of information he was looking for anyway. "I'm a friend of his wife's. I'd like to talk to you about the investigation."

I anticipated a frosty brush-off, but there was a long silence instead, followed by a heavy sigh. "Sure, why not. I haven't seen you all grown up anyway. Bet you're th~ image of your mother. You want to come by this afternoon, say about one?''

"That's fine. See you then.''

The timing was good; it would give me the morning to track down Carla Newcomb. I finished dressing, made sure Loretta's water bowl was filled, then grabbed the map and headed over to the east part of town in search of Ponderosa Place. After considerable effort, I'd finally managed to locate the proper coordinates, but because of a large splotch of catsup in the same vicinity, I wasn't entirely sure of the location.

11

About half a mile from the house, I realized I'd forgotten the photograph of Jannine I needed for my trip to the mall that afternoon. I slowed, preparing to make a U-turn and head back to retrieve it. A white Lincoln was moving up fast behind me, and a convoy of logging trucks was coming in the other direction so I pulled off to the right, onto a private lane instead. A cloud of dust billowed up around the car, leaving a layer of powdery grunge on the shiny metallic finish. I groaned, then groaned again when I realized that the road was narrow and the shoulder on either side soft. Turning around was going to be no easy matter.

By the time I had the nose of the car pointed in the right direction and was ready to pull back onto the main drag, I'd worked myself into a low grade sweat. Which is probably why I didn't see the large white car coming at high speed from my right. I pulled out, then slammed on my brakes. He swerved onto the shoulder at the far side, sending another plume of dust my way, and then sped on.

Shaken, I inched onto the blacktop and crept back to the house, where I gave serious thought to staying for the remainder of the day. But my curiosity about Carla Newcomb was too great. I rechecked the map and started out again.

I would have had trouble finding Ponderosa even if the map hadn't been spotted with catsup. It was one of those narrow, meandering streets that jogs, skips a few blocks, and then winds off in a different direction entirely. Nevertheless, with persistence and a bit of help from an elderly gentleman who seemed delighted to have a captive audience, I finally located the house.

It was a faded blue clapboard, small and shabby. One of many in a run-down neighborhood near the sawmill. The steps were sagging, the lawn a thick brown thatch, the flower beds overgrown with weeds. I doubted Carla had ten dollars to spare, much less ten thousand.

She may not have been the source of Eddie's buy-out money, but I was willing to bet there was still plenty she could tell me. I parked across the street and waited for inspiration. When none came, I did what I usually do in such situations—I forged ahead anyway.

Pots of flowers, all of them plastic and rather gaudy, dotted the front porch. I stepped around a perky pink geranium and knocked. The woman who answered had a head full of curlers and a tense, impatient manner.

"Whatever you're selling, I don't need any."

"I'm looking for Carla Newcomb. Is that you?"

She eyed me suspiciously, took a long drag on her cigarette and asked, "What of it?"

Lust can turn a man's head, and a woman's too I've been told, but I had a hard time imagining Eddie going weak in the knees over this woman. She did have a figure, or rather a bosom, that much was obvious from the way the thin cotton robe clung to her body. But her hair was a straw-like yellow, growing in dark at the roots, her brows plucked to a thin, harsh line, and her mouth tight. She had the same worn-out look as the neighborhood.

"I'd like to talk to you about Eddie Marrero," I said, watching closely to see how his name affected her. It was a technique I used questioning witnesses, especially when I wasn't sure what I was looking for.

But Carla only stared at me blankly. "Who's he?" she asked after a moment.

"The high school teacher who was murdered last weekend."

Recognition flashed on her face. "Right. I didn't recognize the name at first."

It was a good act. "When did you last talk to him?" I asked, speaking in my attorney voice.

"I don't believe I've ever talked to him."

"I understood you were a friend of his."

"Me?" She laughed, a harsh, dry laugh that pierced the morning stillness. "I don't know where you got that. I didn't know the man from Adam."

Now it was my turn to stare blankly.

"Even the name wouldn't mean nothing to me except that Cheryl baby-sat for him a couple of times."

"Cheryl?"

"My daughter. Sassy smart-ass won't lift a finger around the house, but she'll go running off to baby-sit every chance she gets."

Cheryl Newcomb—C.N., initials the same as her mother's. A teen-ager who sat for the Marreros. I felt silly, to say the least.

"She's at school if you want to talk to her. You'll have

better luck finding her there than here. Way she sees it, home's just a place to drop off your laundry."

In Cheryl's case, I thought, the sentiment might not be a bad one. "Sorry to have bothered you," I said. The front door slammed shut before I made it halfway across the rickety porch.

My appointment with Benson wasn't for another hour and a half. Not enough time to drive over to Stone Mountain Mall, but too long to sit and twiddle my thumbs. I decided to drop by the school and see if I couldn't track down Jack Peterson and maybe a couple of other teachers whose names Jannine had given me. I started the engine and was pulling away from the curb when I caught a flash of white in the rearview mirror, a late model American car pulling slowly through the intersection behind me.

Goosebumps rose along the back of my neck. I had the sudden, uncomfortable feeling I was being followed. Either that, or I'd recently become a magnet for large white cars. I waited another minute, and when it didn't reappear, I started off, chiding myself for being paranoid. I watched the rearview mirror all the way to school, however.

Peterson was out, but I managed to talk to two of the other three names on my list. Chuck Wilcox, history teacher and student council advisor, was a gaunt, spectacled young man whose sober earnestness probably earned him the respect of his colleagues, and the ridicule of his students. Don Ramirez taught Spanish and had a face as smooth as silk. Both men knew Eddie; neither was able tell me anything helpful.

The lunch bell rang just as I was leaving the main building, and I scooted over to the corner of the quad to avoid being mowed down by adolescent exuberance. Standing there under the gnarled old oak Jannine and I had used as a meeting place years ago, I was caught in a moment of *déjà vu*. I knew what it was to be fifteen, angry at the world, racked with longings you couldn't understand and thoughts that scared you silly.

On an impulse, I stopped two girls who were saunter-ing down the path and asked if they knew Cheryl New-comb. They giggled.

"We know *who* she is," said the taller one, with the Far-rah Fawcett hairdo, "but we're not, like, friends or any-thing."

The dark–haired girl nodded.

"Can you point her out to me?" I asked.

"She's absent."

"Absent?"

"Like, you know, not at school." They looked at me as though I were from another planet. "She's been out all week."

"You sure?"

"Sure I'm sure. We're in dumbbell math together."

"She's sick?"

Farrah gave me a look which shot daggers. "How should I know. Like I said, we're not friends or any-thing."

"Who *does* she hang around with?" I asked.

"No one. That's part of her problem, right, El?" The dark–haired girl nodded. "She's like a total wannabe, you know."

I didn't. "Wannabe what?"

"A somebody." Farrah snapped her gum. "Is she in trouble or something?"

I shook my head. At least not yet. It might be a different story once her mother found out she wasn't in school. "You sure she's absent?"

"Yo, Madelaine." Farrah hailed the girl who'd been working in the main office yesterday when I stopped by to see Nancy. "This here lady's looking for Cheryl Newcomb."

"She's absent," Madelaine said. "Flu."

Farrah flung her head with I-told-you-so nonchalance, and strutted off. El was close on her heels.

"You're Mrs. Wallace's friend," Madelaine said. "I recognize you from yesterday."

I nodded. "How well do you know Cheryl?"

"Hardly at all. I only know she's sick 'cause I had to take her place in Mr. Peterson's office the last couple of days. She always acts like working in his office is a such a big deal, but if you ask me, attendance is a lot better. I can't wait to get back."

As I climbed into the car, I struggled with the muddle I'd landed myself in. I didn't know Cheryl, and I certainly didn't want to look like a busybody. On the other hand, the girl was playing fast and loose with the rules, which is something I approve of only when I do it myself. There was also the matter of that notation in Eddie's calendar. The more I'd thought about it, the less sense it made. By the time I pulled up in front of City Hall, I'd made up my mind to drop back by the Newcomb house that afternoon and speak to Cheryl. After that, I'd decide what, if anything, to tell her parents about cutting school.

I still had a few minutes before my appointment with Benson, so I found a pay phone in the lobby and called Sara Stewart at our office. I don't know whether I was disappointed or relieved when she couldn't come to the phone. There's an element of truth to that old saying about ignorance and bliss. If the firm was no longer giving out raises and bonuses, maybe I was better off not knowing. Then I took a deep breath and asked to be transferred to Ken's line. Our conversation Monday evening had left a sour taste in my mouth. We hadn't been going out long enough to have had any real fights, but Monday felt awfully close. And equally unsettling. I didn't want to leave it that way.

Ken, it turned out, had flown to D.C. for a last minute settlement conference.

"He tried to reach you yesterday," his secretary said, turning the announcement into something of a reprimand.

"I was away most of the day."

"I know," she snipped. "He left a message though, in case you called in. He said he hoped you'd 'reconsider about the weekend.' " She said this last part rather stiffly. "I presume you know what that means."

I felt a smile beginning. He wanted me home for the weekend. Apparently I wasn't the only one uncomfortable about the tone of our last conversation.

"Well?"

"Well what?"

"What," she said airily, "shall I tell Mr. Levitt?"

"Why don't you give me his number in D.C., and I'll tell him myself."

"You won't be able to reach him. He's going to be in meetings from early morning till late at night."

I couldn't tell if this was Ken's line or merely another example of his secretary's resourcefulness, and I didn't have the time to find out. "When's he coming back?" I asked.

"Friday night." She paused. "Shall I tell him you've reconsidered?"

"Tell him," I replied, "that I'll talk with him when he returns." It sounded good, but I don't play hardball very well. I dialed again, his home this time, and left a message on his machine. I wouldn't be able to get back by the weekend, but I'd take a rain check. I considered adding something a bit more personal, but when I tried to think what, I came up blank. It was probably just as well, since there was a good chance I'd end up unintentionally offending him. Ken is funny like that.

To my surprise, Daryl Benson was available and waiting for me when I made it upstairs. Helga ushered me into his office with a thin-lipped scowl, then left abruptly, leaving the door slightly ajar. Benson rose from behind his desk to greet me.

"Goodness, how time flies," he said, giving my hand a hearty shake. I'd seen him hesitate for just a fraction, not knowing whether to offer a hug or a hand. I was glad he'd chosen the latter. Still, seeing him brought back a flood of memories. Benson had been a part of the happy period of my childhood. Those years before my mother's death, when the house was filled with conversation and laughter and my father's whistling; with comforting kitcheny smells and the bustle of lives being lived.

"Just look at you," he bellowed, "all grown up. And so lovely, too. You're the image of your mother."

He offered me a seat, then perched on the edge of his desk facing me. He'd put on weight over the years, and his head was almost completely bald. He looked more like a jowly Kojak than the lighthearted, loose-limbed man I remembered.

"I can see why your dad was so proud of you," he said after a moment.

"He never acted like he was. In fact, most of the time he acted as though I were invisible."

Benson raised an eyebrow at my tone, then dropped his gaze to study his hands. They were thick and gnarled, but neatly manicured like the rest of him.

"He loved you, Kali."

"He had a funny way of showing it." The words came automatically. But when I thought of the shoe box filled with letters, I felt a tug inside my chest. Maybe, in his own way, he had cared. For a moment the cloud of bitterness parted, and I was able to recall the pleasant roughness of his cheek against my own, the strong, solid arms that had so often swung me off my feet and high enough to touch the ceiling.

"Yeah, probably so," Benson said. The hint of a shadow darkened his face. "Your mother used to say the same thing."

I looked up.

"Your dad was never very demonstrative, even before he started drinking."

"That's pretty much all he did these last few years, isn't it? Drink and brood."

"I didn't see him very often. Couple of times a year we'd get together and shoot the breeze, but that's about it. Your mother's death hit him hard. He never got over it."

My mother's death hit a number of us hard, but my father had overlooked that part. And in so doing, had compounded it.

"But that's not why you're here." Benson stood and

reached for his jacket. "Come on, let's go get a cup of coffee while we talk about the Marrero case."

We climbed into his car, an unmarked black Buick, and drove to the Denny's near the edge of town.

"So, what about Marrero?" Benson asked, pouring half a pitcher of cream into his coffee.

"Is it true that his wife is a suspect?"

"She is indeed." He added two packets of sugar. "You her attorney?"

"Does she need one?"

He stirred the milky brown liquid with his finger. "She might."

"She didn't do it."

"What makes you so sure?"

"I know Jannine. I've known her practically my whole life. She's the warmest, most gentle person I know."

Benson stirred his coffee, took a long swallow, then looked me in the eyes. "I'll tell you something, Kali. I've been a cop practically *my* whole life, and every person I've arrested has at least one friend or relative who says he couldn't have done it." Benson paused, offering a good-natured smile. "I'm not trying to give you a hard time, but you have to look at this objectively. Everything we've got points to the wife."

"You mean the gun? It was in her dresser drawer, for God's sakes. Almost anyone could have taken it."

"She never reported it missing though."

I was ready to argue that one, but Benson didn't let me. "Anyway, there's more. Hers are the only prints we found on the gun. She has no verifiable alibi for Saturday afternoon. She and her hubby had a big fight that morning."

"Jannine told you that?"

"The neighbor did. She heard them yelling at each

other from all the way inside her house. Your friend apparently threw a vase or something at the guy and called him some pretty vile names. Said he was gonna get what he had coming."

"That's hardly a threat. Besides, every couple fights at some point."

"Maybe, but one of them doesn't usually wind up dead a few hours later."

Their quarrel was clearly not the "little spat" Jannine had led me to believe it was, but that didn't make her a killer. Not necessarily anyway. Nonetheless, her half-truth to me chafed uncomfortably. "It's your theory she killed him because of a fight?"

"We leave the motive stuff up to the D.A.'s office. I'll tell you though, we've got a source that says their marriage was headed south."

I interrupted. "You mean the neighbor?"

"Someone else. You got a situation like that with a dead body, and nine times out of ten you've got yourself a pretty solid motive."

I knew the statistics, but I also knew Jannine. Or I'd thought I did. "What you've got is circumstantial, and tenuous at best. You can't arrest her on that."

Benson set his cup down in front of him, then pressed his fingertips together and looked me straight in the eye. "We could and you know it, but we haven't." He paused. "We may be small time, but we're careful."

Arguing wasn't going to get me anywhere. What I really wanted was information anyhow, so I tried a different tack. "What about physical evidence? Did you find anything besides the gun?"

Benson leaned back in his chair. "Not really. An outdoor, wooded area like that makes it hard. Sometimes you'll get lucky and find a footprint or loose button, but usually not."

I nodded and let him talk.

"He was shot in the chest," Benson continued, "from a distance of about twenty feet. No sign of a struggle, no attempt to flee. That makes it likely he knew his killer. From the trajectory of the bullet I'd say the assailant was standing, Marrero sitting. We found blood on a nearby log, so that's probably where he was shot. Looks like the assailant then dragged his body about ten yards and hid it under some leaves and brush. Coroner puts the time of death at three o'clock Saturday afternoon, or thereabouts."

"Did you check for fingerprints on the body?" I knew this was possible because our firm had once defended a client who'd left his bloodied fingerprint on the shirtsleeve of his victim. It took know-how, though, and some pretty sophisticated equipment.

Benson smiled. "We're not as backward as you city types like to think. Yes, we looked for fingerprints, even on the body; no, didn't find any. We checked for hairs and fibers, too. Only thing we found was a strand of dark hair, like the wife's. 'Course it could have been there for days."

"You have any idea what he was doing out by the South Fork?"

"Nope. We checked his credit cards, ATM withdrawals, that kind of thing, to see if there'd been any activity that morning, but nothing showed up."

"He went by the high school after he left home," I said, "Did you know that?"

Benson shook his head. "I don't see that it makes a lot

of difference, but if you want to give me your source, I'll send someone out to check on it."

I told him about the night watchman, omitting the circumstances surrounding our meeting. Then I thought of something else. "What about tire marks? Unless the killer rode with Eddie, wouldn't there be a second set of marks?"

"There's about a hundred sets, all jumbled together and superimposed. That road's so dusty you can't tell a thing."

"If Jannine had been out there, her car would show traces of the same kind of dirt, wouldn't it? Did you check?"

"She took it to the car wash Saturday afternoon." He paused, watching for my reaction. "The Prestige Special, with Wheel Bright and everything." The sick feeling must have shown on my face, because Benson leaned forward. "Look," he said, "we don't really know who whacked Marrero. Maybe it was your friend, maybe it wasn't. But fact is, there's a lot says she did it, and at the moment she's all we've got."

"So you're going to pin it on her just because it's convenient?"

Benson straightened, crinked his neck to the left and rubbed his shoulder. "We're not pinning it on anyone just yet. And when we do, it won't be for convenience. I know you lawyers don't like to admit it, but when it comes to murder, the obvious answer is also most often the right one." He paused, swallowed a mouthful of coffee, then leaned across the table and continued. "You want to help your friend, you talk to her about cooperating with us. Maybe she just meant to scare the guy. Or maybe it was self-defense. Hell, maybe they were taking target practice, and it was all an accident. There's reasons and there's ways, but it'll be a whole lot better for her if she meets us halfway."

"She can't, though, if she didn't do it."

Our eyes met, and held.

"No," Benson said, after a moment. "She can't."

Still, I had a few questions to put to Jannine. I had the sinking feeling she'd been less than totally straight with me.

12

Stone Mountain Mall is a large discount complex located about forty miles west of Silver Creek in what had been, only three years earlier, open grassland. Now, in addition to the mall, there's a Best Western Hotel and half a dozen fast food franchises. I guess that's so you can make a weekend of it and literally shop 'til you drop.

The stretch of highway between there and Silver Creek is on the main route to the Sierras, and it can be a real bottleneck. But mid-day, mid-week, in a season somewhere between winter skiing and summer escapes, the road was practically empty. I slipped a tape of Beethoven's Third into the player and turned up the volume. With an eye on the lookout for the California Highway Patrol, I breezed along through the afternoon sunshine, hoping the zen of driving would help me unwind.

I could see the sign for Stone Mountain Mall from the highway. But by the time I'd found the exit and wound my way through the grid of frontage road turn-offs, I'd just about given up hope of actually getting there. Even the parking lot was something of a maze. Although it wasn't crowded, I had to loop around a long concrete partition and a one-way drive in order to find a spot.

Parking aside, the mall made a real effort at being "user friendly." The shops, ninety-four in all, were arranged in clover–like clusters trimmed with fountains and flowers. Along the periphery were wooden benches for the weary, mostly men. And off to the side was one of the most elaborate play structures I'd ever seen. My semi-annual excursion to Macy's seemed pretty bland by comparison.

Armed with a photo of Jannine and a description of the clothes she'd been wearing on Saturday, I began my trek with the Dansk store at the far left. From there, I worked my way around each cluster and then on to the next, stopping midway for a gourmet chocolate chip cookie. The mall's claim to super-savings did not extend to the food.

By the time I'd finished, several hours later, my voice was growing hoarse, and the muscles in my face ached from the effort of constant, forced smiling. Nobody remembered seeing Jannine. Nobody even paused or showed the faintest glimmer of recognition at seeing her picture. I found myself wishing she'd broken a china cup, or better yet, a whole rack of them. But she hadn't, and I came up empty–handed.

Just so the trip wouldn't be a complete waste, I went back to Grifficcio and bought a soft calfskin wallet for Ken, whose birthday was coming up in a couple of weeks. The peevishness I'd felt earlier had dimmed considerably. I knew that by the time I got home and found myself on the receiving end of his smile, my bad feelings would be nothing but a distant memory. In fact, by then I might even wish I'd bought something less mundane, like the monogrammed red satin pajamas I'd passed up so quickly, or the matching his-and-hers black silk G-string briefs. I smiled at the thought of the latter. My last boyfriend would definately have approved, but Ken probably would not.

Sometimes I wondered whether we were a good match, whether there was any future in the relationship at all. Ken was so different from me, so different from anyone I'd dated before that it was hard to judge.

The sun was dipping low into the west by the time I started home. Traffic was a bit heavier, but moving along at a good clip. I left the tape off this time and tried to figure out what I was going to say to Cheryl Newcomb. When I pulled up in front of the house, I still didn't have a clue.

Carla answered the door with the same snappish expression she had that morning. But a black spandex miniskirt had replaced the robe, and her hair was done up in some fancy top-knot instead of rollers. The cigarette was there in her hand again, along with a glass of something that smelled like whisky. The light of the television flickered in the background.

"Sorry to bother you again," I said, "but I'd like to speak with Cheryl."

Carla cocked her head and regarded me with amusement. "She isn't here."

"When will she be back?"

A shrug. "When she feels like it."

"Do you know where I might find her?"

"With friends, probably." She leaned against the door jam and took a swallow of her drink, then wiped her mouth with the back of her hand. "Like I told you, you'll have better luck if you check at school."

"I did. Cheryl wasn't there."

The news didn't seem to trouble Carla much. She sighed in frustration, but her response was nonchalant. "She wasn't, huh?"

I didn't like the feel of this. "Mrs. Newcomb, when was the last time you saw your daughter?"

"Uh, Sunday I think."

"You think?"

She dropped the cigarette onto the porch and crushed it with her foot. "It was Sunday, I remember now. I worked that evening, and Cheryl was moping around the house when I left. She'd been in a snit all weekend."

"And you've no idea where she is now?"

"With friends, I told you."

"Which friends?"

"I'm not sure, exactly." She hiccupped. "Kids these days, they don't check in with you every time they step out."

And mothers, these days, apparently didn't ask. "I don't want to alarm you, but your daughter hasn't been at school all week. They seem to think she's home with the flu. They haven't seen her. You haven't seen her. Nobody's seen her since Sunday."

She frowned. "It's only been a couple of days."

"Why don't you call around to her friends tonight, then check with the school tomorrow? If she doesn't turn up, I think maybe you should notify the police."

"The police? That's a bit extreme, don't you think?"

A burly, dark-haired man wandered in from the other room and joined her at the door. He had a skinny little mustache that was all wrong for the size of him. "What's this about police?" he grumbled.

Carla sidled up next to him and ran the toe of her shoe up his leg. "This lady's from the school. She says Cheryl's been cutting classes all week."

"I'm not actually *from* the school, I . . ."

"The little bitch," the man said, interrupting my attempt to set the record straight. "You ought to whip that butt of hers. You're too soft on her, Carla. You let her walk all over you."

"Come on, Hal, you know what she's like. It's not a matter of my *letting* her do anything."

Hal grunted.

"Did you check with Miss what's her name, the drama teacher?" Carla asked. "Cheryl's real involved with the production they're doing. I bet she wouldn't cut *that* class."

There was gunfire in the back room—television, I assumed, because it was followed by an equally appalling round of canned laughter. "I don't think she was in drama either," I said, stretching my limited knowledge to fit what I was sure was the reality. "I'm afraid she might be in trouble."

"She'll be in trouble, all right," Hal said. "You let me have a go at her this time, Carla. I'll knock some sense into that head of hers one way or another."

Carla tweaked his chin. "Mr. Tough Guy. You remember what happened last time you had a 'talk' with her." Carla turned back to me. "I'm sure it's nothing to worry about. Cheryl's done this sort of thing before. But I'll call around like you said. Thanks so much for letting me know."

The door clicked shut just as the Energizer Bunny was beginning his long march across the TV screen.

The minute I got home, I called Nancy Walker and explained the situation. "Will you check on it and make sure something is done?" I asked.

"First thing in the morning. I hope everything's okay. Cheryl's a sweet kid, shy and a little awkward. The kind who fades into the woodwork if you're not careful."

"You know her?"

"She's in my fourth period creative writing class. I don't think she said a single word all first semester, but she's loosened up a bit since. Not a great student by any means, but at least she goes through the motions, which is more than I can say for some of them."

Loretta was wiggling around between my legs, and I almost lost my balance. "What about the parents?"

"It's just the mother. One of these 'if there ever was a father he was gone the minute the pregnancy test came back positive' situations. From what I understand, there's never any shortage of men in the house, however."

"I met one of them tonight. A real sweetheart. What about this drama production? Her mother said she was very involved with it."

Nancy snorted. "I don't know where she pulled that one from."

"Will you check on it anyway?"

"Sure, but I'd know if she was. I hope nothing has happened to her."

"Yeah." I was developing a surprising fondness for this girl I'd never met. Maybe because in some little way, she reminded me of myself at that age. I knew what it was to feel alone and adrift in a world where everyone one else seemed safely anchored.

"Anyway," Nancy said, "I'll follow through and make sure it gets reported."

"Thanks."

With the Cheryl situation in good hands, I turned my thoughts to more immediate problems—my stomach and my career, but not in that order.

Ignoring Loretta, I dialed Sara's number again and left a message. Then I waded through the maze of boxes and checked the fridge.

Empty, just as I'd feared, except for a wilted head of lettuce and the remnants of Monday night's pizza, which was now stiff and lumpy. It would have to do though; I wasn't getting in the car again.

I'd kicked off my shoes while talking to Nancy, and slid out of my skirt while conversing with Sara's machine. I was unbuttoning my blouse on the way to the bedroom when the doorbell rang. Hastily, I grabbed my father's old rain coat from the top of the Goodwill pile and slipped it on, securing the front with my arms. Then I answered the door.

"I brought you some flowers," Tom said. Loretta abandoned her post by my legs, and started prancing around Tom's. He reached down and scratched her head.

"What for?" I asked.

"To apologize for waking you so early." He held out a magnificent spray of mountain lilac.

"You already apologized, this morning."

Grinning, Tom held out a large paper sack with his other hand. "I brought dinner, too, and wine. Nothing fancy."

The tantalizing aroma of garlic and herbs drifted in my direction. "You might have called," I observed coolly.

"I did. Your line was busy."

"Did it ever cross your mind I might have plans for the evening?"

"Do you?"

I hesitated. "No. But I'm tired. I've had a busy couple of days."

"Then you ought to be especially grateful you don't have to cook." Tom stepped through the door and headed for the kitchen as though he owned the place. "I just have a few last minute preparations to take care of."

I followed at his heels. "I *never* cook."

"Never?"

"Almost never."

"You should. It's good for the soul." He set the wine on the counter, then began unloading plastic-capped bowls. He took another look at the raincoat and frowned. "You want to slip into something cooler? It was eighty-five degrees in the shade this afternoon."

I was beginning to understand what had prompted Tom's wife to run off with the contractor. Even if the guy did nothing more than grunt and watch TV all evening, he was probably a lot easier to live with than her ex.

"Go on," Tom said, sifting through my carefully boxed crate of kitchen giveaways. "I can handle things in here." He retrieved a frying pan and a medium–sized saucepan. Then he turned again to his bag and pulled out a glass bowl filled with the most scrumptious looking salad I'd seen in a long time. Crisp lettuce, avocado slices, mushrooms, bright red cherry tomatoes.

Soggy pizza seemed suddenly a most unappetizing alternative. "I'll just be a minute," I told him.

He grinned again, and his eyes crinkled. "Take your time."

I didn't make a big deal of it, but I didn't exactly rush either. I took a shower, freshened my make-up and slipped into jeans and a jersey shirt. I realized only after the fact that I'd chosen my favorite shirt, the one every one tells me clings in just the right places and turns my eyes an enticing emerald green.

Loretta, who'd been watching my *toilette* with bland in difference, followed me back to the kitchen and cozied into the space between Tom and the stove.

"Hope you like garlic," Tom said. "This is a pasta sauce I learned to make when Lynn and I were living in Italy. Very authentic. There's not a tomato in it."

It smelled divine. My stomach was already nudging me in anticipation.

"When were you in Italy?"

"Before Los Angeles. My daughter was born there, but we left when she was still a baby."

"How many kids do you have?"

"Two. A girl and a boy." Tom handed me a spoon. "You want to stir this while I toss the salad?"

"They're with you on weekends?"

"Every other weekend. And some Tuesdays." For just a moment a shadow crossed his face, then the cocky look dropped back into place. "I think we're about ready. You *do* have a couple of plates that aren't packed away, don't you?"

I did, and I got them out, along with silverware and candles and real cloth napkins embroidered by my mother. The pasta was every bit as good at it smelled, the salad as fresh and crisp as it looked, and the wine so

smooth I began to think Tom's wife might have been a
fool to leave, after all.

By the time we'd finished dinner, and the entire bottle
of wine, we'd just about caught up on the past twelve
years. We'd also exchanged a lot of surreptitious glances
as we sized each other up, and laughed at a lot of things
that weren't all that funny.

"I'm out of coffee," I told him, "unless you're fond of
instant made from gluey crystals."

He smiled. "I'll pass."

We were clearing the table when the phone rang.
"Hi," Sara said, "I got your messages. I'd have called you
earlier, but I didn't want to add to your troubles."

I glanced over my shoulder at Tom. "Can I call you
back?"

"I'm going out again in about half an hour. I, uh, probably won't be back till late."

"How late?"

She laughed. "Tomorrow morning. Why don't you call
me at work? The stuff that's going on around here isn't
anything you want to rush to hear anyway."

Tom was wiping cheese crumbs from the table when I
hung up. "That your boyfriend?"

I shook my head.

"What's his name?"

"I told you, it wasn't him."

"I didn't say it was."

I gave him a sour look, which I had to cut short because
the phone rang again. It was Jannine this time, sounding
as though she were teetering on the edge.

"The police were here this morning."

"Again?"

"With a search warrant." Her voice was thin and tight.

"There were three of them. They went through the whole house, closets and everything. It was awful."

"Did they find anything?"

She made a low moaning sound. "I don't know. We didn't exactly have a conversation."

Benson had to have known. All the talk about cooperation and meeting him halfway, and he hadn't even been completely honest with me. But then, I reminded myself, neither had Jannine.

"You're coming tomorrow?" she asked abruptly.

The funeral. "Of course I'm coming."

"Will you ride with us? I need somebody strong like you, or I'll never make it through."

"Do you want me to meet you at the house?"

"Would you? I'd really appreciate it. You've no idea how difficult this is going to be."

"How about tonight? Do you want me to come by now?"

"I'm okay. But thanks."

She didn't sound okay.

"Kali?"

"Hmm?"

"How'd you make out at the mall?"

I bit my lip, wavered, then opted for the hard truth. "I couldn't find anyone at all who remembered seeing you."

There was a moment's silence. "I was afraid of that." Her voice caught, and she took a deep breath to even it out again. "So what do we do now?"

"We keep looking, picking at things until something begins to unravel."

"And if it doesn't?"

It was my turn to take a deep breath. "We shoot holes through their case in court. If it comes to that."

She made a wheezing sound, deep in her throat. "It won't . . . I can't . . ." Her voice was thin and high-pitched.

"That's a long way off," I told her.

She mumbled something I couldn't make out and then was quiet. "I went through Eddie's things," she said, after a moment. The frantic overtones had faded. "I've got a box of stuff to give you tomorrow. Everything was kind of jumbled. I guess the police don't care how they leave things. It all looks pretty ordinary though."

It probably was. I told her I'd take a look anyway.

"And I called the bank," Jannine continued. "You were right about the ten thousand. It's right there in our account."

"Can they tell you were it came from?"

"Eventually, unless it was cash. But it will take time. Maybe a week or so. Do you think it might point the police to someone besides me?" Her voice was strained.

"Let's talk about it tomorrow, Jannine. Get through the funeral first." I caught myself on the brink of telling her everything was going to be all right, but I stopped short because I wasn't so sure myself. Instead, I mumbled a few generic encouragements, then hung up.

"The Marrero murder?" Tom asked.

"How'd you come up with that?"

"Jannine, funeral, court. It wasn't hard." He was rinsing the plates and loading them into the dishwasher. "I'm a journalist, remember? That's the kind of stuff I pick up on."

I sat down at the table and stared at my hands. "The

way you guys in the press are going after this, she'll be convicted before she's ever arrested."

He raised an eyebrow. "Don't tell me you've forgotten about the First Amendment."

"Oh, come on. This isn't about freedom of the press. It's about selling papers. *The Hadley Times'* picture of Jannine was bigger than the one they ran of Eddie."

Tom turned off the faucet, then dried his hands with a paper towel. "I wouldn't judge all newspapers by *The Hadley Times.*"

I was being unfair, and I knew it. That morning's *Mountain Journal* hadn't even run the story on the first page. And Jannine's name had been mentioned only as a possible suspect in an ongoing investigation.

"In fact, some of us take our responsibility rather seriously." Tom had been rooting around in the back closet. He came up, finally, with an old bottle of brandy. "You want some?"

"Make yourself right at home," I muttered.

He smiled. "I will, thanks." He set the bottle on the table, then started going through boxes until he found glasses which met his approval. "I have a friend who's a cop," Tom said, over his shoulder. "An inside source. If I wanted to get into a spitting contest with those folks at *The Hadley Times,* I could, easily. That's not my style, though. Official department line is the investigation's still open. That's my approach, too."

He offered me a glass of brandy, and even though I was already sailing comfortably along under the rosy glow of wine, I accepted.

"*Is* the investigation still open?"

"For the moment. Daryl Benson is a cautious man. He's had run-ins with the D.A. before. Now that he's only a couple of years from retirement, he's treading lightly."

A confession would certainly make it easy for him. No wonder he was pushing so hard for Jannine's cooperation. "Nothing the police have, including the gun, proves she did it."

"Not conclusively. You have to admit she's a pretty logical suspect, though. In light of everything."

She was, but I wasn't going to admit it. Even to Tom.

"You acting as her attorney?"

"Friend, mostly. But attorney too, I guess."

Tom sipped his brandy. "What have you come up with?"

"A lot of pieces that don't fit."

For a moment, I debated the wisdom of talking with a newsman. But as long as Tom had the inside dope from the police, I figured he might as well have a look at the other possibilities as well. Besides, I trusted Tom. Trusted him even though he'd been a pain in the ass when I was a kid, and was still able to raise my hackles. Maybe it was just the wine and the warm spring evening, but I was willing to bet that underneath, where it counted, he was about as honest as they come.

While we finished our brandy, I told him what I'd learned, which sounded as disjointed in the retelling as it did in my mind. We tossed ideas around for a bit, then Tom looked at his watch.

"I need to get going," he said. "And I promise, no early morning hammering."

We walked to the door, stepping over Loretta who lay sprawled in the center of the hallway.

"Thanks for having dinner with me," he said, and

knuckled my neck like he'd done years ago when he and John were trying to stir up trouble.

It didn't smart the way it used to, though. In fact, it felt kind of nice.

13

Eddie's funeral was a well orchestrated affair, tastefully somber without being at all mawkish. There were innumerable references to his standing in the community and efforts on behalf of the town's young people, mercifully few to God and His mysterious ways, and none at all to the violent manner of the death we were there to mourn. The minister had been acquainted with Eddie, however peripherally, so we were spared the vague platitudes and hesitant tones of those paid-by-the-hour ministers who usually sound as though they're auditioning for a role they don't want. Even so, I had trouble reconciling the shiny black coffin near the front of the church with the pictures of Eddie that played in my mind.

Because I'd been sitting up front with Jannine and her family, I didn't realize what a crowd there was until the service ended and we left the church. The funeral procession stretched for blocks. Like a long, slow–moving string of ants, we wound our way through town and out to the cemetery, passing first through the older section where the headstones read like a history book, and then finally into the newer, more manicured portion. The headstones there are polished granite, all of a uniform size and design, much like the housing tracts going up at the edge of town. Even the trees in this section, evergreens undoubtedly planted by cemetery designers, have a clipped, orderly look to them. A marked contrast to the gnarled old oaks that dot the surrounding hills.

We parked, then drifted onto the knoll, where we stood silently, and a little awkwardly, in the bright noon sun until everyone was assembled. I listened to the mockingbird off in the distance and tried to keep my gaze from drifting to the spot farther on where the grass was newly patched from my father's burial a week earlier. That day there had been only four of us—Sabrina and I, my father's younger brother who'd driven up from Fresno, and the mortuary chaplin in his dark three–piece suit. I'd focused on the business of getting him buried, one more detail to cross off my list. Today I let myself dwell on life and death, and that single point in time when they join. And I stared out at the sea of faces around us and wondered if anyone there knew what it was that had brought Eddie to that moment.

While we waited for stragglers, the minister mopped his brow and ran a finger under his collar. He murmured something to one of the representatives from the funeral home, who in turn said something in Spanish to another man. Off to one side, I caught a young woman staring hard in our direction and wondered fleetingly if she was the other woman in Eddie's life.

When the last of the mourners had finally joined the group, the minister said a few words, then asked us to bow our heads in prayer as the casket was lowered into the earth. Jannine was standing between her mother and me, with her children assembled in front. I heard her breath catch when the ceremonial spade of soil struck the casket, but she held her head level and her eyes were dry. Somewhere she had found an inner strength that amazed me. After the minister said a few more words, a woman with tight blonde curls and visible streaks of pink blusher sang an off–key solo of "Amazing Grace."

And then it was over. The crowd dispersed, and we made our way individually to the Langleys' for bodily nourishment and spiritual fortification.

The Langleys' house was a fairly new, excessively fancy ridgetop villa that looked to me more like a mausoleum than the place we'd just come from. But Marlene was right. It was spacious and ideally suited for entertaining, something at which Mrs. Langley seemed quite proficient. While Mrs. Langley greeted guests and directed them to the various tables of food and drink, Marlene took Jannine off to the side and settled her onto a comfortable couch. There were a couple of chairs angled next to it, presumably for those who wished to offer words of comfort.

"Thank goodness this day is almost over," Nona said, joining me in the alcove off the dining room.

"Jannine seems to be holding up remarkably well," I observed.

"She didn't really want any of this foofaraw, particularly with people saying the things they're saying about her, but you know how it is. Sometimes it's hard to say no."

"Especially for Jannine."

"Yes, she's a great believer in peace at all costs." Nona started to say something more, then stopped, pulling her mouth tight. "Have you managed to see Benson yet?" she asked, after a moment.

"Yesterday."

Nona looked at me expectantly, her expression an odd mix of hopefulness and dread. "What did he say?"

I looked over at Jannine in the far corner, surrounded by a small group of women. Her head was bent, her hands clasped tight in her lap, but she managed to look up every now and then, and nod at one of her companions. With the exception of a few bleak moments, she'd managed to hold herself together. But I wasn't sure how long she could sustain it. An arrest, the ensuing trial, I hated to think what it might do to her.

I looked back to Nona and sighed. "The police don't have anything concrete, but they've got enough to make them think they can build a case. And I haven't found anything so far to blow it apart. No one remembers seeing Jannine at the mall last Saturday, and she has no proof her gun was stolen."

Nona drew in a sharp breath. "This isn't going to work, is it? You're not going to be able to stop them." Her voice was tight. Her hands twisted and kneaded, mirroring the panic inside. "Dear God, I don't know what to do next. I don't know what to do at all."

I took her hands in mine and held them steady. They were frailer than I remembered, the skin soft and loose like worn flannel. "It's going to be all right. I'll find something. It's just a matter of digging. I've already come up with a couple of things that may lead somewhere."

It wasn't much, but it was enough for Nona. She pulled herself together, mentally dusting off the places that had scraped bottom. She gave me a feeble smile. "Thank you, Kali. I don't know what we'd do without you."

I smiled back, reassuringly. After a moment, I said, "I need to ask you some touchy questions. I hope you don't mind."

She raised a brow, curious.

"Did Eddie and Jannine have a good marriage?"

The curious look gave way to a frown. "Jannine doesn't talk to me about such things."

"From what you've seen, though, did they get along?"

"People work things out in their own way, you know." There was a pause. "Anyway, Jannine just sort of let things roll over her."

"Let what roll over her?"

It took a moment for Nona to answer, but she finally stopped biting her lower lip and looked at me. "You know, the sarcasm, the insults. I can't remember any specifics, but the gist of it was that she was fat and stupid and dull. Seemed like lately Eddie found fault with everything she did."

"How did Jannine take it?"

"She acted like she didn't even notice." Nona glanced over at her daughter. "I'm sure she did, though."

I nodded. As Nona had said earlier, Jannine was a great believer in keeping the peace. "Do you think Eddie might have been involved with another woman?"

Nona laughed self-consciously. "Goodness, Kali, do you think *I'd* know something like that?" I looked at her levelly, and she sighed. "I suppose it's possible. Eddie always did have a tendency to cast himself in the leading role. He was a good man, but I don't think he was ever as devoted to Jannine as she was to him. There was a restlessness about him I never understood." She smiled thinly. "But then, I've never had a great deal of luck trying to understand men, or marriage."

That made two of us.

"I'm going to take the kids home," Nona said, after a moment. "Would you mind giving Jannine a ride when she's ready?"

I gave Nona a hug, mumbled a few words of encouragement, and promised I wouldn't let Marlene and Mrs. Langley smother Jannine with their compassion and good intentions. Then I went off in search of food and refreshment.

There was an abundance of the former, a wide assortment of crustless sandwiches, nut breads and cookies, but a rather limited offering when it came to the latter. Coffee, tea and a sickly pink punch. It was nothing like the last of these affairs I'd attended, the funeral of my firm's founding father, where there'd been so much heavy drinking the widow had had to call cabs for half her guests. Maybe Mrs. Langley had been to a few funerals like that herself, or maybe this was simply the way church ladies in Silver Creek did things. Still, decorum aside, I could have used a real drink.

Instead, I settled for tea with lots of sugar. It was a poor substitute, and a silly choice for a hot afternoon. My body temperature skyrocketed with the first sip. From the looks of it, Nancy had made the same mistake. She was standing by an open window, fanning herself with her free hand.

"Whew," she said when I'd finally threaded my way through the crowd to her side of the room, "what a day for a funeral."

"Quite a turnout, though."

"Amazing, isn't it? I don't think I even *know* this many people. There are some fairly big guns here, too. Look, over there with Jack Peterson, that's Franklin Mooney, the CEO of Sierra Hospital and one of the big local contributors to the Republican Party.''

"What's he doing here?"

"His son was our star quarterback a few years ago. And see that blonde woman with them? That's Lorna Mulford, Jerry Mulford's wife."

"Who's Jerry Mulford?"

"The developer. You know, Mulford and Banks, they're the ones putting in those posh new planned communities—everything you need for authentic 'executive living.' Peterson doesn't miss an opportunity, does he? Out there pressing flesh, rounding up support, even at a good friend's funeral. Though he did announce yesterday that the school is setting up a trust fund for Eddie's family. You can bet he got a lot of press out of it, too."

"I take it you're not one of his supporters?"

"Me?" She laughed. "Hardly. Oh, he's okay as a principal, though he's a bit of a prig. And he's barely got the brains to keep one jump ahead of the students. I shudder to think that he might have a hand in running the state." She shuddered, to show me she meant it. "Speaking of students, I checked on Cheryl Newcomb. Nobody's seen her all week, and she doesn't take drama. Never has. I told Peterson about it first thing this morning, but he kind of brushed it aside. Like I said, the man can't focus on too many things at once."

"Will he call the police?"

She shrugged. "I wouldn't count on it. But I also put in a call to the county office of Attendance and Welfare. I'm sure they won't let it drop. Though to be honest, there's not a lot anyone can do. We've had other kids run away. Usually it's a matter of waiting until they come back of their own accord."

One of the church ladies came by with a tray of miniature cheese puffs, each topped with a red pimento. When Nancy and I both declined, she looked crestfallen. "You're sure?" she asked. "I made them myself."

We were sure, we told her. They looked divine, but we were both on diets.

Nancy looked at her watch. "I'd better get going. Canceled classes or not, the final pages for the yearbook are due at the printers first thing Monday morning. I've got kids at school right now proofing and making last minute changes." She gave an exasperated sigh. "This yearbook is more trouble than all my other classes combined."

Nancy wandered off looking for a place to deposit her tea cup, and I went to check on Jannine, who looked ready to wilt but insisted she was just fine. "Half an hour longer," I said, "then I'm taking you out of here. Anyone who hasn't said their condolences by then can send you a card."

Just as I was leaving, Marlene bustled up with a fresh glass of punch for Jannine and another of her reassuring little hand pats. Giving comfort was apparently one of her specialties.

Across the room, Jack Peterson was exchanging a hearty handshake with a portly, well-manicured older gentleman. I eased in behind them and waited until the older man had moved on.

"Your wife has done a wonderful job with this," I told him. "It was good of her to take it on."

He smiled. "She's a born organizer."

"I've been trying to get a chance to talk with you," I said, stepping away from the woman behind me, whose handbag bounced against my back. "About Eddie's death. I was hoping you might have some ideas."

"Me?"

"You were a friend of his. If there was anything troubling him, or if he was involved in anything unpleasant . . ."

Jack interrupted. "Please. This is a funeral."

"Maybe I could set up an appointment for tomorrow then."

"You'd have to check with the school secretary. I don't think there's much I can tell you, though. My conversations with Eddie tended to be more of a philosophical nature."

"What about . . ."

Once again I was interrupted, this time by the minister. He held out a hand to Jack, then clasped Jack's shoulder with his other hand. I turned and left.

I grabbed a cookie, shaped and decorated like a football, and went off to join Susie, who was holding a glass of punch against her forehead and scanning the room with her eyes.

"Damn Al anyway," she said. "He was the one who was so anxious to leave, and now I can't find him anywhere. He's probably found himself a TV somewhere and gone into hibernation. Either that, or he's off dreaming about how he's going to spend 'our' inheritance."

It sounded like Al was as much fun in the flesh as he was on the phone. "You settled things with your uncle, then?" I asked.

She snorted. "In a manner of speaking. You know what that creep did? Not only did he renege on the couple thousand, he *lowered* his basic offer. Twenty grand total for Eddie's share and mine!"

"You could always hold onto them."

"Uh-uh. With Al not working and everything, we need

the money now. George knows that too, which is why he figures he can get away with buying me out so cheap."

"Is he here?" I asked.

She nodded sullenly. "That's him over there with the maroon shirt and the dark, shifty eyes."

George Marrero wasn't what I expected. He was short and round, with thinning hair parted low on the left side and swooped over the considerable bald space on top. He wore a polyester plaid suit which showed signs of strain across the back, a string tie, and a large silver belt buckle you couldn't miss from across the room. The shirt *was* maroon, but his eyes were small and protruding rather than shifty.

"The woman next to him is his wife, Gloria," Susie continued. "She's a peach, always has been. She and George don't have children, so she kind of took a special interest in Eddie and me while we were growing up. She's tried hard not to get embroiled in this controversy about the tavern. I know it's upset her, especially coming when it did."

"Coming when it did?"

Susie lowered her voice almost to a whisper. "Gloria has cancer. About fifteen years ago she had a hysterectomy. Then, five years ago she developed breast cancer. She went through all the treatment, and just when we thought she was home free, they discovered a lump in her other breast. Apparently it had progressed pretty far." Susie glanced again at her aunt. "Life isn't fair. Gloria is one of the kindest people in the world."

My gaze followed hers. I've often wondered how a person can carry on day after day with the specter of death grinning in the shadows. I'm not sure I would be able to pull it off, myself.

After a moment, George caught us staring. He made his way over to the archway where we were standing, greeting Susie with a cordial, one–arm hug. "You holding up okay, honey?" he asked.

Susie frowned slightly and twisted away, then apparently remembered her manners. "Yeah," she said, her tone stiff. She introduced us, and we shook hands. George's palm was soft and sweaty, but he pumped my arm like we were old friends. "Kali is a friend of Jannine's," Susie explained as we were exchanging condolences.

George's expression shifted ever so slightly. "That so?"

Susie's gaze was still directed across the room. She raised her arm and waved. "Finally, there's Al. Gotta go."

She darted across the room and linked up with a ruddy–faced young man who could have been a stand-in for the Incredible Hulk. George watched for a moment, then mumbled a "pleasure meeting you" and turned to go.

I scurried along beside him. "I'd like to talk to you a moment, if I could. About Eddie."

"What about him?"

"He mentioned something to me before he died about needing a lawyer. I was hoping you might have some idea what it was about."

George's expression was unchanged, but the muscle in his cheek twitched. "I'm afraid I don't."

"I thought it might have something to do with the tavern buy-out."

He shook his head. "Simpson was handling that."

"I'm trying to help Jannine work through the financial tangles following Eddie's death," I explained. "Anything you could tell me about the business arrangements would help."

The muscle jumped again. "The Mine Shaft is really not her concern. Eddie's interest passed to his sister when he died."

"I'm aware of that. But he'd come up with ten thousand to buy Susie's share. Jannine can't figure out where the money came from. I thought you might know."

"Sorry. That wasn't the kind of thing he'd have told me. As you must know, we were not on the best of terms over this."

I nodded. There was an awkward silence.

"Seems to me Jannine's got more important stuff to worry about anyway," he said, not at all kindly.

It was his tone more than his words, but it got to me just the same. I set my eyes on his. "It must have been hard for you," I said, "knowing you were going to have to take Eddie on as a partner when you didn't want to."

"We'd worked it out."

"Really? Susie seemed to think you were pretty upset at the prospect."

He smiled thinly. "Look, I don't know what this is all about, but Eddie and I settled our differences last week. There'd been bad feelings all the way around, and I didn't like it any better than he did. I'm set in my ways. I wasn't any too excited about having a partner again, even someone I was as fond of as Eddie. But, well, sometimes young blood's a good thing. He had some darn good ideas, really."

"He must have been very persuasive."

Another thin smile. "We kind of agreed to meet each other halfway."

"But now you don't have to."

The smile turned sour. "What, exactly, is that supposed to mean?"

I shrugged. "You'll end up as sole owner of the tavern, and for a good deal less than it would have cost you originally."

George's expression was hard to read. "With Eddie's interest as well as her own, Susie will end up quite a bit better off than she would have originally. Under the terms of the partnership agreement, I could have bought her out for even less. Not, I must remind you, that this is any concern of yours."

Before I had a chance to reply, his wife joined us. She was a frail, bird-like woman with skin so pale it looked almost paper white. Yet there was a graciousness to her manner that gave the impression of strength.

"Oh, here you are," she said, taking her husband's arm. "I lost track of where you'd gone to." Then she turned to me and smiled warmly. "Hello, dear, I'm Gloria Marrero, Eddie's aunt."

"Kali O'Brien, a family friend."

Nancy passed by just then and gave my arm a friendly brush. "I got side-tracked, but now I'm leaving for real. I'll let you know what I hear about Cheryl Newcomb."

I waved, then apologized to Gloria for the interruption.

She smiled again, reassuringly. "Funerals are such a mixed bag, anyway," she said. "There you are feeling like shattered glass on the inside, and yet going on visiting and making plans and getting on with the business of life. But maybe that's the purpose, don't you think? A kind of transition process." Her soft, round eyes looked into my own and then her husband's. "What do you think,

George?" she asked, tilting her head toward her husband.

He mumbled a vague agreement, then, with an icy glance in my direction, turned on his heel and left.

"Goodness, what got into him, I wonder? Of course, we've all been under such stress these last few days . . ."

"I'm afraid it's my fault," I said. "I wanted to talk to him about Eddie and the tavern, but I did it rather badly."

"He'll get over it, dear. That business with the tavern is a sore spot anyway. I don't understand why he fretted over this whole thing the way he did."

"I understand you've just returned from a trip to Arizona," I said, seeking a less awkward topic of conversation.

"Yes, my family has a place there. We'd only just arrived Sunday afternoon when we got the news about Eddie."

"Sunday? Somehow I'd thought you left Saturday morning."

"We had planned to, but then something came up. George thought I should go on ahead by myself, but of course I wouldn't dream of going without him."

So George hadn't been out of town at the time of Eddie's murder, after all. What's more, he had both financial and personal motives for wanting Eddie out of the way.

I felt a sudden unsteadiness, as though I had a bubble at the back of my brain. I nodded politely, but I was plumb out of small talk.

14

On the drive home, Jannine stared woodenly out the window at the passing countryside, her reserve of inner strength drained. After several miles of silence, she sighed, a thin, sharp-edged sound like that of an injured animal.

"I used to wonder how people got through something like this," she said. "I've discovered you get through because you feel so dead inside nothing penetrates." Her dark eyes looked at me. "Late at night, or in those odd, empty corners of the day, the pain is so great it takes my breath away, but sitting at the funeral today, I had to force myself to remember what it was all about."

"That's called coping," I told her gently.

"And then talking with all those people afterwards . . ." She drew in a breath. "There I was, holding up my end of the conversation, speaking Eddie's name as easily as if we were at an ice cream social." She paused, and snapped the clasp of her purse several times. "Everyone knows what the police think, too. I could see it in their eyes."

"You handled it very well."

"At least it's over."

The funeral part was over anyway. I was afraid the police part might have just begun. "Have you come up with any new ideas?"

She looked at me, confused.

"About what might have been going on with Eddie."

"No, I can't even think about it. Every time I try, my mind just kind of freezes over."

"What about the ten thousand?"

She shook her head. "The man at the bank said he'd call me when he knew something."

"And your gun. Any new thoughts about that?"

Another weary shake of her head.

There was a part of me, a big part actually, that wanted to comfort Jannine and tell her I understood. But there was another part of me that felt like giving her a good, hard shake. I drove in silence for a couple of minutes while my two selves reached a truce.

"How well do you know Eddie's uncle George?" I asked finally, keeping my eyes on the road.

"Until Eddie's dad died, we saw him and Gloria pretty regularly."

"Eddie and George were close then?"

She gave a noncommittal little shrug. "Not really close, but they got along. Mostly we'd get together at family gatherings."

"What about his sister?"

"Susie? About the same. You'd think we would have seen more of them since we were about the same age and all, but she and Eddie were never very close. Susie has a bit of chip on her shoulder, thinks Eddie got all the breaks. Her husband's like that, too." Jannine ran a finger across her forehead, kneading the crease between her eyes. "Why all the questions?"

"Both George and Susie profited from Eddie's death."

"Are you suggesting one of them killed him?"

"It's possible."

"Kali, you can't be serious."

"I can be. In fact, I am. Sometimes I think I'm more serious about this whole thing than you are."

"What's that supposed to mean?"

"It's your neck, Jannine." It was a nasty thing to say, especially under the circumstances, but I was hot and tired. My good angel had about run out of patience.

"I got you that box of Eddie's records and everything, didn't I? It wasn't easy going through that stuff, you know."

I looked over my shoulder at the carton in the back seat. There hadn't been time for more than a quick glance at the files, but from what I'd seen, she'd done a thorough job of pulling things together. What was really eating at me, I realized, wasn't simply her passivity; it was the fact that I didn't honestly know that I believed her anymore.

I pulled over to the shoulder, stopped the car, and apologized. Then I got out, went into the 7-Eleven across the street and bought two cans of Coke. I held mine to my neck and savored the sensation of cool metal against my sticky skin. After a moment, I took a long, slow swallow.

"We need to talk," I told Jannine, who had opened her can and then done nothing but stare at it. "Maybe this isn't the best time for it, but I can't do anything more to help you until we do."

Her fingers traced the letters on the side of the can.

"I talked with Benson yesterday."

She bit her lower lip and focused all of her efforts on the letter "O." Slow, concentric circles. "I can tell from your tone it isn't good."

"He says you got your car washed Saturday afternoon."

"That's a crime?"

"Under the circumstances, he finds it suspicious. Any car that had been down by the South Fork would show traces of dust."

She swallowed hard as recognition dawned. "I hadn't had it washed in months," she protested. "It needed it."

"Benson also told me you and Eddie had an argument Saturday morning."

Jannine nodded. "I told you about that."

"You told me you had a bit of a spat. That's different than a fight so heated the neighbors could hear you through closed doors."

"How did he find out about that?" Her voice sounded hollow.

"From one of the neighbors.'

"Probably Mrs. Willard. She's the neighborhood busy-body. I wouldn't be surprised if she had binoculars, too." At least Jannine had looked up and met my gaze.

"What was the fight about?"

"You know, everyday stuff."

"Give me some examples."

Her eyes shifted back to the Coke.

"Mrs. Willard, or whoever it was, said you threw a vase and told Eddie he was going to get what he had coming."

"What is this, the Inquisition?" The words may have been sharp, but there was nothing sharp about Jannine's voice. It was thin and broken.

"If I'm going to help you, I need to know what happened."

There was a long silence.

"Jannine?"

She pulled in a long breath. "I had an abortion," she said, addressing the soda can. "And I didn't even tell Eddie I was pregnant." She let the breath out slowly and looked at me. "He wanted a son so bad, he would have kept me having babies forever. But I just couldn't go through all that again. I want to go back to school and finish my degree. I want to do something with my life, be someone in my own right. I should have gone on the pill, but I was afraid Eddie would find out, so I just kind of tried to work around the fertile days. My period's always been regular as clockwork, so it was pretty easy."

I don't think I said anything, but something in my expression must have shrieked loud and clear.

"I know," Jannine said. "It's the kind of thing a feather-brained teenager would say, but sometimes I think that's about where my mental development stopped. Anyway, Eddie was going through the stack of bills. He'd *never* paid the least attention to them before, but I guess he wanted to check on something . . . and he found the invoice."

"This was Saturday morning?"

She nodded.

"So you had a big fight, and he stomped out of the house."

"Not exactly. We yelled and screamed for awhile until the kids came downstairs. Then we didn't talk. Eddie puttered in the garage while I cleaned up around the house. About eleven, he came into the laundry room to tell me he had to go out. That was it. He didn't say good-bye or when he'd be back or where he was going, just 'I'm going out for a bit.' "

"That was after he got the telephone call, right?"

She nodded. "But I can't say for sure there's any connection."

"He apparently stopped by school. Any idea why?"

"No. That's not unusual, though." A smile appeared, then vanished. "Football is more than a sport, remember. It's a way of life."

I swished the soda around in my half–empty can, thinking.

"Jannine, I have to tell you something I've learned. Something unpleasant. I wouldn't do it if I didn't think I needed to."

Jannine had stopped tracing the letters on her own can, and had begun rolling it between her palms instead. Brown froth trickled down the side of the can and dribbled onto her lap.

"Eddie never spent nights at the tavern. The upstairs apartment is rented to one of the bartenders, a young man who swears Eddie never slept there. In fact, he says Eddie wasn't around much at all." I spoke slowly, making my voice as gentle as possible, then waited for the rush of raw emotion.

Jannine's response wasn't what I expected. She looked me level in the eye for a moment, then dropped her gaze. "I know," she mumbled.

"You *know*?"

"Going to the tavern was the excuse he used when he would spend the night with Vicky."

"You knew he was seeing another woman?"

She nodded. "I found out about a month ago." The words came out slowly, with effort. "They say the wife is always the last to know, right? We had a big scene. I'm sure Mrs. Willard was in seventh heaven listening to us.

Eddie swore it was over; he said he loved me and didn't know what had gotten into him. He actually cried, Kali, and begged me to forgive him."

"And you did?"

"I forgave him. Part of me even understood. But I was having a devil of a time forgetting."

"Who was she?"

"Does it matter?"

I thought Jannine had to be pretty addled not to see it. "A scorned lover has the classic motive for murder," I told her. "At the very least, it will give the police someone else to nose around after."

Jannine turned to look at me again. "Vicky didn't kill him," she said.

"What makes you so sure?"

"Oh God, Kali, this is so sordid." She squeezed the can between her hands. "I'm sure, because I followed her that afternoon."

"You mean you didn't go to the mall?" I thought of the afternoon I'd wasted parading through shops, talking myself hoarse.

"I *did* start for the mall. I was upset about my fight with Eddie, angry with myself for a whole list of things, and I just wanted to get away. You know, wander aimlessly and blend in. But there was something about the way Eddie looked at me when he left . . ." She shrugged lamely. "I started thinking maybe it wasn't over with Vicky after all. That maybe I'd been a bigger fool than I thought and sent him right back into her arms. So instead of going to the mall, I drove to her house and sat outside in the god-damn car eating candy bars and playing like Kinsey Mill-hone. Only I was crying so hard I went through more tissues in five hours than she probably does in a whole year."

"You're sure this Vicky was home?"

Jannine nodded. "She came out to check the mail right after I got there."

"When was that?"

"A little after noon."

"And she never left?"

"Not till later. About six o'clock some guy pulled up in one of those customized trucks with rows of spotlights across the roof. He honked, and they drove off. By that time I felt like such a jerk, I went by the carwash just so the day wouldn't end up being a total waste. And then I went to my mom's."

Jannine looked over to gage my reaction, then turned back to her Coke can. "I told you it was sordid. Now maybe you can understand why I wanted to keep it to myself. I'm sorry about the mall though, really. I tried to tell you it would be a waste."

My head was spinning, trying to sort this new information into neat little piles. So far it all fit. Not that it would hold much water with Benson. "If you knew Eddie wasn't with Vicky, why weren't you worried when he never came home that night?"

"I really expected he'd be there waiting for us when we got back from Mom's. And then when he wasn't, my imagination started in again. Maybe he'd been there at Vicky's all afternoon, and the guy with the truck was just her brother or something. Maybe he was seeing someone new. Maybe he was so angry with me he'd just walked out for good. It sounds weird now, but at the time I'd worked myself into a real snit."

We sat for a moment, neither of us speaking. Jannine

went back to squeezing her soda can, sending another cloud of fizz cascading over the side and onto my lovely leather upholstery.

Finally Jannine said, "The thought of losing him was more than I could bear. I spent all Saturday night rehearsing exactly what I was going to say when he came home, how I was going to convince him to give me another chance." Her voice faltered. "But he never showed up. The police came instead."

My can was empty. I crushed it with my fist. "Is there anything else you've neglected to tell me?"

She shook her head, wiping at her eyes. "I'm sorry. I should have told you the whole truth in the beginning, but it's just so . . . so embarrassing."

I thought that being embarrassed paled in comparison to finding yourself a prime suspect in the murder of your husband. In the end, though, it didn't really matter. The truth was as hard to substantiate as the fabrication. Assuming we'd finally reached the truth.

I squeezed her hand, which was now damp and sticky. "You have no reason to be embarrassed," I told her. "Human nature isn't the tidiest force in the universe."

In return, she gave me a weak smile. "So what are you going to do now?"

"I guess I'll start by going through that box of stuff you got together for me. And I'll probably pay Benson another visit."

"You're not giving up on me then?"

"Oh, come on, you know me better than that."

I took Jannine's can, which hadn't once touched her lips, and emptied it onto the asphalt. Then I crushed it too, and deposited both cans in the overflowing trash bin outside the 7-Eleven. Sticky upholstery or not, my car was still new, and I wasn't about to let it become the littered heap my old VW had been.

"By the way," Jannine said as we pulled onto the road, "if you find anything in Eddie's papers having to do with the tavern, would you set them aside? George asked me about them just this afternoon. He's got a meeting with his accountant or something and wants to make sure his records are complete."

I made some noncommittal response. My mind was busy trying to align the pieces of the puzzle. I wondered again whether George had wanted the tavern enough to kill for it.

15

Loretta met me at the door with her usual tail-thwacking enthusiasm. I started to make excuses—I was too hot, too tired, too grumpy, but she was having none of it. She followed me into the kitchen, alternately dancing a freeform jig, then sitting tight like the star pupil in obedience class.

"All right already," I grumbled, "we'll go for a walk, but I have a few phone calls to make first."

Walk was the operative word here; Loretta went berserk. I grabbed a handful of Kibbles and tossed them onto the floor to keep her occupied while I placed a call to Lawrence Simpson, attorney-at-law.

He was in, and willing to talk to me. But as the saying goes, willingness and a quarter will buy you a cup of coffee. At least he was able to confirm that Eddie was going to purchase Susie's share and become half-owner of The Mine Shaft. The papers had all been drawn up and were to have been signed that week.

"And George Marrero was willing to go along with it?" I asked.

"He didn't have a lot of choice."

"He was upset then?"

"No, not really. As I understand it, he'd originally wanted to keep the place to himself, but by the time I got involved, he seemed resigned to the fact he wasn't going to be able to."

"Did he say *why* he wanted the whole thing?"

"Not that I recall. Makes sense, though. A guy's been his own boss for a number of years, I can see where it might be kind of unpleasant to have a new partner."

"What about Eddie? He was pretty determined himself."

There was a laugh on the other end. "That he was. Reminded me of myself when I first got out of law school. Heavy on theory and vision, and short on practical knowhow. He was busting at the seams to give it a go, though."

"Where was he getting the money?"

"Beats me. It never seemed to be an issue. Sorry I can't be more help. The only thing I did was draw up the papers. They already had matters pretty much worked out between themselves."

I left my name and number in case he thought of anything else, then dialed Sara Stewart. She answered the phone herself, on the first ring.

"Ah, you're there," I chided. "I was afraid maybe you hadn't rolled in yet."

"It was a hot date, but not *that* hot. In fact, I've been here waiting for your call since ten o'clock this morning."

"Sorry, I got tied up at a funeral."

"*Another* one?"

"I know. It's not something I hope to make a habit of, believe me. Do you have time to talk?"

While I kicked off my shoes and peeled my pantyhose from my sticky skin, Sara filled me in on the firm's woes. The last year had been even less profitable than expected, and this was on top of several already tight years. The client base was down, receivables were up, and one of our major outstanding accounts had gone into bankruptcy. The bottom line was that there would be no new partners in the foreseeable future. No promises of partnership and no bonuses, either.

"They've even done away with the morning donut and coffee tray," Sara sniffed.

"Do you think they'll start laying people off?"

"That's certainly been the pattern at other firms. For now, there's nothing but a lot of closed doors and long faces. And enough rumors to launch a tabloid. Mr. Goldman has been holed up in his office all week, won't talk to any of us. He even canceled tomorrow morning's staff meeting. Nobody really knows how bad it is because the partners aren't talking."

My stomach twisted into a knot. I'd had friends who'd been down this road. It wasn't easy to find a new job in a tight market, particularly as a senior associate.

"Heck," Sara said, "you have a direct line to the inside. What does Ken have to say?"

"We haven't really had a chance to talk, what with my being away and all."

"You mean the phone lines have been down or something?" she asked.

Sara has never been particularly fond of Ken, and she gets her jabs in where she can. There were times I thought she might be closer to calling it right than I was. But there were also times I was certain she was wrong.

"It's a difficult position for him," I added, out of fairness to Ken. "A lot of what goes on among the partners is confidential."

Sara snorted. Her point made, she changed the subject, and we spent the next ten minutes catching up on less weighty matters. We even found things to laugh about, but the knot in my stomach stayed tight.

By the time Loretta and I actually made it out the door, the air had already turned brisk. The sky was a shimmery, indigo blue, fading at the western edge to crimson. In the distance, the trees were a black silhouette, as though they'd been painted flat against the sky. I took a deep breath, filling my lungs with the fresh scent of mountain grass and wild mustard weed, and silently thanked Loretta for talking me into a walk.

I'd placed classified ads in the local paper, listing my father's truck and power tools, but I'd somehow neglected to run the "Free to good home" blurb about Loretta. I'd have to make sure, when I did, to mention how much she liked getting out for walks.

We cut across the open field and down to Sycamore, where a wide dirt path runs by the side of the road. Loretta trotted along, sticking her nose into cracks and crevices. At one point, she caught a ground squirrel by surprise and started after him, only to stop a few steps later. She was getting fat, no doubt about it. I was going to have to cut down on her Kibbles, or she'd soon be too wide to fit through the doggy door. Then I sucked in my stomach and made a similar promise to myself.

I hadn't been paying much attention to where we were headed, and I was surprised to find myself passing by the foot of Tom's long driveway. It wasn't the path I'd intended to take. I gave some thought to stopping off to thank him again for last night's dinner. Then I caught myself grinning. Okay, so I wouldn't. Even Miss Manners would probably say that a personal visit for such a purpose was overkill.

But as I was turning to leave, Tom pulled up.

"Hey," he said, "fancy meeting you here."

"I was walking the dog," I explained. Loretta did her part to corroborate this.

"Come up and have a drink with me."

I hesitated. The drink sounded good, especially after my conversation with Sara. But there was something about Tom that piqued my interest in ways I didn't want to consider just then. All in all, I thought it better to decline.

"Come on," he nudged, "just a quick one. I've got to leave for a meeting in about forty minutes anyway." He shut the door of the truck with a hearty thud. "Cub Scout night."

I tried to picture the rowdy and rakish Tom I remembered teaching eight–year–old boys to weave potholders and wash behind their ears. It was enough to make me chuckle. But it also, oddly, warmed my heart. "Okay," I said, following him into the house. "A quick one."

"Beer okay?" Tom asked. He removed his jacket and tossed it over the back of the couch. "I've got wine if you'd prefer."

"Beer's fine."

He rolled up his sleeves, dug out some chips and salsa, and then opened two bottles of Anchor Steam. We sat on deck chairs in an unfinished room at the back of the house. The decor wasn't much, but the view of the valley at sunset was spectacular.

"I did a little nosing around for you today," Tom said, scooping a mound of salsa onto a too-small chip.

"For *me?*" I tried for an understated sarcasm.

Apparently I succeeded, because Tom raised an eyebrow. "For me, then. That better?" He took another scoop of salsa. "You want to hear?"

I nodded.

He was suddenly serious. "It isn't all good."

"I still want to know."

"I was talking to a police friend of mine. Seems the search of Jannine's house turned up nothing."

That much was good news, anyway.

"Also, they found a couple of kids who remember hearing what sounded like shots about three o'clock Saturday. They said they were looking for frogs down by the creek, but the suspicion is they were smoking dope—which is why they were reluctant to say anything before now." Tom paused and looked at me. There was an unexpected softness to his gaze. "The kids also remember seeing a blue car turn onto the county road a little before that. It had one of those bumper stickers, 'If you can read this, thank a teacher.' "

I looked away and took a long swallow of beer. Blue cars were pretty common, and the bumper sticker wasn't exactly a special issue. I'd seen several of them out at the school. Turning onto the county road didn't mean much either, since it was a natural turn-around for people who missed the entrance to the bridge. But it didn't help Jannine any that her car was a blue Ford with the same rear bumper sticker.

"You think she's guilty?" I asked.

Tom shrugged. "I'm just reporting what I heard. You

obviously have reason to believe she's not." His voice was kind, and not at all patronizing.

"I'm not sure what I think anymore."

"Maybe I shouldn't have said anything."

"No, I'm glad you did." I managed a smile. "And thanks for asking around." I began peeling the label from my bottle. "Are they going to arrest her?"

"I don't know. They might."

The police still didn't have a strong case, but I could see that it might be enough.

"At the funeral this afternoon I talked to George Marrero and his wife. They were supposed to have left for Arizona last Saturday morning, but they changed their plans at the last minute and didn't leave until Sunday." Tom looked perplexed, and I realized I'd jumped ahead of myself. "He and Eddie were involved in a dispute over control of The Mine Shaft. In essence, George lost. Now that Eddie's no longer in the picture though, he gets full control of the business."

"Are you suggesting he might have killed Eddie?"

"It's possible. He's got a motive, and he probably had access to Jannine's gun."

Tom looked skeptical. "George Marrero's been a member of this community for a long time. Past president of the Rotary Club, member of the Silver Creek Business Association . . ."

"Jannine's been a member of this community for a long time, too," I said, cutting him off. "It hasn't prevented anyone from thinking *she* might be a killer." I rubbed my head, suddenly weary of the whole business. "Anyway, George and Eddie had apparently reached an agreement. According to the attorney involved, George was more or less reconciled to taking Eddie in as a partner."

I rolled the bits of peeled label between my fingers. When I looked up, I caught Tom eyeing me. A small, lopsided smile pulled at his mouth.

"What?" I asked.

The smile grew till it pulled at the corners of his eyes as well. "Nothing."

There was a fluttery sensation somewhere in my chest. I looked away, remembering again why I'd been hesitant to join him for a drink.

Tom glanced at his watch. "Cripes," he said suddenly. "It's later than I thought." He stood and tossed the empty bottles into the trash. "Sorry about the rush. You want a ride home?"

I shook my head. "I can use the exercise, and Loretta's getting downright fat."

Tom threw his head back and laughed. It was a rich, wonderful sound that ran across my shoulders like the tickle of a feather. "She's not fat, Kali. She's expecting."

"Expecting?"

"Puppies. From the looks of it, I'd say she's due in a couple weeks. You'd better get the whelping bed together, and anything else you need."

I looked over at Tom to see if he was joking, but he was busy gathering up his jacket and car keys. Apparently he was serious.

What little I knew about birth, animal or human, I'd learned in eighth grade science class. I had steadfastly refused to add to that knowledge, and I certainly didn't want to change the pattern now. I had enough to worry about already.

Tom climbed into the truck and started the engine. "You sure you don't want a ride?"

"I'm sure." Pregnant or not, Loretta had walked there, and she could damn well walk home.

Tom was backing down the driveway when he leaned out window. "How about going dancing with me tomorrow night."

Dancing. The word had the same effect on me that *walk* did on Loretta. Only I'd learned not to be so obvious.

"Nothing fancy," Tom said. "There's a country western bar about twenty minutes up the road that usually gets some pretty good local bands."

"Sounds like fun," I told him. I could already feel the twang of the steel string guitar reverberating in my bones.

Back at the house, I cooked up some frozen hamburger meat for Loretta, which she wolfed down in no time. I also poured her a bowl of milk, which she sniffed and then ignored.

For myself, I dug out a fork and began eating leftover noodles, cold and straight from the fridge. It was a habit which drove Ken crazy. He likes his meals warm, preferably served on real china in at least three courses.

The box of papers Jannine had given me was on the floor by the front door. I hauled it onto the kitchen table and began sorting through it while I finished off the noodles. I started with the phone bills, which were on top of the stack. There were only a couple. I scanned them quickly, finding nothing that caught my attention. Canceled checks and bank statements came next. The mortgage company and Save-Mart were the big winners, but the gas and electric company, the county assessor, and the church all got a sizable share, too. Again, there was nothing that struck me as questionable. I went through the MasterCard statement with the same result.

At the bottom of the box, I found a large envelope which Jannine had labeled "tavern." The word was followed by a string of question marks. When I looked inside I could understand her confusion. There were loose papers, blueprints, pages filled with columns of numbers, and an assortment of odd-sized notes in Eddie's own writing. I pulled everything out and spread it across the table, then focused my attention on a small stack which appeared to be copies of balance sheets. Diligently, I went through them line by line.

The columns totaled up, that much I could tell pretty easily. The individual entries and the total monthly revenues looked reasonable, as well. Of course, back in my idealistic days as a law student I'd opted to take *Policies for Effecting Change* instead of *Accounting for Lawyers*, so my analysis wasn't airtight by any means. I put the whole mess back in the envelope and began plowing through the rest of the box. I was into last year's tax return when Nancy called.

"Finally, you're home."

"Well, ex-cuse me!"

"Oh for goodness sake, Kali, this is important."

Properly chastised, I tried again. "Sorry. What's up?"

"It's about Cheryl. I went back to school right after I left you at the Langleys. A couple of kids were there working on the layout for the yearbook, and we got to talking. Anyway, to make a long story short, one of the boys saw Cheryl Newcomb with Eddie last Saturday morning."

"Where?"

"Right here at school, just before noon. They were

walking from the athletic field toward the front of the school.''

"What happened?"

"That's it. Erik, that's the boy, was getting something out of his locker. They kind of nodded at each other, and then he went off in the other direction. You think her disappearance is somehow connected with Eddie's death?"

"I don't know what to think. Her phone number's on the missing page of Eddie's calendar, Eddie's dead and Cheryl's missing. It's an awfully strange coincidence.''

"I just can't imagine Cheryl mixed up in anything violent. Cutting class, maybe smoking in the bathrooms, but that's about the extent of it.''

"What do the police think?" I asked.

"I haven't talked to them yet. So far, they've been treating it as a simple runaway. Seems some of Cheryl's clothes and a little over a hundred dollars of her mother's money are missing.''

"The big question here is, why did she run away? It might be that she's afraid. Or it might be that she's in trouble.''

"Cheryl's a confused kid, but she's a good girl at heart.''

"Even good people get into trouble,'' I said. "Add a little youthful inexperience and confusion, and who knows what the outcome will be.''

"Cheryl didn't run away until Sunday though, the day after Eddie was killed. If she was somehow mixed-up in all this, wouldn't she have left before that?"

I agreed, it didn't make a lot of sense. "At the very least,'' I said, "she may have been the last person to see

Eddie alive. Did she ever mention a friend or relative, someplace she might go in a time of trouble?"

"No."

"What about her writing?"

"Cheryl's stories weren't like that. They tended to be fabrications, usually about wealth and glamour and excitement. She wrote a whole string of them about being a famous model in San Francisco."

"You think she might have gone there?"

"It's possible. I don't see her running off to Placerville. It just isn't the same."

"What about her friends?"

"Cheryl's kind of a misfit, the type of kid who tends to seek out adults more than her peers. Makes her feel important, I guess."

"Tom knows someone connected with the police. I'll see if he can find out if they have any leads on her."

"Tom?"

"Tom Lawrence. He was one of John's friends, a couple of years ahead of us in school. He used to be a hotshot reporter for *The L.A. Times.* Now he's back here working for *The Mountain Journal,* of all things."

She laughed. "He doesn't *work* for the paper, honeybuns, he owns it."

"Well," I humphed, "it still strikes me as a major step *down* the career ladder."

"I don't know. He's done some pretty interesting pieces. Built up quite a following, even down in Sacramento. Besides, there are some of us who find that particular ladder much too narrow for comfort."

It was a thought I'd entertained once or twice myself, but as one now clinging on for dear life, I found I'd forgotten why.

After I hung up, I started going through the box of papers once again, but my mind was jumping off in twenty different directions at once. I put the box away and got out my pads of lined yellow paper instead. With Loretta snoring lightly at my feet, I began writing out what I knew—without order, without trying to make sense of any of it. That would come later.

There are people who swear by index cards. They can arrange and rearrange the pieces like a jigsaw puzzle. Some people use an elaborate system of color coding as well. I've tried it, but I find I spend more time selecting the appropriate color than thinking about the case. Besides, the lines on paper are better suited to my scrawling and often slapdash handwriting. With all my arrows and notes in the margins, the page looks pretty messy by the time I'm finished, but it somehow flows the way my mind does.

When I'd finished putting everything on paper, I poured myself a glass of wine and looked at my notes. Nothing made sense. I tried thinking of motive, means and opportunity. The last two didn't get me very far. Neither did motive, but it seemed like my best chance. If only I could figure out why Eddie had died, maybe I could figure out who was responsible. He'd spoken to Nancy about something "unpleasant." He'd spoken to me about needing an attorney. I shut my eyes and tried to imagine the dark corners of Eddie's life. Other than Vicky, there wasn't a shadow or smear to be found.

16

There was nothing in the morning paper about Cheryl Newcomb's disappearance, and by the time I called Tom, he'd already left. But Nancy's news had been gnawing at me all night; I couldn't simply let it drop. I called Beverly Silverstein, a therapist I'd met during my ~~~~~~~ internship with the San Francisco Family Law Center. Beverly works with troubled teens, and I figured she might be able to tell me a little about runaways.

She told me more than a little, none of it encouraging.

"Unfortunately," she said, "the city's full of them. Sad kids, abused kids, scared kids, hateful kids—they run away for all sorts of reasons. Most of them end up worse off than they were. Of course, for some, the street's an improvement."

"How do they manage?"

"Hand–to–mouth, mostly. They beg, steal, get into drugs or prostitution. Girls especially, they take up with some guy they think is going to watch over them, and before they know it they're in so deep they have trouble getting out."

I'd seen the hard–edged hookers, the glassy–eyed ad-
dicts, the cold and hungry souls who wandered the city's
streets. I couldn't imagine how a fourteen–year–old kid
from a hillbilly town could make it there. "She wants to
be a model," I said.

Beverly laughed without humor. "Don't they all? If the
family is serious about getting their daughter back, their
best bet is to hire a private detective. It'll cost them, but
the police just don't have the manpower to deal with
something like this. These kids are smart, too. It's not
easy finding someone who doesn't want to be found."
She gave me the number of a runaway hotline, and the
names of a couple of social service agencies. "I'll keep my
ears open," she added. "I've got a few street connections
myself. You should try the Silver Creek area, too. Most
runaways don't get far from home."

I agreed to send her a description and a picture,
though we both knew it was a long shot. Then I got into
the car and headed for Vicky's, which was an even longer
shot.

The address Jannine had given me turned out to be a
duplex in the old section of town. A green stucco box
with two doors and four windows. The two on the left
were hung with starched lace curtains, the two on the
right with sheets, a pink floral design which did nothing
to improve the building's curb appeal. Vicky's number
matched the windows on the right.

To the side of the door, the buzzer dangled loosely
from a single wire. I knocked instead. When no one answered, I tried peering through a gap in the sheets, which
is something like threading a needle by moonlight.
There wasn't much I was going to learn anyway, except

that Vicky's chosen profession was not that of interior designer. Sheepishly, I tried the knob.

Locked.

I turned to head back down the front walk and just about collided with a willowy blonde in pink spandex running tights. Her lips and nails were a complimentary shade of iridescent fuchsia.

"Miss Fairlaine?"

She looked as though she wanted to deny it, but was having trouble coming up with a suitable story. Finally, she nodded.

"My name's Kali O'Brien. I'd like to talk to you about Eddie Marrero."

Vicky's face went through a succession of contradictory expressions before settling into a tight mask of indifference. Then she did a slow, deep stretch, as though she'd just finished a healthy workout. Only she wasn't even sweating.

"I'm investigating his death. I understand you knew him."

She shook her head, but got only as far as the "No, I . . ." before she stopped her stretching and burst into tears. "Oh, shit," she said, wiping her eyes, "you might as well come in while I find a Kleenex."

I followed the tight little derriere down a narrow hallway to the kitchen at the back, then stood silently while Vicky poured herself a glass of orange juice and dabbed at her eyes. I had been prepared not to like her, and I didn't. She was attractive, but more flashy than beautiful, and about as genuine as a three dollar bill. And she had an annoying habit of tossing her head and shoulders as though she were readying herself for the click of a camera.

"You a cop?" she asked between tosses.

"A lawyer." The answer didn't make a lot of sense, but it seemed to satisfy her.

"He was so deep," she said, blinking hard. "So intense. Nothing like the Neanderthals you generally find around here. And those eyes—all he had to do was look at me, and I was putty."

I could understand the part about the eyes. The rest of it didn't sound much like Eddie. Of course, Vicky's and my ideas of deep were probably a bit different. "How well did you know him?" I asked.

She gave another pert toss of her head. "*Very* well, if you get my drift."

I did. "Was he in any kind of trouble that you know of?"

The artfully penciled brows furrowed, but Vicky's face remained expressionless.

I tried again. "Anyone angry at him?"

"Yeah, me." The furrow became a full-fledged crease. "Turns out the guy was married."

"You didn't know that?"

"Not until I called his house and found myself talking to his goddamn wife. Jeannette or whatever her name is. Kids, even. The bastard." A fresh round of tears gathered at the corners of her eyes. Vicky was an emotional roller coaster.

"When was this?"

"Four weeks and three days ago, exactly." She dabbed at her eyes. "I thought I'd finally met Mr. Right, you know, wedding bells and picket fences, and then it turns out the creep was cheating on me."

That was certainly a novel way of looking at it.

"For a while I was so mad I couldn't see straight, but I loved the guy, too. I kept hoping we could work it out." A sniffle. "It was just awful to pick up the paper and see his picture right there on the front page. I've never before dated a man who was murdered." Vicky's voice trailed off. "Married, murdered—jeez, I really know how to pick them, don't I?"

I tried to work up some sympathy, but I couldn't. Too many people I cared about had been hurt. Were hurting still. "When you found out he was married, what then?"

She set her empty juice glass in the sink, adding it to the existing assortment of crusty cups and bowls. "He said he was going to leave his wife, that I just had to be patient until he worked it out. Then he told me we had to lay low for awhile because his wife knew about us." Vicky's eyes narrowed. "It took me awhile to figure out that if she already knew, and he was going to leave her anyway, we shouldn't have to sneak around. God, men are such shits."

That sentiment I could sympathize with. "How long had you known him?"

"Not long." She actually sounded embarrassed. "A couple months is all. But it was intense." The fuchsia mouth quivered. "Intense and very, very special."

"Did you meet at The Mine Shaft?"

"Oh no, nothing like that." The quiver was gone. The habitual head toss was accompanied by a breathless laugh. "I work for Baker Janitorial and Maintenance. Part-time. I go to cosmetology school, too."

Baker Janitorial—the name sounded vaguely familiar, although I couldn't think why. It still didn't explain Eddie though, so I waited.

"One day he came in to talk to Mr. Baker about an account. It was just like out of the movies. He stopped by my desk and said, 'Hi, gorgeous.' "

Eddie was deep all right.

"The next time he came by, Mr. Baker was tied up, so I suggested we have lunch while he waited. It kind of went from there."

"What, exactly, is Baker Janitorial?"

"Commercial cleaning, floors, windows . . ." She did a little shuffle. "You name it, we do it, and do it right!"

It may not have been the job of her dreams, but she gave it her best, I had to give her credit for that. "What was Eddie's connection to Baker Janitorial?"

Vicky shrugged. "All I know is Mr. Baker wasn't any too happy to see him."

"Didn't you ever ask Eddie about it?"

"No, he didn't like to talk about everyday stuff like that."

That was Eddie—deep with a capital "D."

I'd figured out that Vicky wasn't going to be able to give me much, but I had one more question. "Where were you last Saturday?" I asked.

She thought for a moment. "Home for the most part. Why?"

"You didn't go out at all?"

She shook her head. The blonde mane bounced around her shoulders. "I went out that evening, though. There's this guy I started dating to get my mind off Eddie. He's got no class at all. Comes to pick me up, and he honks the friggin' horn."

I let go of a breath I hadn't realized I was holding. Her story matched Jannine's to a tee. I thanked her and let myself out.

To the best of my knowledge, Benson didn't know anything about Vicky. I wanted to keep it that way. Jealous wives were a favorite with homicide inspectors, probably with good cause, and Jannine had enough jewels in her crown already.

As I headed back to Silver Creek, I thought about Eddie and Jannine and Vicky. And love. And I pondered the dark irony of the fact that Jannine was able to provide an alibi for her husband's mistress, while she herself had none.

17

I got to the high school just as the passing period bell rang. In an instant, the hallway was empty, its silence almost as deafening as the preceding bedlam.

The student assistant working at the front desk was the same cherubic young lady I'd met on my last visit.

"You here to see Mrs. Walker again?"

"Mr. Peterson first. Is he available?"

"He's got someone with him right now. You want to wait?"

I nodded and she went back to the paperwork in front of her, but not for long. "This is so bor-ring," she said. "And now it looks like I'm stuck here for the rest of the year. I'll never get back to attendance."

"I thought this was temporary, until the regular girl got well."

She smiled, a shy, girlish smile you don't see on many her age. "You've got a good memory." Then her face grew serious again. "I don't think she's coming back. She isn't sick after all. She ran away. Nobody knows where she is."

"Cheryl Newcomb?"

"You know her?"

I shook my head. "Do you?"

"Yes. No. I mean, we've been classmates since kindergarten, but you know how it goes."

"What's she like?"

A shrug.

"Who did she hang around with?"

The girl thought. "Mostly she kept to herself. Last year in junior high she used to hang around with Eva Holland, but Eva's kind of . . ." She made a circular motion with her finger. "You know that expression, her elevator doesn't go all the way to the top. She was in regular classes last year, but high school's tougher. They had to send her to a special school in Northvale. I don't know whether Cheryl stayed friends with her or not."

"Do you happen to know where Eva lives?"

"Sure. The little white house across from the school. Doesn't seem fair. She could practically fall out of bed and roll to school, and instead she has to be bussed clear over to a different town."

Just then an interior door opened, and Jack Peterson ushered out a couple and a freckle–faced boy who was obviously their son. None of them looked happy, including Peterson, who looked even less pleased when he saw me.

"Miss O'Brien," he said. "What a surprise."

"I'd like to speak with you if you have a moment."

"I have another parent conference coming up, and then this thing with Ch . . ." He looked over at the assistant, then caught my eye and mouthed, "the missing girl." He cleared his throat. "Of course, the school is not directly involved, but we're trying to cooperate any way we can."

"That's part of what I'd like to talk to you about."

His smile was gracious, but unbending. "I really don't have the time just now, I . . ."

"It will only take a minute."

He frowned. "Well, just a minute then."

Peterson's office didn't begin to compare to the partners' offices at Goldman & Latham, but I would have been willing to bet it was fancier than any other room at school. It certainly outshone the teachers' lounge by a country mile.

The room was large, probably a remodel of several smaller offices, and furnished with an antique armoire, several easy chairs and a large oak desk. Clearly none of it was regulation issue.

He caught me looking, and smiled. "I want the students and parents to feel comfortable here. No reason for the principal's office to look like the reception area at San Quentin. But I paid for it myself. I'm fortunate to be well enough off that I can afford such indulgences. Now, what can I do for you?"

"I'd like to talk to you about Eddie." I settled into the green wing chair across from him. "How did he seem in the days before his death?"

"What do you mean?"

"Did he seem worried or upset? Anything out of the ordinary?"

Peterson thought for a moment, then shook his head. "No, not that I was aware of."

"Did he talk to you much about his uncle or the tavern?"

"He'd mention it on occasion. 'My ticket out of here,'

is how he referred to it. He was taking business courses, you know, working on his M.B.A." Peterson smiled. "Those of us in education sometimes feel the need to move on to something a bit more . . . challenging. I may be running for State Assembly, myself."

I smiled back and tried to look impressed. "Are you familiar with any of the details of the transaction? Like where Eddie was getting the money to buy his sister's share?"

"No, we never got into that sort of thing."

For a man who liked to talk, Eddie had been surprisingly closemouthed about his business venture. "He apparently stopped by school the Saturday morning he was killed," I continued. "Would there be some record of the time he arrived or left, the calls he made, that sort of thing?"

"No. Teachers aren't required to sign in on weekends, and we no longer have a central switchboard. I'm afraid I can't help."

I hadn't expected much, but I was disappointed all the same. "Cheryl Newcomb was here that morning also," I said, shifting to the second item on my agenda. "One of the students saw her talking to Eddie."

"I hadn't heard that." Peterson swallowed hard. "So many terrible things happening all at once. And it had been such a successful year too, before all this." His fingers drummed the desk top and then stopped suddenly. "Surely you don't think there's a connection?"

"I don't know. It seems odd that they were both here Saturday morning, then suddenly Eddie's dead, and Cheryl is missing."

"I suppose, looking at it that way, it does seem odd. But

teachers and students are frequently here after school hours."

"What do you know about the girl's disappearance?"

"Not much. I got a call from the authorities last evening, pretty routine questions about her attendance record and so forth. And then I phoned Mrs. Newcomb this morning to see if there was anything we could do to help. She was rather reluctant to discuss the matter. Frankly, I don't blame her."

"She isn't worried?"

"The girl is a bit of a troublemaker, I'm afraid. This is not the first time she's run away." He paused for a moment, meeting my eyes. "I probably shouldn't say this, but it's my opinion that Cheryl is a disturbed child. She's dishonest and entirely unreliable. There are a number of schools, usually residential facilities, that are equipped to handle children like that; we are not. I suggested to Mrs. Newcomb this morning that she begin exploring the alternatives."

I'd heard of such places. Some have decent track records, but others are little more than privately operated reformatories. Their charges might learn something about obedience, but I couldn't believe they learned much about love or trust. Then again, I doubted that Cheryl was learning much about them at home, either.

There was a knock at the door, and Peterson stood. "I know you're trying to help Jannine, but sometimes you've got to face facts. All this poking around and asking questions—it's not going to change anything."

"You don't think Jannine killed him, do you?"

"I don't know what to think, to tell you the truth. Jannine's a dear soul. She and Eddie are . . . were, almost like family. But we can never *really* know another person. If the police think she's guilty, then I have to believe she probably is. That's their job, you know, checking the evidence, solving crimes."

He'd forgotten the part about burden of proof and a fair trial, but I didn't feel it was the right time for a civics lesson. I left Jack Peterson to his next parent conference, another grim—looking couple with child in tow, and went off to find Nancy. She was busy typing up a grammar test, but took time out to dig through the yearbook files for a picture of Cheryl.

"I'm glad *somebody's* doing something," she said. "Jack Peterson just about bit my head off when he found out I'd bypassed him and called the county directly. He's not too happy with you either, I might add."

"Me? What did I do?"

"It was you who started all this."

"Because I discovered that she was missing?"

Nancy nodded.

Terrific. A young girl in trouble, possibly injured or dead, and Peterson sees nothing but bureaucratic inconvenience. How do people like that end up working with kids anyway?

I found the white house across from the school without any difficulty. It was a narrow two-story Victorian with yellow climbing roses by the porch and a low picket fence along the front. A swing set and slide took up one side of the yard, a sandbox, the other. It could have been the backdrop for a Norman Rockwell painting.

And Eva's mother, who was short and round and rosy—cheeked, looked as though she belonged there in the painting as well. She greeted me with a dishtowel in her hands and a host of young children hanging on to the hem of her skirt.

She laughed, and spoke before I had a chance. "No, they're not all mine." She rumpled the head of a blond toddler, then added, "Though I'm as fond of them as if they were. Sunshine Day Care. They provide the sunshine, I provide the care. What can I do for you?"

I introduced myself. "I'd like to talk to you about Cheryl Newcomb."

"Oh dear, she isn't in trouble, is she?"

"She's missing." I explained my interest in the case, relying heavily on my association with Nancy Walker. "The police seem to think she's run away."

The oven buzzer sounded from the other room. "Come in, why don't you? I'm in the middle of fixing lunch for this bunch of rascals, but we can talk while I finish up."

She sent the children off to wash up, then led me to the kitchen. "Poor Cheryl," she said, taking a large pot from the stove. "What happened?"

"No one seems to know. She hasn't been at school all week, or at home. Her mother thought she was staying with friends."

"Staying with friends," Mrs. Holland humphed. "I don't suppose that mother of hers ever thought to check *which* friend. You just wonder what a woman like that uses for a brain." She set spoons and napkins on the table, then poured five glasses of milk. "And the string of boyfriends the woman's had! I'm surprised she can keep their names straight."

"What about Cheryl's father? Is he around?"

"She never mentioned him. At least not to me. Eva might know, though."

"Are your daughter and Cheryl still friends?"

"They don't see each other very often now that they're at different schools. Much to my sorrow. Cheryl was always sweet to Eva; she never made fun of her the way some kids did." Mrs. Holland sighed. "Eva doesn't have any real friends at the new school, but at least no one teases her either."

"I get the impression Cheryl wasn't a model child. Weren't you worried about her influence on Eva?"

"Pshaw. There's trouble and there's *trouble*. Too many people can't tell the difference, if you ask me. Cheryl isn't going to be on anybody's list of most likely to succeed, but deep down she's as sincere and decent a person as I've known."

The youngsters returned, hopping and giggling and jiggling every which way. Mrs. Holland scooped spaghetti onto plastic plates, then set a bowl of crackers in the middle of the table.

"Poor, poor child," she said again. "And to think she sat right here in my kitchen only last Saturday."

"Cheryl was here?"

"She stopped by to see Eva. Didn't stay but about ten minutes. She'd been over at the school. Seeing as how it was Saturday, she was pretty sure Eva would be home, so she came to say hello."

"What time was this?"

"A little after noon, if I recall. I asked her to stay for lunch, but she was in a hurry to get home. I can't imagine why. Her mother wouldn't have known whether she was there or not."

"Did she happen to say why she'd been at school?"

Mrs. Holland shook her head.

"How did she seem? Worried, upset?"

"Not really. Mostly she and Eva talked about school and people they knew. I was in and out of the room, so I didn't hear everything. She wasn't all bubbly the way she was last time we saw her, though."

"When was that?"

"Let's see, it was sometime after the first of the year. I'm sure that's when she told me she had a boyfriend. When I asked her about him on Saturday though, she looked at me like I was crazy. 'What boy would ever want me?' is what she said. Just about broke my heart."

"Do you remember anything else about Saturday?"

She shook her head. "I'm sorry."

"Will you ask Eva, see if she does?" I wrote my name and number on a slip of paper. "Anything at all."

Mrs. Holland promised she'd speak to her daughter that afternoon. "I only wish I could do more," she said. "I have a warm spot in my heart for that girl. She deserves better than she's got."

18

Loretta was happy to see me, and even happier to see the box of dog treats I'd picked up at the store on my way home. She pranced at my feet, then plopped herself down near the cupboard and thumped her short tail hard against the linoleum floor.

She was so obviously pregnant I couldn't believe I'd missed it. I felt like one of those women in the supermarket tabloids, the ones who give birth and then utter in amazement, "And I thought it was just the stomach flu." For a person trained in logic and keen observation, it was not an encouraging comparison.

While Loretta chewed on her snack, I put away the groceries, then called the vet and made an appointment for the next day. This was as much for my benefit as hers. Nothing short of a fully–equipped canine delivery room would give me real peace of mind. Lacking that, I wanted advice.

Then I made myself a cup of tea and pulled out the photograph of Cheryl. What struck me immediately was how young she seemed. Fresh and unsophisticated in a way many girls her age are not. She was small–boned, with a pale complexion, thin, almost invisible brows, and straight brown hair that hung limply to her shoulders. Her eyes were an unusual shade, almost teal, and her smile so tentative you wanted to smile back in encouragement.

While I sipped my tea, I studied the photo, trying to unlock its secrets. I squinted through half-closed lids, as though that would enable me to read her soul. Then I put the picture into an envelope, hastily scribbled a note to Beverly Silverstein and walked down to the mailbox at the end of the road.

Was I building a castle of sand, finding design in mere coincidence? Possibly. Probably, in fact. After all, it wasn't the first time the girl had run away. And there were dozens of plausible reasons why she and Eddie might have each, independently, ended up on campus that day.

But then why had Eddie jotted Cheryl's phone number on his desk calendar that Saturday?

The phone was ringing when I returned from my trip to the mailbox. I scurried to catch it in time, but I might as well have saved my energy. There was a brief moment's silence, followed by a click. Telemarketing, I thought with disgust. Phones dialing other phones, automatically.

As if to prove my point, the phone rang again. This time, however, it was a honest to goodness call, the woman from Goodwill Industries calling to arrange a pickup date. I'd told her a week ago I would have the boxes ready by Friday. But a week ago the only thing on my mind had been the injustice of Sabrina's hasty departure.

"I'm sorry," I told her, "I've been so busy with . . . with

other things that I haven't finished going through all the rooms yet."

"You take all the time you need, darling. You only have one father. Saying good-bye is always harder than we expect."

I thought of the upstairs bedroom I'd been avoiding, the desk I hadn't gone back to since finding the cache of letters my father had been saving. The situation with Jannine had kept me busy, but in all honesty, I had to admit it wasn't the only thing holding me up.

"It shouldn't be much longer," I told the woman. "I'll get on it this afternoon."

But instead of running off to sort through my parents' old bedroom, the one my father had abandoned the day my mother died, I pulled out the box Jannine had given me and went through the tavern papers a second time.

The numbers added up, just as they had the night before. Maybe an accountant would see something I'd missed, though. It was worth a try. There was a chance I could find somebody in town who would be willing to take a look that afternoon. I started to put the pages in order. The two year-end statements, followed by half a dozen sheets of random monthly figures.

It was when I was putting the monthly accounts in chronological order that I noticed Baker Janitorial and Maintenance. It was listed under the column of expenditures for September. $95. That's why the name had seemed familiar to me when Vicky mentioned it; I'd undoubtedly seen it when I'd gone over the accounts before.

As I was clipping the whole pile together, I happened to glance at the statement for this past April. Baker was no longer listed. Instead, there was an entry for Foothill Cleaning, at a monthly charge of $600.

I believe the old adage "you get what you pay for," but that was quite a jump.

Out of curiosity I unclipped the sheaf of papers and once again pulled out September. Expenses for April, the most recent month I had, were nearly eight hundred dollars higher than for the previous September.

And this in a period of economic recession.

I got out the phone book and called Baker first. Luckily it wasn't Vicky who answered, but a gravelly-voiced male who turned out to be Baker himself.

"I'm a lawyer going over the books for The Mine Shaft," I explained. Another statement which was technically true but not entirely accurate. "I was wondering . . ."

Baker cut me off gruffly. "We don't do work for them anymore."

"Yes, I know that, but . . ."

"Ten years we have, Marrero and me. Ten years of hard work and trust, and he tosses it out the window the minute he gets a better deal. Won't even give me a chance to see if we can work it out." Baker snorted. "I don't have to talk to no lawyer of his. I don't owe him nothing."

He hung up with a deafening clunk.

I tried looking up the number for Foothill next, and came up empty-handed. The listings jumped from Foothill Acupuncture Center to Foothill Florist. It took me only a minute to come up with an alternate plan, however. I called the tavern and held my breath, praying I would reach someone besides George. My good angel was looking out for me.

"Hi," I said to the voice that wasn't George, "my husband and I are opening a small deli in town. We're looking for someone to clean up a couple of times a month, you know, a janitorial service. Well, my husband talked to somebody over there at your place and got a recommendation, but then, well, he lost the slip of paper he wrote it down on. Do you think you could give me the name and address again?"

"You need to talk to the owner. I don't know much about that stuff." There was some commotion on the other end, then the voice said, "Wait a minute. Hey, Wally, what's the name of the guy who cleans up on Sundays, Jose something."

Wally didn't know the last name either, but he knew the address because he'd given the guy a ride once when his truck broke down. I thanked him effusively, which wasn't an act, then headed over to pay a visit to Foothill Cleaning.

I had trouble finding the place at first because Foothill's office wasn't an office, but a tiny, rundown shanty in the hills outside of town. The woman who opened the door was young, Hispanic and very pregnant. She didn't understand English, and she didn't understand my fractured Spanish either.

"Un momento," she said finally.

That I understood.

She left and returned a few moments later with a man whose grasp of English wasn't much greater. He, at least, could make some sense of my Spanish.

"George Marrero, The Mine Shaft," I said, articulating carefully.

"Sí."

"Do you clean for him? *Límpia?*" I made a sweeping motion with my arms as though I held a broom.

The man looked at me warily. *"Es migra?"*

"No," I answered, *"amiga."* I was no friend of George's, but I didn't want Jose worrying that I was from immigration either.

He grinned broadly. *"Sí. Limpío."* He rattled off something else I couldn't make out.

"Es su patron?" I asked. Is he your boss?

The man nodded. *"Trabajo mucho,"* he said, and continued speaking rapidly, gesturing with his hands to make his point.

That was the extent of our conversation, and I'd understood only parts of it, but it told me all I really needed to know. George Marrero had replaced a reputable, long-standing cleaning service with cheap, probably illegal, labor. Jose might very well do a top-notch job, but I was willing to bet he wasn't getting paid six hundred a month for his efforts.

What's more, I had a pretty good idea where the money *was* going.

California businesses using a name different from that of the owner are required to file a fictitious name statement. This is public information that can be obtained through either the county or the Secretary of State's office in Sacramento. The road to Sacramento is four–lane interstate a good part of the way, but it was still a long drive. I decided to head for Jacksonville, the county seat, instead. I thought it would be quicker, but I'd forgotten what Friday afternoon is like. By the time I made it to the courthouse, having poked along behind every tractor and Winnebago in the county, I was in ill–humor.

The two women behind the front counter were busy

chatting. I waited politely for a couple of minutes while they discussed someone named Milo, whose first wife was bleeding him dry. When the story showed no signs of winding down, I cleared my throat and asked to see the records for Foothill Cleaning. The woman closest to me took the information, snapped her gum, then went back to talking to her friend. Finally, they moved together toward the record area at the back. When they returned, they'd moved on to discussing a Mike, whose finances seemed in better shape. He'd apparently just purchased a large and expensive boat.

While they debated the best attire for boating, I glanced at the listing of fictitious names. It was just as I expected—George Marrero doing business as Foothill Cleaning. He was skimming money from the bar into his own pocket. He probably paid Jose in cash, a *de minimis* amount at best. The healthy check to Foothill Cleaning went into an account of his own. There was a good chance the janitorial scam wasn't the only one he was running, either.

It wasn't a pretty picture, but it explained why George had been so eager to keep Eddie from becoming involved. Duping Eddie's father had probably been fairly easy. It was my guess he'd never looked at the books, just taken what his brother doled out. George had skimmed cash off the top, an easy thing to do in a business like his, and then divvied up the remaining profits.

But with Eddie in the picture, things changed. He was young and enthusiastic, ready to jump in with both feet. Eddie wanted to understand the numbers; he wanted things to add up.

No longer able to pocket cash, George had set up a dummy business or two. Everything looked fine on paper, but the money still found its way to George's pocket.

That much fit pretty comfortably. The next step was a big one, though. I let it play out in my mind slowly.

George hadn't simply wanted to keep the business to himself. He'd wanted to cover up the fact that he was embezzling funds.

Had Eddie caught on?

Had George killed him to keep him quiet?

Dead men don't talk. It's about as common a motive for murder as you can find.

Without more, it wouldn't convince a jury. But I was hoping it would be enough to convince Benson. Or at least get his attention.

19

After my experience with afternoon traffic on the way over, I was afraid I wouldn't make it back to Silver Creek before Benson left for the weekend. In person might be better, but by telephone was definitely quicker. I found a pay phone in the lobby and called.

I might as well have saved my quarters.

"You're grasping at straws," Benson told me. "Trying to deflect attention from your friend."

"I'm not grasping at straws," I replied evenly. "I am trying to find out who really killed Eddie. If you ask me, it looks like George has a pretty good motive."

"Kali, if you look hard enough, you can find any number of people with motives of some sort." It was the same mildly indulgent tone a father might use when explaining to his son the necessity of daily bathing.

"Bilking your partner, cheating the IRS—covering up something like that is pretty substantial."

"It could be a legitimate business, you know. Nothing says a guy can't use the services of one of his own companies."

"Unless it involves fraud. He'd probably know about Jannine's gun too, since he's family. And he postponed his Saturday departure for Tucson at the last minute."

Benson sighed. I could imagine his heavy jowls vibrating with the effort. "All right, I'll make a note of it and have someone look into the possibility next week. That make you happy?"

I would have been happier if I hadn't had the impression he was doing it strictly as a favor to his old friend's daughter. "There might be a couple of other suppliers he's doing the same thing with. You want me to check them out?"

"No, we'll take it from here." There was a pause. "I don't suppose you've managed to convince Jannine she'd be better off cooperating with us?"

"She *is* cooperating."

"You know what I mean."

It was my turn to sigh. "Haven't you been listening to me? She didn't kill him."

"We've got a pretty good case, Kali. I'm only trying to make it easier on her."

After I'd hung up, I realized I should have asked about Cheryl. Not that he'd have told me anything. Not that I was so sure it mattered any longer. With what I'd uncovered about George, the pieces fit rather nicely. Eddie running into Cheryl at school Saturday morning now seemed irrelevant.

The only thing was, Eddie's murder aside, I found myself caring about the girl. I knew what it was to feel alone in the world, to have a parent who wouldn't acknowledge your pain or confusion, a parent who looked right through you, as though you weren't there at all.

But I also knew that on the streets, feeling unloved wasn't the worst thing that could happen to you.

By the time Tom arrived that evening, I'd managed to work myself out of the funk I'd fallen into after my call to Benson. If the police weren't willing to investigate George Marrero, I'd do it myself. That thought, plus a short walk, a long, hot shower, and my favorite scooped neck blouse did wonders for my disposition.

The notion of spending the evening with Tom didn't hurt either.

"Don't you look spiffy," he said, eyeing me in a way that made my skin tingle.

He looked rather spiffy himself, I thought. Snug jeans, plaid flannel shirt, and his proverbial cat-who-ate-the-canary smile. He smelled nice too, like a bar of fresh soap, which wasn't surprising I guess, given that the curls on the nape of his neck were still damp from the shower.

"I brought you something," he said, and handed me an off-sized paperback, *Why Dogs Have Puppies and Other Imponderables.* "I debated between that and *The Complete Book of Dog Care.*"

"You're all heart."

He laughed. "You're getting old, Red. Fifteen years ago you'd have thrown the book at me and probably stomped your foot, too."

"I never stomped."

"Oh, but you did. So hard your curls used to bounce." He eased himself onto the sofa, then cocked his head and studied me. "Old, but as beautiful as ever."

"Oh, come on."

"What, you don't think you're beautiful?"

It was my turn to laugh. "No, I don't think I'm old."

The phone rang, and I went to answer it, trying to remember if my hair had ever been curly enough to bounce.

When I picked up the receiver there was a moment's silence, followed by a click. I shrugged and went back to the other room.

"Your boyfriend again?"

"It wasn't Ken who called the other night. I told you that. It was a woman I work with."

"Ken? Hey, that's cute. Ken and Kali."

"Oh, for Pete's sake." I picked up an embroidered pillow and tossed it at him.

Then we both waited to see if I'd stomp my foot.

"Come on," he said, standing with a stretch, "let's get going."

I grabbed my purse and then thought to grab a jacket as well. The evening had turned breezy, with a smell of rain in the air. Already huge, dark clouds were drifting across the sky, cutting daylight short.

"Do you think we could stop by The Mine Shaft?" I asked on the way to Tom's truck. "We don't have to stay long, but I'd like to see it on a busy night."

"This about Eddie Marrero?"

"More or less."

Tom shot me a sideways glance, and waited.

"I think George has been skimming money from the business, and that's why he wanted to keep Eddie out." I filled him in on what I'd found that afternoon. "If Eddie hadn't already discovered what was going on, he was bound to sooner or later."

Tom rubbed his chin thoughtfully. "I don't know, palming a couple hundred a month . . ."

"It could be more."

"Palming even a thousand a month, it's not big time corruption, Kali. Murder is. That's a big leap."

It was the same argument I'd had with myself earlier. "People have been killed over a whole lot less," I observed.

Tom nodded, his forehead creased in thought. "You told me George and Eddie had worked everything out, though."

"Maybe they had, and then George changed his mind. Or maybe George only wanted Eddie to *think* things were resolved."

Tom drove in silence for a moment. "Makes as much sense as anything, I guess. What are you going to do next?"

"I'm not sure. I was hoping Benson would be interested enough that I wouldn't have to do anything."

"And he wasn't?"

"He said he'd have someone look into it, but he wasn't exactly boiling over with enthusiasm."

"Maybe he'll turn up something all the same."

"Maybe. But I'd better not count on it. If George killed Eddie, there's *bound* to be something that ties him to it. I just have to find what it is."

Tom kept his eyes on the road, squinting into the growing darkness. "You'll be careful?"

"I'm always careful."

"I'm serious, Kali. This is murder we're talking about."

"What are you, my keeper?"

He looked over at me, then shook his head and laughed. "You always were stubborn as a mule."

The Mine Shaft wasn't my kind of establishment, but it clearly had no shortage of enthusiasts. The place was packed, the air thick with smoke and booze and sweat. We found stools at the bar and ordered beer, shouting to be heard over the din of laughter and the sharp, penetrating crack of dice.

It was a man's bar, the kind of local hangout which attracted a regular, steady clientele, in this case mostly middle-aged and paunchy. There was a good deal of calling out to friends across the room, and an equal measure of amicable joshing. It was the sort of place you could almost call homey, if you were inclined to think of a bar in those terms. I wasn't, but I could understand how some people might, and why George hadn't been eager to embrace Eddie's plans for live music and fried zucchini appetizers.

At the other end of the bar, George was listening to the animated retelling of a story with countless repetitions of "And then I says to him." When the tale ended, both men laughed uproariously. George leaned across the bar top to add a final thought. Then he saw us, and straightened.

I gave him my best smile, but he turned away so quickly I doubt he saw it. "That's him," I whispered to Tom, who turned and followed my glance.

"I don't know what he does with the money he skims," Tom whispered back, "but he sure doesn't spend it on clothes."

Or, as far as I had been able to tell, on fancy cars or a fancy lifestyle. "His wife has cancer," I said. "He might need money for medical bills."

Then again, some people didn't need a reason. They simply couldn't see the point in taking any less than what they could get away with.

We finished our beers and headed back to the truck. "You find what you were looking for?" Tom asked.

"I wasn't looking for anything in particular. Sometimes it helps just to get a firsthand impression." Although I had to admit, in this case, it hadn't. In all honesty, I couldn't even say that Foothill Cleaning did anything less than a first–rate job.

Then I sent all the ugly, uncomfortable thoughts packing, and focused on enjoying myself.

The RoundUp was more my kind of place, lively and funky, and homey too, in a different sort of way. We drank beer, and munched on chips and guacamole while we waited for our burgers. Then we switched to French fries and onion rings, and a second pitcher of beer. At nine, the band came on and the place began to buzz with a high–keyed energy. Intermittent whoops and hollers rang out from around the room. And occasionally a long coyote-like howl.

The band was surprisingly good. Their songs ranged from foot-stomping bluegrass to soft ballads, and we danced and laughed like a couple of teenagers. Later in the evening, the crowd thinned out, and the songs became slower.

Our dancing slowed, too. I found myself draped against Tom, feet barely moving. I could feel his breath on my neck, his hands anchored against the small of my back. It was a nice sensation. Hell, more than nice. And I felt it through my entire body, like ripples in water.

It was after midnight when we left. The rain, which had been threatening earlier in the evening, was coming down now in earnest, pelting the roof as though it were being dumped from the sky by the bucketful. The hum of the heater, the regular rhythm of the wipers, the windows clouded with mist—it was the kind of night that makes you feel that time has stopped, that the rest of the world doesn't exist.

Sliding over, I rested my head against Tom's shoulder. I had that warm, fuzzy, delectable feeling, like the weightlessness of a dream. I thought of the several foil packets of Trojans I'd slipped into my purse earlier that evening, and smiled.

The smile was short–lived, however. Tom pulled into my driveway, walked me to the door and kissed me lightly. He was gone before I had a chance to invite him in.

Talk about wounded pride. I kicked open the door, slammed it shut behind me and hurled my purse, with its damned packets of Trojans, against the floor. The warm, fuzzy feeling evaporated somewhere in the process.

In the corner of my mind, I remembered seeing something on the porch. Something I'd overlooked in my anger. I flipped on the light, and sure enough, there off to the side of the doormat was a long florist's box. Guiltily, I thought of Ken, who had a way of surprising me sometimes. Maybe he wasn't as aloof and insensitive as I'd begun to think. Maybe he simply had a different style.

I took the box inside and ripped open the card.

"Bon Voyage." And it wasn't signed.

I felt a flicker of disappointment. The flowers weren't from Ken after all. They weren't even for me. How could a delivery get so fouled up when there were only three houses on the entire road? And then I opened the box.

And screamed.

I ran to the bathroom and vomited. When my stomach had stopped rolling up into my throat, I rinsed my mouth and splashed water on my face and tried to think what I should do about the pulpy, bloody mess in the box.

I could try the police, although it was hardly an emergency. In any case, I would rather wait until morning when I could reach Benson directly. I could call Ken, who might or might not offer solace, and who would certainly be annoyed at being woken from a sound sleep. Or I could swallow my pride and call Tom. Which is what I did. But Tom wasn't in, or wasn't answering. I cursed him anew and hugged my arms tightly across my chest.

Loretta wandered into the room and peered at me with deep brown eyes. Then she put her head in my lap, gently nuzzling me with her nose, and whimpered in commiseration. I scratched her head and whimpered back. When the phone rang, we both jumped.

After an initial silence a voice said, "Did you get my message? Better start packing, missy. Unless you're waiting for a formal sendoff." And then the line went dead. The words were faint and muffled, but they sent ice through my veins.

I tried Tom again, and he answered on the second ring.

"Tom. Something awful . . ." I blurbled, not at all lawyerlike, not at all ladylike. "I got this package, this . . . this . . . oh God, and then this phone call. Would you mind coming over? Please?"

He was there in less than a minute, clearly worried, but unruffled at the same time. It was the kind of stoic, take-charge attitude the situation required.

"Fish guts," he said, inspecting the florist box and then dropping it into a large plastic sack. "Lots of them."

I swallowed hard and tried to force a laugh. "Oh, only fish guts." But the laugh caught in my throat and came out as a croak instead. I'd stopped shaking, but my insides felt like Jello.

"Tell me again what happened." Tom sat down opposite me and cupped my hands in his, giving them a quick, reassuring squeeze.

I told him about finding the box and the card, and then about the phone call.

"What about the voice?"

I shook my head. "It was disguised. I couldn't even tell if it was male or female."

"And you didn't hear anything as you were coming into the house?"

I shook my head again. "It has to be tied into my investigation of Eddie's murder, though." I suppose I should have been feeling pleased. Threats were usually a sign you were on to something. But logic lost out. There was nothing at all good about the way I felt. "It's the only explanation that makes any sense," I added. "Jose must have told George about my visit this afternoon, and now George is trying to scare me off."

"Even that doesn't make a whole lot of sense, though. You've already uncovered the fact that George was lining his own pockets. Scaring you off now isn't going to change that."

I nodded numbly. Tom had a point.

"Unless," he said slowly, "it isn't simply the fact that George was taking money, but what he was *doing* with it."

That made sense, too. But what sort of trouble could he have bought himself into? And what sort of trouble was grave enough to lead a man to murder?

I shivered, thinking of the possibilities.

"You sure you don't want to call the police?" Tom asked.

"I'm sure. There's nothing they can do tonight except take a report. I'll talk to Benson in the morning."

"How about some brandy then? You look like you could use it."

We each had a glass of brandy. And then another. Somewhere along the way we moved from the kitchen chairs to the living room couch, and from supportive hand-holding to more amorous snuggling.

At one point I nuzzled my head into the crook of his neck and asked where he'd been the first time I'd called.

"I took a walk," Tom said.

"In the rain? Whatever for?"

An embarrassed smile. "It seemed preferable to a cold shower."

"There was another alternative, you know."

"That was the problem," he said. "I didn't really know."

So I showed him, and in the end we made use of the Trojans after all.

20

" "You got a florist box containing *what?*" The young desk sergeant had that fresh, all-American look you find in Pepsi commercials, but his eager smile had given way to wary skepticism.

"Fish guts," I said for the second time, handing him the plastic sack. Benson wasn't going to be in until Monday, and I wasn't eager to hold onto the evidence in the interval.

The sergeant opened the bag, then closed it again quickly. His Adam's apple bobbed up and down a couple of times as he held off a choke. "You want to make a report?"

I nodded. The young man rolled a printed form into his typewriter. When everything was adjusted to his satisfaction, the sergeant cleared his throat and blinked at me. Then he took down my story, typing carefully, one painstaking word at a time.

"I think it might be related to the Marrero murder," I told him when we'd finished.

His eyes widened, and his Adam's apple bobbed again. "What makes you think that?"

"It's a long story. Chief Benson knows all about it. You'll make sure he gets a copy of this as soon as possible?" I hoped that was enough to keep the report from finding its way to the bottom of the processing pile. "I'm a lawyer. Jannine Marrero is my client."

"Ah," he said, sitting up straighter, "I see." But his expression said he didn't see the connection at all.

"You want my fingerprints or anything, for comparison?"

'Someone will contact you later if that's necessary." He smiled another wholesome American smile. "You have a nice weekend now, ma'am, and thank you for coming in."

At least he hadn't added, "Hope to see you again real soon."

He turned back to the baseball game he'd been watching when I came in, and I went off to retrieve Loretta. I'd left her tethered to a tree in the plaza in front of the station. She was curled up contentedly on the warm cement, but she lifted her head when I approached.

The vet had given her a clean bill of health, and me a list of dos and don'ts - *don't worry* being number one on the list. Easy for him to say. Until a week ago, I'd never so much as walked a dog, and now, suddenly, I would be responsible for a whole family of them.

Loretta, who seemed to be taking the vet's advice to heart, sauntered blithely along behind me on the way to the car. She climbed in and settled herself by the window, then whimpered softly until I rolled it down a crack. I backed out of the parking space, trying hard to ignore the nose smudges on the windows and the muddy paw prints stretched across my lovely leather upholstery.

Back home, I poured her a bowl of Kibbles and made myself a cup of instant coffee—vile–tasting, fully caffeinated stuff that I hoped would keep me awake through the afternoon. It had been late when Tom and I made it to bed, and a whole heck of a lot later by the time we made it to sleep. And then Tom had bounced out of bed at 6:00 that morning.

"Cub Scout camping trip," he explained.

"At this hour?"

He looked at his watch and grinned. "I guess if I skipped breakfast, I could wait till seven."

He did, though we hadn't used the extra hour for catching up on our sleep.

I yawned and wrapped myself for a moment in the pleasant memory of Tom. As long as I didn't *think* about it, didn't try to make sense of it, I was okay. The thinking part left me feeling shaky and a little short of breath. Without really reflecting on the matter, I'd sort of gone with the moment, yielding to what felt good. The fact that it still felt good was troublesome.

Then I took another gulp of the brown swill, got out the phone book and went to work.

There are a limited number of financial institutions in the towns neighboring Silver Creek, and I got lucky on my fourth call. The woman at Great Northern Savings was happy to verify that Foothill Cleaning did indeed have an account there, but she was unable, or unwilling, to tell me anything further.

I didn't actually expect to be any more persuasive in person, but I was running out of ideas. I hopped into the car, which now smelled decidedly doggy, and drove to the Sierra Vista branch of Great Northern, a different and smaller branch than the one I'd called. Along the way I tried to figure out what it was I was after, and how to best go about getting it. I had only a murky idea about the first part, and none at all about the second.

Sierra Vista is a sleepy little hamlet about twenty minutes from Silver Creek, and far enough off the main highway that it's been more or less overlooked in the great rush of development. Great Northern, situated at the far end of the town's main street, was housed in a narrow masonry building that looked as though it had been there since the Gold Rush days. The interior had been refurbished, but none too recently. The floor was uneven, the desks wooden, the walls painted a dingy gray. If it hadn't been for the massive grill at the vault entrance and the computer terminals posted about the room, you'd have thought you'd stepped into an authentic assayer's office rather than a modern-day bank.

The teller, a gentleman almost as old as the building itself, suggested I speak with Mrs. Lee and pointed me in the direction of an open office at the back.

Mrs. Lee was a tiny Asian woman with a dusting of gray at her temples. Looking up from the pile on her desk, she greeted me with a smile. Standard banking practice, I know. But hers was a genuine, from-the-soul smile that caused me a momentary tremor of guilt. Nice people deserve better than I was about to deliver.

"Lovely children," I said, nodding at the large photograph on her desk. That part was sincere. They were two girls, one about three, the other maybe nine or ten. Both had the same chin-length hair, dark eyes and exquisite doll-like features as their mother.

Mrs. Lee laughed. "They're lovely sometimes, not so

lovely others. Those angelic faces fool everybody. Now, what can I do for you?"

And here is where it got hard.

"I'd like to verify an account," I said, taking a seat across from her. Start with what you already know and build momentum. It's an old lawyer trick. "Foothill Cleaning. They're a new customer of ours. They want to purchase supplies on an open account and, well, we've had some trouble in the past collecting from these small, family-owned businesses. They always have the best intentions, but things don't work out quite the way they expect. Cash gets short, you know how it goes."

She turned to the computer on her left, flipped on the screen, hit a few keys, waited and then typed in a name. "Yes," she said, smiling, "they do have an account with us. No problems to date."

"Could you give me a ball park figure on the balance, and maybe some feeling for overall activity?"

The dark eyes grew darker. "I'm so sorry. I can't do that without a written release. Do you have one? Or maybe a letter from them authorizing us to give you the information?"

"Yes, I do. Or did." I began to fidget, which wasn't a hard act to pull off under the circumstances. "But that's the trouble. See, I was supposed to do this yesterday, and I forgot. The file is at the office." I lowered my eyes. "I've only worked there a couple of weeks. If I don't have this information for Mr. Gregory by Monday morning, he'll be really angry. And with my being a new employee and all . . ."

Mrs. Lee smiled sympathetically. "I really am sorry. I wish I could help, but I can't. Not without a signed release."

"Maybe you could ask your supervisor?"

She looked dubious.

"Please? Then I'll at least know I've done everything I can."

She dimmed the screen and went into an office at the back. Quickly, I scooted my chair closer to the screen, and turned it up again. There seemed to be regular deposits of $600, then withdrawals of an equal amount one or two days later. There were always exactly one hundred dollars left in the account, probably the minimum required by the bank. There were no other deposits or withdrawals.

It confirmed what I'd already suspected. Foothill Cleaning was a shell, a vehicle for skimming money from the tavern.

Mrs. Lee still hadn't reappeared. I hit the "page up" key and scanned the screen. The names on the account leapt out at me almost immediately, George Marraro and Carla Newcomb. It was the second name that gave me a jolt. What connection could there possibly be between Cheryl's mother and Eddie's uncle?

I turned the screen off again and slid my chair over just as Mrs. Lee returned with her supervisor, an older man with a stern face. I repeated my song and dance, although I had trouble sounding as desperate as I had the first time around.

"Sorry," he said, when I'd finished. "The rules are clear."

Another person might have gloated, not Mrs. Lee. She looked at me with those soft brown eyes of hers, and I felt like a real heel.

"I'm so sorry," she said. "You come back first thing Monday morning with the letter and I will get you the information you need. We will do it quickly, and you can get back to your boss right away. He will never know you let it slip on Friday."

As I stepped outside into the bright afternoon sun, my head was swimming. Carla Newcomb. What did *that* mean? What *could* it mean? I wound the information through my brain and came up with nothing. I was pretty certain Foothill Cleaning wasn't a legitimate business. Not with only one deposit and one withdrawal each month. But I had no idea what it was.

I started with the one thing I was sure of. George Marrero was skimming money. And he wasn't in it alone. So what was he up to? Drugs? Gambling? Was he feeding the money through Carla or was he paying her off? And where did Cheryl fit into all this? I was, by now, convinced her disappearance was no coincidence.

It was only mid-afternoon, but I felt drained, ready to settle in with a mind-numbing evening of television. Or better yet, skip the television and head straight for bed, diving into the soothing nothingness of sleep.

But I must have something of the Puritan in me, because instead of heading home, I drove straight to Carla's.

She was sitting on the top porch step, next to her collection of plastic pink geraniums, painting her nails and getting an early start on her tan. The radio was pulsing out a tune about love gone bad, and Carla was humming along between drags on her cigarette and chugs of her beer. She didn't hear me approach, and looked up only when my shadow darkened the steps. The hand holding the nail brush jerked, sending a streak of scarlet up the back of her finger.

"Geez, you scared me," she said, squinting into the sun. "I didn't see you until just now."

"Sorry, I didn't mean to."

She dabbed at the errant polish with a tissue, then finished the fingers on her left hand.

"Remember me?" I asked, in competition with a radio commercial for Pizza Hut. "I'm the woman who spoke with you last week about your daughter."

Carla looked up and squinted again. "That's right. I thought you looked familiar."

"Any word from her?" I took a seat one step below.

Carla fanned the wet nails and took a long swallow of beer. "You want one?"

I shook my head. "Thanks, though."

She reached over and turned down the radio to a level that almost permitted conversation. "No word. The police sent her description out over the wire. They've got some kind of network, and they're checking with her friends, that sort of thing. But they say it's mostly a waiting game. Nobody fitting her description has taken a bus out of here lately. 'Course that doesn't mean much. Cheryl'd be the type to hitch a ride anyway."

Carla recapped the polish, shook the bottle and then began on her right hand. I was fascinated by the process. My nails are relatively short, more square than tapered, and almost always bare. Not by choice, but because I've never mastered the art of doing them myself and have neither the time nor patience for trips to a manicurist. Carla made it look so easy. I thought maybe I should give it another try.

"She took my money, you know. Money I was saving for a new dishwasher. The one we've got's been busted almost a year."

"Did she leave any kind of note?"

"Nope, nothing. Just took some clothes and stuff, and ran off like she was Miss High-and-Mighty. That's the way she is, always has been."

I listened for the fear in her voice, for the anxiety you'd expect from the mother of a missing girl. If it was there, it was buried deep beneath the anger.

"Aren't you worried?" I asked.

Carla had finished with the right hand and held it out to dry. "Yeah, a little. But I'm also fed up. You don't know what it's like, having a daughter like that. There's things I go without 'cause of her, breaks I can't take advantage of, but does she appreciate it? No. She thinks the world revolves around her and her alone."

"Hey, Poochie," a male voice called from inside the house.

"I'm out front," Carla called back, then turned once again to address me. "And the lies! Every Thursday night, sometimes more, she's off to drama. Stays out real late too, but I figure what the heck, she's involved in something, thing means something to her. Come to find out she's never even been to one class. God knows what she was doing out until all hours. Trouble, that's for sure."

I'd forgotten about the drama class.

"She's run away before, a couple of times."

"Where'd she go then?"

"Once to a friend's, once to my sister's in Reno."

"You've checked with your sister?"

"Yeah, she hasn't seen Cheryl since that time she ended up there last year. My sister's hardly someone you'd want to run *to*. I think Cheryl figured that out pretty quick."

"Hey, Poochie." The voice was at the door this time. "I

need twenty bucks for the . . ." He saw me, and his voice trailed off.

Carla yelled over her shoulder. "There's money in my purse, but don't you go taking more than twenty. You owe me enough as it is." Then she finished off her beer, lit a cigarette and began painting her toenails. "Seems sometimes like everybody thinks I owe them a living."

I couldn't speak to her relationship with Mr. Charm, but I thought she had overlooked the fact that she *did* owe Cheryl a living, and a whole lot more. But I could understand her frustration, too.

"Mothers and daughters usually have a rough time of it," I told her. Although, interestingly, my own mother and I hadn't. I liked to think it was because of the kind of person she was, but it may simply have been that she died before I'd reached a difficult age.

"Other people have nice things to say about Cheryl. As a mother, you get most of the grief and none of the good." What I was trying to say, diplomatically, was that Carla's take on her daughter was probably skewed.

"What good?"

"Mrs. Walker, her English teacher, thinks Cheryl is a hard worker. And Eva Holland's mother . . ."

"Eva, now there's a good one. Last year Cheryl was over at Eva's every chance she got. Wasn't until this fall I find out Eva's a retard. Can you believe it, my daughter's best friend is a retard? Now that says something, don't it?"

She expected easy agreement, which she didn't get, but my silence didn't make a dent.

"She'll come home fast enough," Carla said, "once she finds out there's no one there to cook her meals and pick up after her." She finished with one foot and began on the other. "You got news about Cheryl, or is this just a social call?"

"Neither actually. I wanted to ask you about George Marrero."

The hand with the brush stopped mid-nail. It was one of those moments, those almost imperceptible flickers in time, when everything stands still. Then Carla gave me a bewildered smile and was suddenly absorbed again in her nail–painting. "Who?" she asked.

"George Marrero. He owns The Mine Shaft."

She shook her head. "Sorry, doesn't ring a bell."

"And Foothill Cleaning."

She shook her head again, but her face froze up. "Never heard of him."

"That's funny, the two of you have a joint account at Great Northern Savings."

"I don't know what you're talking about." Her eyes were riveted on her feet.

"I think you do."

Carla straightened and recapped the polish. The little toe on her left foot was still bare. "I think you'd better leave. I have stuff to do."

"Look, I said, "I don't know what's going on here, but Eddie Marrero is dead, and his wife isn't the one who killed him He and his uncle locked horns over the tavern. I think George was trying real hard to keep Eddie from finding out what you two were up to. If he's guilty of murder,   ere's a good chance you're going to get dragged into it. Maybe if you level with me, I can help."

She'd grabbed her pack of cigarettes and headed, barefoot, for the door, but she stopped short and turned to look at me. The expression in her eyes was hard to read, but whatever it was, it was genuine.

"Who did you say was dead?"

"Eddie Marrero, the coach. I spoke to you about him the other day."

"Great Jesus." Her voice was a thin, flat whisper. "Marrero . . . I never . . . I didn't . . ." The words came in spurts, as though she were having trouble breathing. Then she turned abruptly and went into the house without meeting my eyes. I heard the deadbolt slip into place behind her.

So much for the easy, innocent explanation I'd half–expected. "Why, yes, George hired me to do their book-keeping," or, with a laugh, "Gracious, George's wife and I are old friends, and we got this bee in our bonnet about starting our own cleaning business."

Not that I'd *really* expected it. But I've found that sometimes the quirkiest things are, in truth, quite simple. It was foolish not to look for those explanations first.

Now I knew. It wasn't simple. And I had the feeling it wasn't clean. But I didn't know much more than that. And what was worse, there wasn't a whole lot more I could do without invoking the powers of the law, which in this case were not mine to invoke. I could try leaving still another message for Benson, but I knew I'd have to wait until Monday morning when he was back at work.

I had just kicked off my shoes and sprawled out on the couch for a moment's rest when the phone rang. It was Ken.

"When did you get back?" I asked.

"Last night. I've been trying to reach you since early this morning."

Ken's idea of early is some time before ten. Remembering what I'd been doing at six, I was glad he wasn't an early riser. "How was D.C.?" I asked.

"You know how it is. I was pretty busy."

"Was this about the Quigley case?"

"Not directly."

I waited. Ken is one of those attorneys who can go on and on about a case and think he's had a meaningful discussion. But this time, apparently, he had nothing more to say.

"I got your message," he said, instead. "You're sure you can't come back for a couple of days?"

"Not right now."

"I need to see you." Ken's words seemed to surprise him as much as they did me. He cleared his throat. "I mean, it's been awhile."

I smiled to myself. He'd actually missed me. Then I remembered Tom, and felt a wave of guilt. I'd been trying all day to sort out my feelings. I hadn't made much progress.

"I'll be home by your birthday," I told him. "Think about what you'd like to do, and I'll make reservations. I could throw a party if you'd prefer."

"At my age birthdays are best forgotten." He laughed lightly, then lapsed into silence. "They have services that will come in and clean out the whole estate, you know. You don't have to do it all yourself."

"I know, but I want to. Besides, that's not all that's been keeping me busy."

"You're not still rummaging around in that murder business, are you?"

Silence.

"Isn't that a job for the police?"

"Except the police seem ready to pin it on my friend."

"They must have their reasons."

"Cops make mistakes, Ken. That's what the legal system is all about."

Ken humphed. "They don't make them very often."

As a litigator, Ken knows things are rarely black and white. Like many of his colleagues, however, he tends to forget that fact when it comes to issues of criminal defense.

We talked for a few minutes longer, about baseball, the weather, the cut of his new suit. I hung up feeling disjointed and unsettled. Or maybe I was simply tired.

Before I could make it back to the couch, though, the phone rang again.

"I think you should get over here," Mrs. Holland whispered. "Right away."

21

" " I found this in Eva's room," Mrs. Holland said, handing me a large manila mailing envelope. "She said Cheryl gave it to her last Saturday. For safekeeping."

Mrs. Holland's voice had a tight, breathless quality to it. Her usually expansive face was pinched and stiff. She looked from the envelope to my face, and then back to the envelope again.

"I could tell there was something bothering Eva the moment I mentioned Cheryl's name. Eva's almost childlike in that respect. Hasn't learned to guard her thoughts or feelings the way most us of have. But she wouldn't tell me what it was until today. Even then I had to pry it out of her. Cheryl made her promise not to tell anyone."

I turned the envelope over and looked at the front. It bore the official Silver Creek High School logo and return address, but was otherwise unmarked.

"It was sealed," Mrs. Holland said, twisting her hands in nervousness. "I opened it when Eva was in the other room. I thought it might be important, but I never expected anything like this."

Opening the tab, I slipped out the contents—a collection of eight by ten full color photographs. They weren't actually pornographic. By *Penthouse* standards, they were probably even tame. But they weren't family album snapshots either.

There were six photos in all. Each of a unclothed pubescent girl in a suggestive pose.

"That's Cheryl," Mrs. Holland said, pointing to the photograph on top.

The expression on Cheryl's face was so different from that of the photo Nancy had given me, that I'm not sure I'd have made the connection on my own.

"What about the others?" I asked. "Do you recognize any of them?"

"Only one." Mrs. Holland pulled a second photo from the pile. "Janet Harrington. She was a couple of years ahead of Eva and Cheryl. I knew the family because I used to baby sit for the younger brother. They moved away last year. The boy was a hellion, but Janet was so shy she wouldn't look me in the eyes when she said hello."

"This isn't a recent picture, then?"

"No, I'd guess it was taken a couple of years ago."

Sickened, I slipped the photos back into the envelope.

I've looked through my share of girlie magazines, and while I wouldn't pose for one myself, I don't fault those women who do. But this was something altogether different.

These were girls. Maybe not children exactly, but not grown women either. Not in body; not in mind. Despite the provocative stances, there was an innocence about them, a wide-eyed vulnerability that made the pictures especially offensive.

I turned to Mrs. Holland. "Did Cheryl say anything to Eva about what was in the envelope?"

She shook her head. "Not that I've been able to determine. She just told Eva to keep it for her, that it was a secret, and that she'd be back for it soon. Would you like to speak with Eva yourself?"

"If you wouldn't mind."

"She doesn't know about the pictures. You'll be careful what you say?"

I assured her I would, then followed her out back. A young girl sat on the grass, her head bent over a drawing board.

"Eva, honey, this is the lady I told you about. The one who's a friend of Cheryl's."

Eva looked up and smiled shyly. She was like a storybook nymph, slight and fragile, with pale skin and fine wispy hair so blonde it was almost transparent.

"She wants to ask you a few questions, honey. You just answer the best you can."

I sat down on the lawn opposite Eva. Mrs. Holland pulled an aluminum lawn chair over to the side and sat, too. "You and Cheryl are pretty good friends, am I right?"

Eva nodded.

"Your mom told you that Cheryl left home without telling anyone where she was going?"

Eva nodded again.

"We were hoping you could help us find her."

Eva looked over at her mother, then back down at the drawing board. "Is Cheryl going to get in trouble?"

"It depends. But I want to help her. So do others. We're worried about what might happen to her while she's away." I too looked over at Mrs. Holland, and she gave me a reassuring nod. "Sometimes when kids get angry or upset about something, running away seems like a good idea. But it's hard to make it on your own. It can be dangerous as well. We want to find Cheryl before anything bad happens to her."

I thought again of the photos, and wondered at the meaning of bad.

"Cheryl said there might be trouble."

"Trouble how?"

Eva shook her head. "Trouble, that's all I remember."

"I know Cheryl asked you not to tell about the envelope she gave you. She may have asked you not to tell other things, too. Sometimes, though, we have to break promises in order to help our friends."

From the next yard over came the squeals and laughter of children. I wondered if Eva was ever invited to play with them.

"It's like when you're in school," I continued. "You aren't supposed to speak out in the middle of class. The rule is you raise your hand and wait for the teacher to call on you. Right?"

Eva nodded.

"But if you saw that something dangerous was about to happen, a fire for instance, or something about to fall, it would be better to break the rule and yell out a warning, wouldn't it?"

Another silent nod.

"It's like that now, with Cheryl. It's okay to tell us what you know, even if she told you not to. It's a way to help her."

Eva picked up a colored pencil and went back to her drawing. I wasn't sure she'd understood what I was getting at.

"When she was here last Saturday, did Cheryl say anything to you about leaving or going away?"

Eva took her time erasing something in the corner of the page. "She had to leave to go home," Eva said at last. "She couldn't stay because she had to be there for the call."

"The call?"

"The phone call."

"Did she say who was calling her? Or what the call was about?"

Eva thought, then shook her head. "She had to be there, though. So he could tell her what to do."

"So who could tell her?"

Eva looked at me and sighed. "I told you, I don't know who."

"Did Cheryl ever mention a Mr. Marrero?" At that point I didn't know if I asking about George or Eddie, but I figured either one would be something.

"I'm not very good with names," Eva said. "I have trouble remembering things."

"How about teachers at school? Did she talk about them at all?"

"No, but they don't treat you like babies, Cheryl said. I wish I could have gone to Silver Creek, too."

I offered a sympathetic smile. "About the envelope Cheryl gave you. Did she say where she got it, or what she was going to do with it?"

Eva's face clouded over. "She's going to be mad at me, I know. It was very, very important, she said. It proved she wasn't stupid." Once again, Eva looked at her mother. "Cheryl kept talking about how dumb she was, but she *isn't* dumb. Cheryl is smart. I'm the one who's dumb."

Mrs. Holland gave her daughter a gentle smile. "You're

not dumb, honey. I've told you that. People are all different."

"Then how come everybody *says* I'm dumb?" Without waiting for an answer, Eva threw down her drawing board and ran into the house.

I looked at the drawing, a unicorn in a field of brightly colored flowers. It was surprisingly good. "I'm sorry I upset her."

Mrs. Holland shook her head. "It's not you," she murmured, her eyes following her daughter. Then she sighed deeply and turned her attention back to me. "So what do you think it all means?"

It was my turn to shake my head. It was obvious Eva didn't know anything about the photographs or about why Cheryl had run away, but that was only one piece of the puzzle. There was also the connection between George and Carla, whatever it was, and the fact that Carla's daughter, now missing, had been with Eddie only hours before his murder.

There were enough tie-ins there to make me think I was onto something, although none of the pieces fit the way I wanted them to. Especially the part about the photos. I didn't want to believe that Eddie, with daughters of his own, could be part of anything so unsavory. Yet the pictures were in a school envelope, and Cheryl had given them to Eva right after meeting with Eddie.

Then too, there was the matter of the ten thousand which had mysteriously appeared in the Marrero's checking account. Unsavory business was sometimes quite lucrative.

I continued to ponder the matter on the drive home. Short of confronting George or finding Cheryl, I couldn't think of a thing I could to that would bring me any closer to the truth. I wasn't sure I even wanted to know the truth. Except, of course, that it might save Jannine.

I spent the afternoon cleaning the large downstairs closet where my father had stashed everything from old linens to a broken toaster. Among the stash I found the silver-plated bread tray he and my mother won in a dancing contest. The tray had become something of a family joke almost immediately. Sabrina and I, always on diets, refused to eat bread. John, who ate a loaf a day, preferred it three slices at a time, straight from the plastic bag. But my mother had claimed, only half jokingly, that the bread tray was the most elegant gift she'd ever received. For a while there, it had adorned our dinner table every night, amid much light-hearted banter. It's one of the last recollections I have of my mother. I wrapped the tray in tissue and set it aside.

By the time I'd finished packing everything away in boxes, dusk had fallen. My body ached, my mind was a muddle and my four–footed friend was getting impatient. I washed the grime from my hands and arms, changed shoes, and took Loretta for a stroll.

It was that time between sunset and nightfall, when the sky is a deep indigo, seeming to stretch on forever. A quarter moon hung on the horizon, and a single star flickered overhead.

Star light, star bright, first star I see tonight . . .

If only it were that easy.

I thought about George and Carla and Cheryl, and wished for answers. I thought about Jannine and Eddie, and wished there was some way to undo all that had happened. And when that didn't get me anywhere, I thought about my own life, about where it was headed and where I wanted it to go. No shortage of wishes there either.

It wasn't wishes that troubled me, however, so much as questions.

And they did nothing but lead me in circles.

I ambled along, my mind a hundred miles away. Which is why I didn't see the car until it was almost on top of me.

It was coming from the opposite direction, on the same side of the street I was walking along. A large, light–colored model that seemed to appear out of nowhere. Its engine accelerated, then it swerved in my direction, heading off the pavement and onto the wide shoulder. The headlights flashed on, blinding me. I froze.

The rest is a blur. Instinctively, I must have leapt out of the way, tripping over a fallen tree in the process. I tumbled onto the jagged rocks beyond the roadway. My shoulder and face hit first, bare flesh scraping against the hard, rough surface. My left leg twisted under me, and a searing flash of pain shot through my knee.

I heard a dull thud as the car collided with the stump of the tree. The impact was like a small earthquake. A cloud of dust rose up, stinging my eyes and filling my mouth and nose with grit.

For a moment, there was an eerie silence. Even the pine branches overhead, illuminated by the car's headlights, were still. Then the car gunned its engine and shot backwards, momentarily spinning out in the soft dirt at the edge of the pavement before swinging onto the road.

I lay without moving while my heart dropped from my throat and my insides unscrambled. Finally, I began to test the extent of my injuries. I ran my tongue around my mouth. Although I could taste blood, my teeth appeared to be secure. I could move my fingers and toes, and recite

the names of the last four presidents in reverse chronological order. My left eye was already beginning to swell,
giving me a somewhat distorted angle of vision, and my
knee throbbed, but as far as I could tell I was in one piece.

I was trying to garner the strength to move when I
heard a soft whimper behind me.

Loretta. Had she been hurt?

Twisting my head, I looked around, straining to see in
the growing darkness. Nothing. And then I twisted the
other way. Almost immediately, I met up with a cold, wet
nose. It prodded and poked and then nuzzled against my
neck. "Hello, girl," I said, running a hand along her
back and legs. Her tail thumped hard against my ribs.

I wrapped my arms around her plump, warm body and
buried my face in her fur. For a long time, neither of us
moved.

When I finally stood, my legs were weak and shaky.
Nonetheless, I managed to limp home, taking frequent
rests along the way. I made myself stop thinking about
the pain, but I couldn't make my mind stop reliving the
incident.

Had the driver been some reckless teenager out for a
wild Saturday night? Or had he deliberately swerved in
my direction?

Was I right in thinking the car had been a white American full-sized model like the one I'd noticed at Carla's?
And the one that had doubled back and nearly collided
with me earlier that same day.

After my experience with the fish guts I was under-
standably nervous. Was I also paranoid?

I let myself into the house, stripped out of my clothes
and took a long, hot shower. The water stung my face and

hands, but it felt wonderful on the rest of me. I dried myself gingerly and applied ointment to the scrapes and
cuts. Then I pulled on a pair of loose–fitting sweats, gave
Loretta another once over, checking for injuries I might
have missed, and sat down with paper and pencil to see if
I could make sense of the day's events. I doodled my initials in the right-hand margin, a flower in the left, got up
to get a glass of wine, then changed my mind and put on
a kettle for tea instead. My mother had been a tea
drinker. I could remember coming home from school
winter afternoons to a warm house that smelled of lemon
and spice. She would fix us a snack and then sit at the
table with us, sipping her tea and listening to the chroni-
cles of our day.

I paced the kitchen, checked the lock on the back
door, hugged my arms across my chest. The water was
taking forever to boil. I picked up the pencil, doodled
some more, then put it down again when I noticed my
hand was trembling. Despite the heat of the day, the
house seemed suddenly, inexplicably, cold. In fact, I was
shivering so hard I was actually shaking. Then it dawned
on me that what I felt was scared. Scared and alone.

I turned off the stove, reached for the phone and invited myself to Jannine's.

22

"Holy cow, Kali, what happened to you?"

I hadn't told Jannine about my encounter with tree limbs and hard granite. Now I thought maybe I should have prepared her.

"I was walking the dog," I explained. "A car almost ran me over."

"Are you okay? What did the doctor say?"

"I didn't call a doctor. I'm fine, just sore is all."

She looked dubious. "Was the guy drunk or something?"

"I don't know. I never saw him."

"You mean he didn't stop to help?" She let the screen door flop shut behind us. "That's a hit–and–run, isn't it?"

"He didn't exactly hit me. It just seemed like he was about to."

"Still, you should report it."

I'd seen enough of police headquarters, and I thought they'd probably seen enough of me. I wasn't anxious to go waltzing in with still another complaint. Besides, there wasn't a lot I could tell them.

"It all happened pretty fast. And it was getting dark, so I didn't see much anyway." I considered sharing my suspicions about the driver aiming for me, then decided against it. Jannine had enough to worry about. "I'm fine," I told her, "really. I just didn't feel like being alone right now."

"Of course you didn't," she soothed. "Come on, I'll make you a drink, a stiff one." She settled me into one of the kitchen chairs, guiding me as though I were a decrepit old woman. "How about food, have you eaten?"

I remembered I hadn't.

Jannine set a glass of straight Scotch in front of me, then poured herself a heavily watered version of the same. "The kids and I had boxed macaroni and cheese for dinner. There's some left. Or I could make you a sandwich. The only bread we have is the squishy white stuff, but I've got some good salami."

"A sandwich sounds wonderful."

She opened the fridge and began pulling out ingredients. "I hear you were out with Tom Lawrence last night."

"How'd you hear that?"

"Eddie's uncle." She began shaving off thin slices of salami. "He said you stopped by the tavern for a drink."

"He called just to tell you that?"

"Of course not. He dropped by this afternoon to see how we were getting along. He offered to lend me money until I get my feet under me. Isn't that generous?"

I'd spent a good part of the last two days thinking about George Marrero. Generous was not a word I'd have used. In fact, it made me wonder about the timing of his visit.

Jannine handed me my sandwich and took the seat across from me. "So tell me," she said, elbows on the table, an eager, school-girl expression on her face, "was it a *real* date or an old friends kind of thing?"

That was a question I'd asked myself, although not in quite those terms. "A little of both, I guess." I bit into the sandwich hungrily. The bread formed a layer of paste on the roof of my mouth, and I had to pry it loose with my tongue. Even so, it was delicious.

"I see him around town now and then. He's a good-looking guy, kind of sexy in a way."

My mouth was full so I smiled blandly. I thought it was a bit more than "kind of."

Jannine stared off into space while I chewed. "You know," she said, after a moment, "there've been moments when I really envied you. Single, no one to answer to, all those glamourous and exciting men, the fascinating adventures."

I laughed. "It's not quite the way you make it sound."

She laughed back. "Maybe. 'Course I never did have your pizazz, and now, on top of that, I'm fat and dumb, and I've got four kids."

"You're not—"

Jannine cut me off with a feeble smile. "You can't deny I've got four kids." The smile vanished, and her face closed down. She stared hard at the golden liquid in her glass. Finally, she sighed. "Now that I'm single, I can't imagine why I ever found the idea attractive."

I reached across the table to squeeze her hand. Before I could say anything, Erin strolled into the room, a set of headphones plugged into her ears. She glanced briefly in my direction, turned away and then turned back. She removed the headphones and draped them around her neck. "You run into Godzilla or something?"

"Erin!" Jannine screeched the way mothers do.

"It's okay." I gave Erin one of my all-purpose smiles. "I tripped over a fallen tree and landed on some rocks. It looks worse than it is."

Erin pulled a can of diet soda from the refrigerator and popped the tab. "Maybe you should get glasses or something."

"Erin." Jannine tried again, but Erin had already left. "Sorry," she said, turning to me. "Erin's in one of her moods."

"Don't worry about it. Seems like only yesterday I used to pull stuff like that myself. Besides, my face *has* looked better."

"Eddie's death hit her pretty hard. Harder than the others, I think. She's at that age—the two of them were quite close."

The photographs I'd seen that afternoon were etched in my mind. Girls only a year or two older than Erin. Eddie couldn't have had anything to do with it, I was sure. The school envelope didn't necessarily mean anything. Cheryl could have picked it up while she was working in the office.

But if I was so sure, why did the very idea cause my stomach to knot up?

Jannine took my empty plate and stuck it in the dishwasher. Then she poured us each a second drink and suggested we move into the living room. She directed me to the sofa and settled me into the downy pillows, tucking and plumping them around me.

The Scotch had helped. My body still ached, but the

pain was muted, as though it were calling to me from a great distance. Even the growing tightness around my left eye didn't bother me much.

"Tell me about Cheryl Newcomb," I said. "She sits for you, doesn't she?"

"Occasionally, when Erin is busy. Eddie and I never went out all that often."

"She a family friend?"

Jannine shook her head. "Eddie knew her through school. One of the few advantages of being a teacher. We never had trouble finding a sitter."

"Has she been here recently?"

"Not for about a month. She was supposed to help out at that party Friday night, the one you were at. She cancelled at the last minute, though."

"Did she say why?"

"I didn't talk to her. Eddie did. I guess she got sick or something. Usually she's pretty reliable."

"She's run away from home. Nobody's seen her since last Sunday."

Jannine frowned. "I heard. Cheryl always struck me as an unhappy kid putting up a brave front. The kind you worry about because you know she can't keep it up forever. I feel bad that I didn't try harder to reach out to her."

"You ever talk to her?"

"A couple of times. She and Eddie got on pretty well, but she never said much to me."

"She was at school last Saturday morning. One of the students saw her walking with Eddie."

Jannine nodded and shrugged at the same time.

"Eddie also wrote her phone number on his desk calendar that day."

A simple nod this time. "Eddie was always making notes to himself."

I paused and took a swallow of my drink. I'd thought I was working up to telling Jannine about the photographs, but I found I couldn't. Not while there was still the possibility that Eddie was somehow involved.

"You're sure Eddie knew her through school and not through some tie-in with his uncle?"

"George?" Jannine looked at me as though I'd sprung antlers. "What makes you ask that?"

"George and Cheryl's mother have a . . . a business connection."

"You sure? I remember one time Cheryl sat for us. George dropped something off here just as we were leaving. Eddie introduced them, and George was barely polite. You'd think he'd have said something if he knew her mother."

I nodded absently. You'd certainly have thought so. Unless George's connection with Carla was something he wanted kept quiet.

"Did George say anything else about me when he stopped by this afternoon? Other than reporting the latest developments of my love life, that is."

Jannine gave me another one of those looks. "He just happened to mention it in passing, Kali. It isn't like he particularly cares who you go out with." She kicked off her shoes and pulled her feet up under her. "He did ask, though, if you'd found anything about the tavern in that box of Eddie's stuff I gave you. Have you had a chance to look through it?"

Here was another chance. Maybe I couldn't bring myself to tell her about the photographs, but I could tell her what I'd learned about George.

"Jannine," I said slowly, "there are some—"

I stopped when Lily walked in. She'd gotten the zipper of her yellow fleece pajamas stuck and needed Jannine's help. When the zipper was once again free, she climbed into her mother's lap and pulled Jannine's arms around her, like a shawl. It was a capture-the-moment picture Kodak would have been proud of, and it touched one of those places deep inside I try to keep hidden.

"I found a couple of loose pages," I said lamely, looking down at my glass. "They were just copies, but I'll get them back to you all the same."

"Did you find anything that was helpful?"

I shook my head, suddenly aware that I felt uncomfortable. It had been a mistake coming to Jannine's. There was simply too much I wasn't telling her.

"I may be on to something, though. I'll know in a day or two." I stood and yawned. My earlier shakiness had been supplanted by bone-deep exhaustion. "I think I'll head back."

"You're welcome to stay here. I have an extra toothbrush."

"I'll be okay. Thanks for taking care of me this evening, though."

"Gracious, Kali, you don't have to thank me for that." She walked me to the door, then hesitated. "Did you talk to Vicky?"

I nodded.

She gave me a funny smile. "I figured you would."

We were silent a moment.

"What's she like?" Jannine said finally. Her voice had an unfamiliar scratchiness to it. "Besides being beautiful, I mean."

"She isn't even beautiful. Blonde and skinny, but that's about it."

Jannine sighed. "That's enough, isn't it?" Then she hugged her arms across her chest. "Vicky couldn't have known him as well as I did, though, or loved him as much."

I had no doubt about the love. But when I thought of the pictures, I wondered if there was a side of Eddie Jannine hadn't known at all.

23

It took me a long time to fall asleep that night, and when I finally did, the quiet comfort I'd sought eluded me. I slept fitfully, like a dog hunting in his dreams. What woke me a little after two, however, was neither my aching body nor the demons I'd been chasing in my mind. It was a sound. A sound so faint, so fleeting, that once I was fully awake, I wasn't sure I'd actually heard it.

I glanced at the clock, using its green glow as a beacon to orient myself. I lay perfectly still, barely breathing, straining to hear through the surrounding blackness.

For a long time there was nothing, then I heard it again. A soft, rhythmic crunching, like footsteps.

The sound stopped. I waited, my heart pounding in my ears. It had seemed to come from outside, by the driveway. I listened hard for other, closer sounds. I thought I heard a creak. And then nothing.

The only telephone was in the kitchen, at the front of the house. The stretch of darkness between here and there was like uncharted space. A void of untold peril.

But I couldn't simply lie there either.

I slid out of bed as if in slow motion, pulled on a pair of jeans and a shirt. As I reached for my shoes, my arm knocked against the nightstand. I froze, anticipating a quickened shuffling in response.

But the house was still.

Then I heard a low hiss, coming again from somewhere outside.

Moving as quickly as I dared, I felt my way along the wall to the bedroom closet where my father kept his shotgun. I'd left it there, out of harm's reach, when I'd learned Goodwill wouldn't accept firearms.

I hadn't fired a gun since my father had taken me duck hunting for my thirteenth birthday. I'd practiced all summer on old cans out back, and I hit a duck almost immediately. I strutted along behind my father when we went to retrieve it. And then vomited as I watched him ring its neck for the final kill. I haven't eaten duck since. Nor, until that night, had I touched a gun.

I felt for the box of shells, slid one into each chamber and another two into my pocket. Not that the extras offered much beyond peace of mind. If I had to reload, it was already too late.

At the closet door I stopped to listen again. Then I carefully tiptoed into the kitchen, checking for unexpected shadows along the way. It was a warm night, and I'd left the windows cracked, but as far as I could tell, none had been opened farther. The back porch door remained locked as well.

It was small comfort, but it was something.

I was reaching for the phone when I heard a frantic scurrying outside, followed by a loud crash. Then car alarm began to shrill. And mingled in with all of it was the yelping of a very agitated dog. I went to the front door and flipped on the outside lights.

There, where I'd parked it earlier, was my lovely, new BMW—with tires slashed, a window shattered, and kindergarten–style splashes of red paint covering the doors and hood. My heart, which had been in my throat for what seemed an eternity, dropped suddenly to the pit of my stomach. Not even a thousand miles on the odometer, and the thing looked ready for the salvage yard.

What with the alarm's wailing and Loretta's yapping and my heart dropping, it took a moment to make out the figure sprawled on the car's roof—George Marrero, hunched on all fours, intent on fending off Loretta with a can of spray paint.

I unlocked the door and stepped slowly out, keeping the gun raised and ready. The alarm continued to wail, and Loretta continued to yap so I had to scream to make myself heard. "I've got a gun here," I shouted, "so don't try anything funny."

"Call him off," George shouted back. "Call the goddamn dog off." His face glistened, and there were dark circles of sweat under his arms.

"It's a *her*," I said, "not a him."

"Call *her* off then, for Christ's sake." In desperation, George flung the can at Loretta, missing her by several feet.

This, of course, only made Loretta bark more frantically. And her tail wag even harder. In spite of whatever guard dog instincts she may have possessed, she was clearly having the time of her life. It was probably the most excitement she'd seen.

George had leaned over to toss the can, and now pulled back as Loretta leapt once again against the side of the car. "Call her off, would you." It came out as an order rather than a request.

I readied the gun, then called Loretta's name, as much to protect what was left of the car's finish as to appease George. In an instant, she stopped her barking and sat, but her body continued to wiggle with excitement.

"Can't you put the gun away, too?" he asked.

"You must be joking."

The car alarm cycled off, and I lowered my voice. But I raised the gun to eye level. I wished now I'd thought to phone the police before coming outside. I was having a hard time figuring out the logistics of keeping my eye on George and calling the cops at the same time. "Slide down off the car now, nice and slow. Keep your hands where I can see them."

"You going to hold the dog?"

"Move it," I said, keeping my voice low and gruff.

George hesitated, his eyes wide and fixed on Loretta.

"Oh, for goodness sakes." I grabbed her collar, and George slid off the roof. There was a sharp grating sound as the metal from his belt buckle scratched the car's finish. I winced.

"I knew this was a stupid idea," he said when he was once again on firm ground.

"Damn right, it's stupid. And a whole lot more."

"It wasn't *my* idea in the first place."

"Whose was it then?" George started to tuck his hands in his pockets. "Hands up," I told him, "on top of your head." The hands went up, begrudgingly.

"It was Carla's idea. I told her it wouldn't work."

"Carla?"

"She was only trying to help me out. I mean, it's not

really her problem. Look, do I really have to keep my hands up like this? I feel ridiculous."

"Is that so?" He wasn't winning my sympathy. "Keep your hands where they are and start moving toward the house."

"What are we going to do?"

"*You're* not going to do anything. *I'm* going to call the police."

"The police?"

"What did you expect, a sit-down meal?"

"Listen, I know you're upset, but do you really *have* to call the police? I'd prefer that this whole thing didn't get out."

George hadn't budged, and I was getting angrier by the minute. "Get moving."

He started for the porch, dragging his feet like a schoolboy. I followed, one hand on the gun, the other on Loretta's collar.

Once inside, I ordered him to sit against the far wall of the living room. There was nothing there he could grab as a weapon, and I could see him easily from the phone in the kitchen. I kept Loretta in tow, as though I were restraining her. Only a person truly terrified by dogs would have been fooled, but George apparently fit the description.

"I'll pay for the damage," he said, lowering himself awkwardly onto the threadbare rug. "The paint is water soluble, and I can have someone out to replace the tires first thing in the morning. The window was an accident. The damn dog was chasing me, so I threw a brick. Only I missed and hit the window."

I backed into the kitchen, keeping the gun pointed at George.

"I was just trying to scare you off, is all," George said.

"Yeah, well you've made your point loud and clear." I held the gun over my forearm, freeing my hands for the phone. "But you're a little late. I've pretty much figured it out. You've been skimming money from the business, probably have been for years. You managed to cheat Eddie's father pretty easily, but you knew it would be hard to pull that kind of stunt with Eddie. That's why you were so anxious to buy Susie's interest and force him out. When she decided to sell to Eddie instead, you got desperate and killed him."

"Killed him?" George mopped his brow with the back of his sleeve. "Surely you don't think—"

"You and Carla have a nice little scam going there with Foothill Cleaning. Tell me, what do you do with the money? Is it drugs?"

"You think that *I* killed Eddie?" His voice had a kind of squeak to it, like a broken record. "Are you out of your mind?"

"We'll let the police decide that. And while we're at it, maybe you can tell them about Cheryl, too."

George stared at me. His face went white, and fresh beads of sweat appeared on his brow. Then he dropped his head to his hands and moaned. "I should have known. You can't keep a thing like that quiet."

It had been something of a stab in the dark, but it appeared I'd been right. "Those photos may not be technically obscene, but that's irrelevant when you're dealing with girls that age." My disgust was apparent in the tone of my voice. "Did you ever stop to think what it would do to them, about the emotional scars something like that would leave?"

George remained hunched over. "' don't know what you're talking about," he mumbled.

"I think you do."

He shook his head. "I didn't kill Eddie. And if you think I'd do anything to harm Cheryl, you're crazy." He looked up. "After all, she's my only child."

24

"Maybe it would be best," I said, hanging up the phone and moving back into the living room, "if you started at the beginning."

George stared glumly at his two thumbs.

"Is Cheryl involved in this scam you and Carla are running?"

"It's not a scam. All I'm trying to do is help support my daughter."

"Opening a phony business account is a funny way to go about it."

"Yeah, well I couldn't exactly write a personal check, now could I? Not without Gloria finding out." He moved his eyes from his thumbs to my face. "Look, can I move to the sofa or something? My back is killing me."

I nodded, but kept the gun ready. George pushed himself off the floor and lumbered to the sofa. He sat heavily, arms crossed against his chest.

"Go on," I said.

He took a deep breath and let it out slowly. "Carla and I had an affair. A long time ago."

"Like fifteen years?"

The look he gave me was biting. "My wife and I were going through a rough time, and Carla was . . . well, there was something almost electric about her. At least I thought so at the time."

George's face no longer glistened with sweat, but he looked uncomfortable all the same. He shifted, uncrossing and then recrossing his arms. "We'd been seeing each other about six months when she told me she was pregnant. I offered to pay for an abortion, but she wasn't interested. I don't know whether she really wanted a kid, or just some hold over me. By then some of the novelty had begun to wear off. I think she realized I was pulling away."

"So she blackmailed you?"

"It wasn't blackmail, really. Carla asked for support, and I agreed. There was always the chance she would take me to court and sue for support anyway. This way I could keep it quiet, keep Gloria from finding out."

Sounded an awful lot like blackmail to me, but I guess maybe, like the glass that's either half-full or half-empty, it's all in how you look at it.

"It was right about then that my wife developed cancer. We'd tried for years to have a child ourselves. Lots of waiting and two miscarriages. Then with the cancer, she had to have a hysterectomy. Learning about Carla would have destroyed her."

"And Carla accepted this arrangement?" I asked. I'd known a woman in a similar situation. She'd gone after the gold band as well.

"Once she realized I wasn't going to leave Gloria, I guess she figured there was nothing to be gained by creating a scene. She was already getting money. And then she met up with some new guy not long after. By the time that died out, there was a lot of distance between us."

I'd taken a seat across the room from George. Although I no longer had my finger on the trigger, the gun was in my lap, within easy reach. As a concession to the easy flow of words, however, I'd left Loretta locked in kitchen.

"But it was no scam," George insisted. "I never cheated my brother. I paid Carla off in cash from the business, but I kept tabs. He always got his fair share."

"Then when he died, you did everything you could to keep Eddie out."

"I offered to pay him fair and square, but he wouldn't give up." George mopped his brow. "Last thing I needed was somebody looking over my shoulder."

"So you phonied the books. You tried to fool him."

"I tried to protect Gloria." George smoothed his hair, looked at me, then looked away. "Eddie wanted to examine the books. He wanted an accounting of everything. So I came up with the idea of Foothill Cleaning. I'd make a deposit into the account, Carla would pull it out. The money flowed as it always had, only now it was accounted for. I didn't want Gloria to find out, especially now, when the cancer has returned."

"But Eddie figured it out anyway, right?"

"If only he hadn't been such a stickler for detail. The guy was obsessed with learning every aspect of the business. I offered him and Susie, both, a fair price. But he got this bee in his bonnet about running the business himself."

"So you killed him."

George blinked and leaned forward, half–rising out of his seat. A vein in his temple throbbed. "I told you before, I didn't kill him. He's family, for Christ's sake. My dead brother's son.''

"You have a pretty strong motive for wanting to see him dead."

"I wanted to keep this thing about Carla from blowing up, but I never wanted to see Eddie dead. What do you take me for anyway?"

When I didn't answer, George sat back and glared at me.

"You're right about one thing," he said finally. "Eddie figured out Foothill Cleaning was phony. Like I told you the other day, though, we'd reached an understanding. I hadn't wanted a partner at first, and Eddie, well, he was full of crazy ideas about expanding the business. But after he found out about Carla, we had a heart–to–heart. He understood. Was real nice about it. He could have held me up for money, or gone all righteous and threatened to tell his aunt. You never know about things like this. But he didn't. 'Course, he knew Cheryl, maybe that made a difference. Anyway, we made our peace. Hell, in the end I was looking forward to having him there. Some of his ideas were actually pretty good. Then suddenly, he's dead."

"You've got your business, and your secret is once again safe." I shook my head in wonder. "How convenient."

"You still don't believe me?"

"What about the pictures of Cheryl and the other girls?" I asked.

His brows furrowed. "What pictures?" He sounded genuinely perplexed.

"Pictures of nude teenaged girls. You don't know anything about that?"

He shook his head. "One of them was Cheryl?"

"One of Cheryl; five of other girls. Cheryl stashed the whole set at a friend's house right after she saw Eddie last Saturday morning."

I watched George carefully. Not a hint that any of it sounded familiar. I ran a what-if by him anyway. "Cheryl's your daughter. Eddie's involved her in something sleazy. Seems like that might be another reason you'd want to see him dead."

He shook his head. "I don't know anything about any pictures, and I didn't kill Eddie. How many times do I have to tell you that?"

I leaned forward. "Why did you and Gloria postpone your flight to Tucson at the last minute?"

"What's that got to do with anything?"

"You were supposed to leave Saturday morning, then you changed plans at the last minute and didn't leave until Sunday."

"Meaning?"

"Meaning you had everyone believing you were in Tucson, while in truth you were still in town when Eddie was killed. That's another convenient coincidence, don't you think?"

George tugged at his pants' leg and coughed. A dry, hoarse cough that brought a pink flush to his cheeks. "I was having prostate trouble," he said, averting his eyes. "We changed our flight so I could see the doctor. You can call him and check."

The guy looked embarrassed enough, maybe that part was true. "And what about me? What about this stuff with my car?"

The pink flush grew deeper. "Like I said, it was a stupid idea. Jannine mentioned that you had Eddie's files, and then at the funeral you started asking all those questions about the tavern. And you mentioned Cheryl. Last night, when you showed up with a newsman, I was already getting antsy, and then this morning I get a frantic call from Carla. I figured you were ready to blow the whole thing. I guess I panicked." He looked at me. "Carla made it sound so simple. She probably got the idea from one of those idiotic television shows she watches."

"Were the fish guts her idea, too?"

"What are you talking about? What fish guts?"

"And earlier this evening, were you only trying to scare me when you practically ran me over? You could have killed me, you know."

George shook his head in bewilderment. "Either you've got a good imagination, or there's something going on here I don't know about. I was at the tavern all evening. Ask anyone there."

"And you don't know anything about a florist's box filled with fish entrails?"

George choked. His complexion turned from pink to green. "You think I'd get involved in something like that? I can't even cut up a raw chicken without feeling sick."

We eyed each other warily.

"What kind of car do you drive?" I asked finally. I was suddenly aware that the answers weren't coming the way I wanted them to.

"A Toyota."

"What color?"

"Maroon. It's parked down at the bottom of the hill." He paused. "Look, if you call police on this, they'll make a formal report and that will lead to all kinds of trouble. There's no way I could keep something like that from Gloria, even if it didn't make the papers." His voice was strained, his tone almost pleading. He looked like a man cornered.

I hesitated.

"Please. Think about Gloria, about what it would do to her. I am sorry about your car, really. I'll have someone come out and take care of everything."

I was angry about the car, but involving the police wasn't going to get it fixed any quicker. And I'd taken a liking to Gloria when I met her. Besides, I was inclined to believe George. As far as his story went anyway. It made sense, though it left a lot of questions unanswered as well.

I looked toward the phone in the kitchen while I weighed my options. George shifted uncomfortably on the couch.

"I'll make it up to you," he croaked. "I promise."

In the end, I didn't make the call. Instead, I had him hand over his wallet and ruby ring, for security in case his story didn't check out. Then we walked together to his maroon Toyota, George in front, me following with the gun. He got in and drove away. I watched until the car disappeared from sight.

25

It had been a long night. I was still asleep when the doorbell rang a little after eleven the next morning. Groggy and sore, I hobbled to answer it.

Ken greeted me with a smug smile and a peck on the cheek. "Surprise!"

"What are you doing here?" I squinted at him with my one good eye.

He looked as though he were on his way to a polo match. Khaki slacks, crisp white shirt, blue pullover looped around his shoulders. It was a look he carried well.

"You couldn't make it to San Francisco, so I came here instead." The tone was jaunty, but there was an unfamiliar tightness to his voice. Even the smile was more restrained than usual. "It was kind of a last minute decision. I tried calling last night, but I guess you were out."

We moved from the doorway into the living room. I got another kiss, but it wasn't any more impassioned than the first. Ken sat and began drumming his fingers on the table top.

"You have any coffee? I could use a cup."

"Actually, I don't. I threw away my father's jar of instant when I cleaned out the kitchen, and I've run out of the good stuff from home. I could make tea, though."

Ken stopped his drumming. "How about I take you out for lunch instead?" He paused and raised an eyebrow. "Or is it breakfast?"

"I had a very late night," I said, deciding to leave it at that. "And I'd love to go out for something to eat. I don't think there's much of anything in the house."

His gaze drifted away and then back again. He'd been casting surreptitious glances at my swollen eye and scraped cheek since the moment I'd opened the door. Finally, curiosity got the better of good breeding.

"What happened to your face?" he asked, staring openly. "An accident? I saw the car window on my way in."

"The two things are unrelated." It was an observation which offered little comfort. If George was telling the truth, there was still someone wandering around who wanted me out of the picture, one way or the other.

Ken scrunched up his face and waited.

I opened my mouth to explain, then shut it again. The truth required more explanation than I had energy for. "The car was an accident," I told him. "As for my face, I fell." I headed for the bedroom. "Just give me a minute, and I'll be ready to go."

I left Ken to his own devices while I took a quick shower and got dressed. My face looked worse than it had the night before, and make-up didn't help much. It hurt too, as did my whole body. I ached in places I didn't even know I had.

When I returned to the living room, I found Ken sitting on the sofa, right where I'd left him. He was rubbing his temples with his fingertips, but glanced up when I came in. "All set?"

I nodded.

Ken hesitated a moment, then stood, offering me a lightning quick smile. It came and went almost in the same instant.

Out front, we passed by the BMW. True to his word, George had had someone out already that morning. The guy must have come and gone while I was still asleep, like the shoemaker's elf. But he'd done his job. The tires had been replaced, the broken window neatly covered with plastic, and the exterior cleaned. I was, however, able to detect a few new scratches.

As we climbed into Ken's car, which had not so much as a single nick or smudge anywhere, I tried to remember that in the great scheme of things, material possessions didn't count for much.

I directed Ken to Betty's Cafe, the only local spot I knew. When we pulled up in front, Ken frowned.

I shrugged. "This is Silver Creek. We don't have a Ritz-Carlton."

The Sunday morning crowd had begun to thin out. Here and there stragglers dawdled over the morning paper, but we had no trouble finding an empty booth. I ordered ham and eggs, and a side dish of French toast, having suddenly discovered that I was ravenous. Ken had an English muffin.

"It was nice of you to drive up here," I said, smiling at the thought of it. I was still having trouble believing he'd actually come. Ken's life is tightly scheduled. It doesn't leave a lot of room for spontaneity.

He reached across the table for my hand and gave it a gentle squeeze. I squeezed back.

I'd been waiting for that fluttery feeling I usually got around Ken, a feeling like butterflies beating their wings against my chest. It hadn't happened, but it was good to see him all the same.

"You want to go on a picnic this afternoon?" I asked. "The countryside is beautiful this time of year."

For a minute, Ken didn't say anything. He simply looked at me, glassy-eyed. Then he withdrew his hand and lowered his eyes. "I'm taking a job in D.C.," he said.

I heard the words, but it took a moment for them to register. "You're leaving the firm?"

"The firm is breaking apart." He looked up. "Wallace and Betts are going off on their own, Latham is retiring, Fisher and I are joining other firms. Turns out Goldman has been dipping into firm accounts, playing fast and loose with the funds. When our receivables went way up, it all came home to roost. He's taking full responsibility."

"What about the associates?"

Ken rubbed his thumbs against the side of his coffee mug. "I don't know. I guess it depends on what they can work out."

"They don't know?"

"We're going to make the announcement tomorrow."

I thought of my mortgage, my car payments, my student debt. I thought of the long hours I'd put into building my reputation. I remembered the horror stories from friends who'd suddenly found themselves jobless in a tight market. I felt sick—truly, physically, nauseous.

"Latham will give you a good recommendation, you

know. And I'll help in any way I can. You could probably even go with Wallace and Betts. They're talking about taking one or two associates with them."

Wallace and Betts were the sort of attorneys people had in mind when they told lawyer jokes. Besides that, they were arrogant chauvinists. I'd wait tables before I'd go with them.

"When are you leaving?"

"I start officially in D.C. a week from tomorrow, but I'll be back and forth quite a bit initially. It's hard leaving on a moment's notice. I've got to sell the house, tie up a few loose ends. You know how it is."

I nodded mutely. Not that I expected him to ask me to go along. I wouldn't have anyway. But it hurt that he hadn't acknowledged leaving anything more than a house and a few loose ends.

"It's a good opportunity," he said, looking enthusiastic for the first time all day. "The firm has good clients and solid political connections. It's the kind of work I've always wanted to do."

Across the room a young family was packing up after their meal. The mother piled stuffed animals and baby bottles into a cloth bag, while the father jiggled an infant in one of those plastic rockers. I pushed away my uneaten food. I noticed Ken hadn't touched his English muffin either.

"I'm sorry it had to happen like this, Kali. None of us had any idea how bad things really were. Not until this last partners' retreat. That's when it all started to unravel."

I nodded again. I couldn't think of a thing to say.

"I wanted to tell you in person, and before you heard it from someone else."

"Thanks." I meant that honestly. A round–trip drive of six hours must have weighed heavily against a simple phone call.

Ken paid the bill. We drove back to my father's house and sat around awkwardly for another forty-five minutes. We talked about other, more pleasant subjects, but there were still long periods of silence.

I was reminded of the first time we met, a recruitment lunch in which we'd struggled to find enough in common to get us through dessert. Ken had been engaged then, to the daughter of one of the firm's major clients. After the engagement was broken, and I never did get the full story, he'd shown up at every firm function with a different woman. Slender, usually blonde, always attractive in that blue-blood sort of way. I never gave him much thought during any of that time; he was a different breed than the sort of man I usually dated, as well as a partner in the firm. But when he invited me to attend a black-tie dinner at the Stanford Court, I did exactly what I'd promised myself I wouldn't do—I fell for the guy. Except that it had always been an uneasy infatuation.

Finally, Ken looked at his watch and announced that he had to be getting back. He put his arms around my neck and pulled me close. I could smell the familiar scents of aftershave and laundry starch. Pressing my cheek against the nubby fabric of his shirt, I closed my eyes and tried to remember the other, better, times.

After a moment, he held me at arm's length and looked me in the eye. "You're a good attorney, Kali. You'll do fine. This may even be a blessing in disguise. You never did fit the Goldman and Latham mold. And what's more important, you're a good person. They're even scarcer than good attorneys."

The words were nice, but they sounded too much like a eulogy to do much for my spirits.

"Maybe you can visit me in D.C.," he said.

"Maybe."

Silence.

"It wouldn't have worked anyway, you know."

I nodded. I did know. I'd probably known all along.

The doorbell rang just then. Ken went to get a drink of water, and I went to answer the door.

Tom leaned against the frame, grinning. He was coated in dust and smelled of wood smoke and pork fat. In an instant, the grin dropped. "What happened to your face?"

"It's a long story."

Before I could begin explaining, Ken returned from the kitchen. The two men scrutinized each other, poker face to poker face.

I cleared my throat. "Ken, Tom." No sooner had I made the introductions, than the phone rang.

I recognized Jannine's voice immediately.

"Kali, I need your help. I've been arrested."

26

I left Tom and Ken to work out the "how-do-you-know-Kali" connections on their own, and headed for the county jail. I'd taken time to put in a brief call to a bail bondsman I'd worked with in the city. He was standing by, but I knew we'd never be able to get a hearing on Sunday. Even Monday might be iffy.

It made me wonder. Had Silver Creek's finest deliberately timed the arrest for a weekend, giving Jannine added time to think about "cooperating"? Or had the arrest come on the tail of some fresh bit of damning evidence? While the first explanation rankled my sense of fair play, the second was by far more worrisome.

The street fronting the Hall of Justice was practically deserted. I parked, and out of habit locked the car. With the driver side window protected only by a flimsy sheet of plastic, it was a meaningless exercise.

The building was relatively new. A three–story structure which looked, from the outside, like the cookie-cutter office buildings which had been springing up throughout suburban areas of the state. The inside wasn't too bad. Austere and colorless, but not dreary. A definite step above its counterparts in San Francisco and Oakland.

I gave my name to the guard, and he had someone usher me to an upstairs room. It was sparsely furnished, with a bare table and four vinyl chairs. Though windowless and stuffy, it was at least clean. A strong disinfectant odor permeated the air.

Moments later, a police matron brought Jannine to the room and sat her at the table. "I'll be outside if you need me," the matron said to me. Apparently, Jannine's needs didn't count for much.

When the matron left, Jannine looked at me and burst into tears. "Get me out of here, Kali."

I sat next to her and hugged her hard. "I will, I promise. But I'm afraid it might not be right away."

"When *will* it be?" Jannine's shapeless prison-issue dress looked to be several sizes too large. Her face was shiny and scrubbed raw, her hair flew out in odd directions.

I took her hand. "Tomorrow maybe. Or it might be a lot longer."

"Tomorrow?" Her voice broke somewhere in the middle of the word. "You mean I have to spend the *night* here?"

"Probably. It might be Tuesday before we can even get a hearing. It all depends."

"On what?"

"The court calendar, the D.A.'s schedule, that sort of thing. They've got forty-eight hours to set a hearing, and weekends don't count."

She drew in a sharp breath. "I don't think I can stand it that long."

"I'll push for something as soon as possible, but I can't promise."

Jannine slumped down in her chair and drew a hand across her cheek, wiping at the tears.

"Have they been treating you okay?" I asked.

She nodded. "It's not that, it's just . . . just that everything is so *awful* here. I want to get out. Please, Kali. I need to get out of here."

"I'll try my best."

"The kids were so upset. They're frightened and worried, and I can't even *talk* to them."

"Where are they now?"

"With Mom. The police were nice about that at least. They let me call her from home."

"Do you need anything?"

She bit her lower lip, then shook her head.

"Tell me what happened when the police came."

"Not much. They said they had a warrant for my arrest, and they were going to take me in. Like I said, though, they were nice about it. We waited until Mom got there."

"You didn't let them question you, did you?"

"No, when they said that stuff about the right to an attorney, I told them I wanted to talk to you. I don't think they were particularly interested in asking questions anyway. They seem to think they already have all the answers." She pulled herself up straight, and sighed. "So what happens now?"

"There'll be a hearing where you are formally charged and you enter your plea. That's also when we deal with the question of bail and getting you out of here. Later, there will be another hearing where the D.A. will show that he has a case. Unless the judge throws it out at that point, there will be a trial."

Jannine blinked hard. "You really think it will come to that?"

"I'm afraid it might."

The tears began gathering again in the corners of her eyes. "But I'm innocent. They can't prove I killed him if I didn't."

They could, though. And that's what made the whole thing so frightening. "They'll put together a scenario that fits with the evidence they have. It's all circumstantial, but they'll use it to paint the picture they want."

I didn't bother to add that, from the state's perspective, the pieces fit rather nicely. Jannine's gun as the murder weapon, a witness who saw a blue car like hers in the vicinity of the murder, the fact she cleaned her car that afternoon, and the fact that she had no alibi. Add to it rumors of a rocky marriage and the neighbor's account of the fight Jannine and Eddic had that morning, and it made a pretty convincing story.

"The thing to remember," I told her, "is that the state has the burden of proof. All you have to do is show that their case leaves room for reasonable doubt, that there just *might* be a different way of looking at the evidence."

She bit her lower lip again and nodded.

"You should start thinking about *your* scenario of what happened. You need to make sure everything's covered and that everything is consistent. You don't want to be tripped up, and you don't want your attorney to be surprised by new revelations."

She nodded again. "I've told you everything I remember."

"I'll handle the arraignment and bail," I told her, "but you'll need someone else for trial."

Her face dropped. "Why?"

"I'm not a criminal attorney, for one thing."

"And *I'm* not a criminal."

"All the more reason you need an attorney with solid criminal experience."

"How am I going to pay someone like that?" She looked up from wringing her hands. "I didn't mean that the way it sounded. I expect to pay you, Kali, it's just that it won't be right away. Not until the insurance is settled and everything."

"It's not the money, Jannine, it's that I haven't handled a criminal case in almost five years. And I've never handled a big murder trial."

She closed her eyes against the tears.

"You have the right to have an attorney appointed by the court, you know."

"A public defender?" Her eyes opened, and her mouth twitched. "Me and the junkies and the bag ladies."

The idea didn't give me a lot of comfort either. There were exceptions, of course, but for the most part, public defenders were harried and overworked, more experienced at arranging plea bargains than aggressive trial defense.

"I'll stay involved," I told her. "I'll meet with the P.D., help out, see that nothing gets lost in the shuffle."

The matron stuck her head in. "Time's just about up. Couple more minutes is all."

"I'll see about getting you out of here today," I told Jannine. "If not, I'll be back first thing tomorrow morning. You hang in there. And don't worry, we'll work it out.

Okay?" I reached for her hand and held it tight a moment.

Jannine smiled, a tentative, sad smile. "I'm sorry to have put all this on you. It's just that I'm so scared. I don't know who else I can turn to."

"I want to help. I'm happy to do whatever I can."

She stood to leave and then turned back. "Oh, I almost forgot. The man from the bank called yesterday, about that ten thousand dollar deposit. It's the strangest thing. You'll never guess where the money came from." She shook her head. A bewildered half-laugh followed. "It was your father, of all people."

"My father?"

She nodded. "I can't figure it out either."

Why would my father give money to Eddie Marrero? I puzzled over the question and got nowhere. I couldn't even venture a wild guess.

I continued playing with it while I trudged downstairs to see the deputy D.A. about bail.

"On a Sunday afternoon?" he said. "Not a chance. Especially not for a felony."

"Tomorrow?"

"That's a possibility. But you'll have to talk to the chief about it. He's handling this one himself."

Which made me think we might very well go the full forty-eight hours.

On my way out, I ran into Benson. "I thought you were off duty this weekend," I said.

"So did I."

"But coming in to arrest a devoted mother with four young children, that was just too great an opportunity to pass up, right?"

"This wasn't my idea, if that's what you're thinking. The timing and the way it was handled, anyway. We took it to the D.A. last week. He was still wavering. Then boom, this morning he's ready to move."

"There's new evidence?"

He shook his head. "That's what's so odd. Maybe he's getting pressure from the higher-ups. I don't really know."

"Well, you guys have gone down the wrong path on this one."

He looked at me. His face was stern, but his eyes were kind. "I'm sorry, Kali, but I don't think so."

We passed through the lobby and into the glare of the afternoon sun. Benson turned to say something more, then stopped. "What happened to your face?" he asked, squinting in the brightness.

"There's a report waiting for you in your office, about a package of fish guts and a threatening note. I think this," I pointed to my eye, "was the past due notice."

"Huh?" While we walked to my car, I told him about both incidents. "And you think they're related to the Marrero case?"

"Why else would someone be after me?"

"No offense, Kali, but there could be any number of reasons. And the reason you're giving me, it just doesn't make sense."

"Unless Jannine is innocent, and the real killer wants to keep me from figuring out the truth."

Benson looked skeptical. "You got any ideas? Besides George Marrero, that is. I looked into that, like I told you I would. The guy was at the hospital all Saturday afternoon having some tests run."

I shook my head. "No ideas." I was plumb out of ideas,

in fact. Yet somebody obviously thought I was close to the truth. It was as frustrating as it was scary.

We arrived at my car, and I pulled out the keys. Benson examined the plastic sheeting covering the window. "Was this part of the past due notice?"

"No, that was something different."

He gave me that *see what I mean* look. "You got a way of finding trouble, Kali. Can't all be related to this case."

"The car that tried to run me over was white," I said, steering the conversation back to productive ground. "An American model."

"That doesn't narrow it down much. How about the phone call, male or female?"

"It was hard to tell."

Benson scratched his cheek.

I decided to let it drop. There wasn't anything he could do at that point. I was getting ready to slide into the car when I had another thought. "Did my father ever say anything to you about Eddie Marrero?"

"Not that I recall. Why?"

"He apparently gave, or lent, Eddie some money. Just recently. That's why Eddie could afford to buy his sister's share of the tavern."

Benson screwed up his face and stared off into space for a moment. It was a long moment, during which his jaw muscle worked furiously, but then his features dropped back into place. "Beats me," he said finally.

Tom was waiting for me when I returned to my father's place. He'd showered and changed, and somewhere along the way he had picked up some steaks. He had the barbecue out on the front patio, already lit, and a pitcher of margaritas, iced and ready to go.

"Didn't figure you'd feel much like cooking tonight," he said.

I wasn't sure I even felt like eating, but I accepted a margarita willingly. I certainly felt like drinking.

"Jannine doing okay?"

"Not great. Under the circumstances, I guess that's to be expected." A warm breeze blew across my skin. I had a sudden vision of Jannine, alone in a dank cell, her young daughters alone too, facing their worst fears without a mother's comfort. I hugged my arms across my chest and shivered.

"Your, uh, friend Ken, he said he was leaving anyway . . . So I thought . . . you know, that you wouldn't want to come home to an empty house." Tom paused to look at me. "But maybe it wasn't such a good idea."

My mind was still on Jannine. I worked to bring it back to the present.

"I mean, we never really talked about this. I guess we should have." He hesitated. "We can pretend Friday night never happened, you know. It doesn't have to be a big deal. We're not sixteen anymore. But if you'd rather I leave right now, I can understand that, too. Steak stays, though. It's yours no matter what."

I'd felt the icy shaft of tequila make its way down my throat and into my stomach. Now I could feel it moving through my bloodstream, like a current of silver bubbles. "It's not the way you think," I said. "Ken just drove up this morning. To tell me he's taking a job in D.C."

"He's leaving?"

I nodded.

"For good?"

"It looks that way."

"Just like that?"

"Yeah, well, the firm's falling apart. It's sort of every man for himself."

"And every woman."

"That, too."

Tom looked at me and then away. He turned the steaks and adjusted the flow of air to the fire, taking his time with both. "The guy wasn't your type anyway," he said, eyes still diverted.

"How do you know?"

Tom glanced my way finally, and I smiled.

He didn't exactly smile in return, but the corners of his mouth turned up ever so slightly, and his gaze softened. Then he turned back to the steaks. "So, you going to tell me what happened with that face of yours?"

I told him. I told him about the midnight episode with George, too, and all that led up to it.

"You believe him?"

I nodded. "Besides, Benson checked it out. He *was* at the hospital Saturday. So now I'm back to square one, with nothing."

"Except that somebody out there thinks you know something."

"Or just plain hates me."

"I don't think that's possible," he said, fixing his eyes on mine.

I ignored the look. "The only other thing is these pictures Cheryl Newcomb gave a friend for safekeeping."

"That's the girl who ran away last week?"

"Right, the same girl who was with Eddie Saturday morning." I explained about Eva and the envelope of photographs. "She must have had them with her at school that morning. It was right afterwards that she stopped by to give them to Eva."

"You think Eddie had something to do with the photos?"

"It makes me sick to imagine it, but yes, I think it's a possibility. A distinct possibility at this point. What it doesn't do, though, is bring me any closer to finding the killer."

Tom took his time testing the steaks. Then he looked at me. "What it does do," he said softly, "is explain why Jannine might have been enraged enough to kill her husband."

27

Monday morning, bright and early, I was back at the county Hall of Justice. I had to wait half an hour for the D.A. to arrive, and another half an hour for him to make room for me in his tight schedule. He laughed at the notion of a negotiated bail, then gave me the same song and dance about cooperation that Benson had, only he couched it in slightly different terms.

"We're going to go for murder one," he said. "We've got a strong case. We win, and we'll ask for the maximum sentence. Jannine Marrero will end up behind bars for the rest of her life." He paused. "There's the publicity of a big murder trial to consider as well. It's bound to be tough on her family. If she pleads to voluntary manslaughter, no trial, and she's eligible for parole in a couple of years."

Tom's words from the night before rang in my ears. I brushed them aside. "She would be pleading guilty to a crime she didn't commit."

He leaned back in his chair and tapped his pencil

against his open palm. "You have her think about it, okay? It would mean she'd be out in time to see those kids of hers before they're all grown up."

I was hoping it also meant the D.A. wasn't as certain of winning as he pretended to be.

I met briefly with Jannine to convey the news about bail and to tell her I'd spoken with Nona. I mentioned the plea bargain, though I advised against it. She nodded wordlessly.

"We have a hearing set for tomorrow morning," I told her. "The D.A. wouldn't agree to bail, but I'm still hopeful we can convince the judge."

I was rewarded with another silent nod. It was as though Jannine herself had flown off somewhere, leaving behind a mere shell. I put away whatever thought I'd had of asking about the pictures.

Downstairs in the main lobby, I found a pay phone and looked up auto glass companies in the yellow pages. A place just on the other side of town offered on the spot emergency repair. My lucky day.

While the window was being replaced, I bought a candy bar and both local papers. *The Mountain Journal* ran a short blurb about Jannine's arrest on page four. She made the front page of *The Hadley Times*, but I was happy to see that that article, too, was rather brief. Then again, there wasn't a whole lot new to report. I figured we'd have press there in the morning, though, and longer articles in both papers the following day.

The candy bar was stale. I tossed it into the garbage and paced around the waiting area until my car was ready. I had the clerk make a second copy of the bill, which I would send to George. I would return his wallet and ring when he paid me in full. I hadn't yet decided what to do about the scratches.

It was five o'clock by the time I got home, but with the summer solstice fast approaching, it seemed almost like midday. I changed into jeans and poked around the house, finding myself unable to relax. I felt the need to accomplish something positive, to take on a finite task and see it through to completion. Finally, I decided to tackle my parents' bedroom. It was the one remaining room I hadn't yet packed up, and with the real estate agent coming out the next day, I wanted to get as much sorted as I could.

The room was at the back of house over the garage, separated from the remainder of the second floor by a narrow stairway. After my mother died, my father moved into the smaller spare bedroom downstairs, and we all more or less forgot the old room existed. I hadn't been up there myself for years, and as I carried empty packing boxes to the landing, I thought with dread of the dust and cobwebs I'd have to contend with.

But the bedroom was spotless. Cleaner by far than the rest of the house. And laid out just as it had been that day my mother put the garden hose to the car's exhaust pipe and breathed her last breath.

Her hairbrushes lined the dresser. The closet and drawers were full of her things. There was even a vase of wilted flowers on the nightstand.

A picture of my parents, framed in heavy silver, rested on the bureau. My mother laughing, her auburn curls loose about her face; my father dark and serious, eyes set lovingly on his wife.

My breath caught, and I swallowed hard to keep the tears from coming. I felt the past envelop me, like a heavy cloak, bulky and cumbersome, but somehow comforting at the same time. As I made my way around the room, I thought I could detect the scent of face powder and lilac cologne, my mother's scent from so long ago.

And sitting on the nubby white bedspread I'd helped her choose, I was sure I could feel her presence.

It took me a moment to notice the depression on my father's side of the bed. When I ran my hand along his pillow, I could feel the hollow there as well. Suddenly I understood. He hadn't closed himself off from her memory at all. He'd made a deliberate effort to keep it intact, alive. He had come here to this room, the bedroom they'd shared, in order to summon up the past, and perhaps to imagine what might have been.

He must have loved her, I thought, although he never spoke of her to any of us, never acknowledged our pain at losing her. "The past is best forgotten," he would tell us. "You can't change what is."

Yet *he* hadn't forgotten at all. I felt the old anger and resentment stirring in my chest, but I felt an overwhelming sense of sadness, too. Perhaps his own pain had simply been too great. Perhaps he'd had to deal with it the only way he could.

Part of me wanted to close the door and walk away, leaving everything as it was. But that wasn't possible. You can't sell a house and hold onto its past. With mixed emotions, I set up the boxes and began to go through the drawers. The contents were carefully folded, and I placed each item just as carefully when I laid it in the box.

I thought about calling Sabrina, then discarded the idea, though I couldn't imagine why neither of us had thought to go through the room before.

I had worked my way down to the bottom drawer when

I found the note, a yellowed slip of paper, creased and well-worn. It was in my mother's hand, but unsigned, on blue bordered stationery I still remembered.

It was dated the day of her death.

Forgive me. There are so many wrongs and I am too much at fault.

I stared at the note, my body frozen, mind numb. What wrongs? What could my mother have done, or thought she'd done, that was so wrong? Was this the reason for her suicide?

The phone rang downstairs. I think I heard it ring several times before I was able to brush the spider webs from inside my head and recognize the sound for what it was. It took another five rings for me to make it to the kitchen.

"She's here," Mrs. Holland said, her voice just barely above a whisper.

"Who?" I found myself whispering in response.

"Cheryl. She came to get her pictures."

My heart was racing by the time I got to the Holland's. I crossed my fingers, hoping that Cheryl had not already fled. Mrs. Holland greeted me at the door, again speaking in hushed tones. "The girls are out back." She led me through the house. "I'm glad you could come. I didn't know what to do. I didn't want to call the police. You know how they are."

"Have you talked to her?"

"Not really. Eva told her you took the photographs, and Cheryl just clammed up after that. At least with me."

The two girls were sitting side by side on an old-fashioned porch swing. They were pushing it with their toes, just barely, so that it was more of a swaying motion than actual swinging. They were drinking sodas, a bowl of chips between them. Their heads were bent close in serious conversation. As we approached, they looked up in unison.

Mrs. Holland introduced me as "the woman who wants to help," then took Eva into the house and left us alone. I wasn't sure where to begin.

"Did you bring my pictures?" Cheryl asked. She looked me in the eye when she spoke, but it wasn't the hostile, accusing glower I expected. It was more like she was testing the waters.

I shook my head. "I'll give them back to you. I just didn't think about it this time."

"You from the police?" she asked.

"No."

"A social worker?"

I shook my head and sat in the seat Eva had vacated, dropping my keys and dark glasses onto the cushion between us.

"I don't get it then. Who are you?"

"I'm a friend of Mrs. Walker," I began. "She's worried about you."

Cheryl brushed a strand of hair from her eyes. The bridge of her nose was sprinkled with pale freckles which hadn't been apparent in the school picture. They gave her something of a pixie look.

"I'm also a friend of Eddie and Jannine Marrero."

She sat forward. "Mr. Marrero sent you?"

"Not exactly, but you apparently saw him last Saturday morning, before you came here."

Her face, which had begun to relax only moments earlier, took on a sudden wariness. "How did you know that?"

"One of the other students told Mrs. Walker. You

might have been the last person to see him alive. I was hoping—"

"Alive?" There was a long, penetrating silence. She obviously hadn't known. "You mean he's dead?"

I felt terrible. "I'm sorry. I thought you knew."

Her eyes widened, and her breathing grew more rapid. "What happened?"

"He was killed Saturday afternoon. Shot. In the woods by the south fork of Silver Creek."

She repeated words, mouthing them silently to herself. "Who killed him?"

"The police have arrested his wife, but she didn't do it." I decided to play a hunch. "I think his death is connected in some way to the photographs."

Cheryl went white. The swing stopped its gentle rocking.

"Did he ask you to hide them for him?"

She shook her head. Her breath was coming in short, uneven spurts.

"Was he the one who took the pictures?"

Cheryl shook her head again, a quick, jerky motion that caused the whole swing to jiggle. Her eyes darted from left to right, settling nowhere.

"But he knew about them?" I asked.

"He was going to call me that afternoon. He *promised.* He said he'd take care of it."

"Cheryl, tell me about the photographs."

"He said . . ."

I waited.

"He said . . ."

"He said what?"

She drew in a deep breath and looked at me. Her eyes were wide and unblinking, as though she had found herself trapped in a burning room. In one quick, fluid motion, she grabbed my car keys from the seat and darted off the porch.

She'd thrust herself from the swing with such force that it pitched back, bumping against the house and knocking me off balance. By the time I was able to extricate myself from the swing and follow, she'd already made it to the front of the house.

I got to the driveway just in time to see my BMW backing onto the main road. The car bucked and then lurched forward, sideswiping a red Honda parked in front of the house next door. The awful crunch of metal on metal was followed by the sharp screeching of tires, and my car flew down the street.

I ran into the house and yelled to Mrs. Holland. "Give me your car keys, quick."

"What's the matter?"

"Cheryl drove off in my car."

Out front again, I caught a glimpse of my BMW at the intersection. I followed, gunning the engine of Mrs. Holland's old station wagon for all it was worth. It was low on power and handled like a truck. It was also, I noticed, almost out of gasoline. I hoped Cheryl wasn't planning any long trek.

Somehow, I managed to gain on her, just a little. Then she careened around a corner, running a red light in the process. I did the same, slowing first to look for oncoming cars. The distance between us grew again.

As I pushed the pedal to the floor, I made some quick calculations. It unnerved me to realize that not only was Cheryl too young to have a license, she was probably too young to have a learner's permit. In either case, it was apparent she didn't have a lot of experience behind the wheel.

Cheryl headed past the interstate and out to the farming country along the river. She weaved from shoulder to shoulder, ignoring the yellow line down the center. She veered around a slow–moving tractor and just barely avoided colliding with the pickup coming from the other direction. Again, my relative caution caused me to fall behind. I saw my car in the distance turn right, off the main road. By the time I got to the intersection, she had vanished.

I turned onto the side road anyway. It was narrow and a good deal more winding, so I took it slow. About a mile in, I spotted my BMW—its front end smashed solidly against the rock wall of a farm house. A cloud of steam rose from the hood. Cheryl was nowhere in sight.

I pulled over quickly and headed for the house. As I passed by the garage, I noticed a white Lincoln, and next to it a blue Acura with a rear bumper sticker.

If you can read this, thank a teacher.

Jannine was apparently not the only owner of a blue car to champion the cause of teachers.

The front door was ajar. I stuck my head in and looked around. Cheryl was crouched inside the door, her hands and face smeared with blood.

"Are you all right?"

She wrapped her arms tightly around her chest and shoulders, and began rocking, moaning softly as she swayed forward and backward.

"Cheryl? Are you hurt?"

Nothing.

"The car doesn't matter. It's you I'm worried about."

The swaying and moaning continued. Cheryl's eyes

were locked straight ahead. Finally I looked to where she was staring and saw the body of a man sprawled out, face up on the floor, a heavy fireplace poker nearby. A pool of deep red blood was forming at his head. It took me a minute to recognize Jack Peterson.

28

"What happened?" I asked, my voice a slow croak. Cheryl stopped her swaying and rocking, but kept her eyes fixed on the pool of blood. "I don't know. He was like that when I got here." She paused. "Do you think he's dead?"

He certainly looked dead. His face was pulpy, and he didn't appear to be breathing. "I think we'd better call the police," I told her.

She nodded but otherwise didn't move.

"You stay here. I'll go look for a phone."

But before I'd finished speaking, I heard an ominous growl coming from the doorway behind me. I turned to look. An enormous German shepherd stood on alert, the fur on his back erect, the sharp teeth bared in a vicious snarl. Next to him stood Marlene, holding a gasoline can in one hand and a blowtorch in the other. Her teeth were bared in a smile rather than a snarl, but the effect was similar.

"Well, well," she said, setting the blow torch at her

feet, "isn't this handy. You've saved me the trouble of tracking you down."

I made a move toward her. The dog lunged, and I pulled back.

"You don't want to mess with Von Baron," she said. "He's a trained attack dog." She turned to Cheryl. "Your friend Jack isn't looking his best, I'm afraid. But if you'd like, you may give him one last kiss." Her voice was cruel. "Of course, he's rather beyond your powers of seduction at the moment."

Cheryl looked again toward the body. She drew in several choking breaths, then started sobbing.

"Hysterics won't change anything," Marlene snipped.

"He said I was special, that *we* were special." Cheryl's words were broken by convulsive sobs. "He said he loved me."

Marlene laughed harshly. "Love. You youngsters walk around half–dressed, flaunting your bodies. You throw yourselves at men, flirt with them, lead them on, and then you want *love*, too." Her lips compressed into a thin line. "Love and sex are not the same, you know."

"He said I was special. And I believed him. I thought we . . ." Cheryl looked at me, her eyes round and frightened. "Then I found those pictures. There were other girls, too."

"Jack Peterson took the pictures?"

She nodded, barely moving. "He said they were for the times when I wasn't there, to help him remember. He said I brought him such joy. He said trust and sharing were important." She dropped her head to her hands. "He said he loved me," she sobbed. "He said it was all about love."

"Well, he didn't love you," Marlene said evenly. "He

loved me. That's why he married me. You girls were nothing to him. Nothing but a meaningless diversion, a simple habit."

"You knew about this?" I asked, incredulous.

She gave me a piercing look. "Of course, I knew. Jack and I had no secrets from each other." She turned to Cheryl. *"That* is love."

"But Mr. Marrero said—"

Marlene snorted. "He's the one who started all this trouble. Got all worked up and made a big deal about it. Said Jack was sick. It wasn't like Jack forced those girls, you know. They were only too willing. Isn't that so?" she said, addressing Cheryl.

The heavy sobs had subsided, but Cheryl continued to weep. Her whole body trembled with emotion. "Mr. Marrero said he'd help."

"Help?" Marlene's voice was sharp. "He wanted to stir up trouble, is what he wanted. He tried to talk Jack into resigning. All Jack had worked for—his career in education, his political aspirations, his whole life—down the drain. And for *nothing.* Just because some stupid little slut didn't get what she wanted."

Cheryl looked up, as though she'd been slapped hard. The pixie face was crumpled and tear-stained. I started to move toward her to offer comfort, but the German shepherd followed with a menacing snarl. I stopped where I was.

"Jack thought he could reason with Eddie. He was sure they could work things out. But after Eddie lifted those pictures from Jack's office, I knew it wouldn't work. Jack would never be safe."

"I was the one who took the pictures," Cheryl said. "I found them in his bottom desk drawer. At first I didn't

want to believe it. All those other girls." Her voice rose a little, then fell. "He said he loved me, but he didn't. Mr. Marrero was right."

Marlene ignored Cheryl. "Eddie Marrero was nothing but a troublemaker, a busybody who stuck his nose in where it didn't belong. Thought he had the right to judge others. I had to stop him before he caused irreparable damage."

"So you killed him." My mouth was so dry the words came out in a scratchy whisper.

She smiled. "Smart girl. Jack said you were smart. He was sure you'd figure it out eventually. I tried to keep you away, but you wouldn't listen. You ignored every warning."

"The *bon voyage* card," I said.

She raised an eyebrow and nodded. "It's a little late to be getting the message."

"And the car that almost ran me over Saturday evening."

"I knew you'd find the photographs eventually. I'd already checked through Eddie's things at the house, and Jack had looked through his office. We didn't know where they were, but once you had them, it would be too late."

So Eddie's office *had* been searched. And it was Marlene, not the police, who'd messed up Eddie's files at home. Only he hadn't taken the pictures in the first place, Cheryl had. Because she knew that without them, it would be her word against Peterson's.

The same reason Marlene had been so anxious to locate them herself.

"Now that you're both here," Marlene continued, "I can wrap everything up at once."

While she uncapped the can and began pouring gasoline around the perimeter of the room, Von Baron positioned himself at the door, venting his impatience with intermittent snarls. Gasoline fumes filled the air, causing my eyes to smart and my throat to constrict. But it was the image of flames, a wall of fire searing my flesh, that made me almost nauseous.

I looked around the room for a means of escape. The only windows were small, high up, and closed tight. And the one doorway was blocked by a drooling hundred pounds of hard muscle and single-minded determination. The situation didn't leave much room for optimism.

Marlene worked her way around the room. When she came to Jack's body, she hesitated for a moment, then continued pouring, dousing his body with gasoline.

"You killed Jack, too?" I asked.

"I had to. He was going to give up, withdraw from politics, resign his position. After all this, after all I'd done, he was going to quit on me." She picked up the fireplace poker, wiped the handle on her blouse, and set it back on the hearth. "Can you imagine the publicity? Why, I'd never be able to show my face in public again. My family has been prominent in this community for four generations. My great-grandfather was sheriff and then mayor. Both my grandfather and father were state senators."

"And you wanted your husband to follow in their footsteps."

"It's not that I'm condoning Jack's weakness for the flesh, but he was a man, after all. These things happen. He asked for my understanding and forgiveness, and he got them. But going public with this, that was unthinkable. A disgrace beyond measure. I couldn't allow it."

"Isn't murder something of a blemish on your family's good name?"

"Not if no one knows," she said. "The police think they've solved Eddie's murder. Even if Jannine's not convicted, they aren't going to come back and start looking for the killer all over again. That's why I was so anxious to keep you from meddling. Everything was rolling along so nicely."

Jannine's arrest. The D.A.'s sudden eagerness to bring her in. "How did you manage to pressure the D.A.?"

"A phone call to a friend, who made a phone call to a friend. A favor repaid. It's what I tried to explain to Jack, connections are so important. You don't walk away and give up when you've spent a lifetime cultivating them."

Cheryl had been sitting quietly, almost trance-like, staring off into space. She turned now to look at Marlene. "You're going to kill us, too, aren't you?"

"You think I'd just let you walk way?"

"They'll be able to tell it's arson," I said.

"Only if they think to look. And that's a risk I'm willing to take. I doubt I'll be on their list of suspects. Especially when I tell them how Cheryl called here last night, hysterical and overwrought, threatening Jack if he didn't change her grades. He's always said she was unstable and given to irrational behavior."

Cheryl leaped to her feet. "You're the one who's nuts!" she screamed. "You're a sick, wicked, twisted old woman."

She started for Marlene, who turned and hurled the gas can at Cheryl, soaking her blouse and hair with gasoline. When Cheryl stopped to wipe the liquid from her face, Marlene stepped away and reached for the blow torch. I immediately dived for Marlene. And the dog leapt for me, sinking his teeth into the flesh of my arm.

"Run!" I yelled to Cheryl.

But instead of running, she grabbed the poker and smashed it across the dog's head. He turned on her, and she whacked him again.

Snarling and frothing at the mouth, the dog crouched, ready to spring. His hind feet had barely left the ground when a shot rang out. The dog yelped and fell short. A second shot put an end to the yelping.

Like a precision drill team, we all three turned and stared in astonishment at the figure in the doorway. The portly highway patrol officer stared back, as stunned as the rest of us.

Finally he returned his gun to its holster. He scratched his cheek and asked, "That smashed up BMW out front belong to any of you ladies?"

29

Daryl Benson was dumping a twin pack of sugar into a styrofoam cup when I flopped into the seat across from him.

"You want some?" he asked, nodding to the cup.

I shook my head. Not if I had any hope of getting to sleep that night. They'd given me a painkiller at the hospital and warned me it would make me drowsy. That had been an hour ago, and I was still wound up tight. I could feel the adrenaline flowing like an electric current.

"Your arm going to be okay?"

"Yeah. Just sore for a while." Like nearly every other part of my body. But at least Marlene had been conscientious about Von Baron's shots. Rabies was one thing I didn't have to worry about.

Benson nodded, then introduced me to the woman seated to my left. "Abigail Roberts," he said, "investigator with the juvenile division."

"Call me Abbey," she said as we shook hands. She had short dark hair and a wide mouth capped with dimples. She didn't look much older than a juvenile herself.

"Abigail's just come from talking with Cheryl," Benson explained.

"How's she doing?"

"Pretty well," Abbey said. "She's a gutsy kid. Even in the face of what happened tonight, she was able to give us a straightforward account, from beginning to end. And one that showed quite a bit of insight for a girl so young. There's a woman from social welfare with her now. She'll have a better idea of how well Cheryl's going to handle all this, but it's my guess that with some counseling she'll come through okay."

I thought about the frail frame hunched close against me in the back seat of the police car, about the smile that came out of nowhere when I gave her arm a gentle squeeze. I thought she'd be okay too, but I'd keep my fingers crossed just the same.

"How about Marlene?" I asked Benson. "Did she admit to killing Eddie?"

"Not in so many words, but she gave us quite a lot before she clammed up and asked to see her attorney. What we've got is almost as good as a confession. I don't anticipate any problems."

"Have you been able to figure out what happened exactly?"

Benson took a sip of his coffee. "We've had to piece things together based on her story and what you and Cheryl told us. But it looks like Eddie had begun to suspect what was going on with Peterson, and confronted him with it. Peterson, of course, denied everything. Cheryl denied it too, at first. But when she discovered that Peterson had been involved with a number of girls, everything changed."

Abbey broke in here, speaking softly, her face clouded.

"You can imagine how Cheryl felt—hurt, angry, be-trayed. And above all else, ashamed. She said she thought about killing herself. I suspect she might have followed through except for the fact that Eddie Marrero had al-ready broached the subject with her, and he was someone she felt comfortable talking with."

"So she went to Eddie and told him everything," I said, thinking that that, in itself, took a fair amount of cour-age.

Benson nodded and picked up the story. "She went to Eddie who in turn went, again, to Peterson. This time, though, it wasn't mere speculation; Eddie said he had proof of what had been going on. I don't know what Pet-erson's reaction was initially, but when he discovered the photographs were missing, he assumed Eddie had taken them, and he panicked. He called Eddie Saturday morn-ing, and they agreed to meet. Marlene was worried that her husband would go along with whatever Eddie sug-gested. She followed them, apparently surprising both men, and killed Eddie."

"Peterson wasn't in on it, then?"

"Not in the beginning, it seems, but of course he knew what Marlene had done, and he went along with it."

"I suppose it was easy for her to get Jannine's gun," I said, thinking aloud. "She's in and out of the house all the time."

"That's the point where she stopped talking to us, but only after she'd admitted dropping by their house Friday night. The Marreros were apparently having a party, and she'd promised to bake brownies."

I nodded. I remembered Jannine saying that Jack and Marlene hadn't been able to attend because Jack had come down with the flu. In retrospect, I could see that it wasn't the flu that had kept them away, but a bad case of nerves.

"What amazes me," I said, "is that Marlene could so readily overlook all that Jack had done, and then go off the deep end because he was willing to admit it was wrong."

"It's hard to figure, but it's not the first time I've run into something like this. I don't know if she fully understood what was going on, or if she'd deluded herself into believing that Cheryl was the instigator, kind of a combination of *Lolita* and *Fatal Attraction*. To listen to her, she certainly seems to believe Jack was guiltless."

"It's not uncommon," Abbey said, nodding in agreement. "People see what they want to see, and that's especially true in issues of sexual abuse. The offenders are often happily married, pillars of the community. The wives simply don't want to know. They either look the other way or fabricate some story which makes it all acceptable."

"What about the other girls? None of them told anybody?"

"We haven't talked with them, so we don't know that for sure, but it's a good guess they didn't. Peterson's type picks on the misfits, kids on the edge of the crowd, kids in need. And he fills that need. Seduction can be a pretty powerful weapon. Cheryl admits he never forced her. At least that's the way she sees it. Of course, we know that physical force isn't the only way to gain control. All she saw, though, was the attention, the charm, the appeal of being loved. Peterson made her feel important, special. That's pretty hard for anyone to turn away from, especially a kid who's never found much in the way of love elsewhere." Abbey paused for a moment, frowning.

"Then too there's the intimidation factor. Peterson convinced her that if she said anything, nobody would believe her. She would be the one in trouble. He held all the cards, don't forget."

"But Cheryl did tell someone finally."

Abbey nodded. "That took a great deal of trust on her part. And when Eddie didn't call as he'd promised, she panicked and ran away, afraid she'd been betrayed once again."

"Peterson's probably been getting away with stuff like this for years," Benson said.

"For years? And nobody knew?"

"We haven't had time to check into it, but he fits the pattern of someone with a history of sex offenses. He's moved around a lot, changed jobs. I'd be surprised if this is the first time."

Abbey nodded. "It happens more often than you'd believe."

She stood then to leave, and I stood, too.

"Stay a minute, why don't you?" Benson said, addressing me.

I gave Abbey my phone number in case she wanted to get in touch, then sat down again. There was a moment of silence.

"About your car," Benson began. "You want to press charges?"

I shook my head.

"I figured as much." He rocked back in his chair. "We'll have it towed to a shop for you. They ought to be able to tell you whether it can be salvaged. You'll have to check with your insurance company, see what they'll cover in a case like this. Technically it's a stolen car, and you can identify the thief."

I hoped they'd cover enough to get me out from under my payments. I was beginning to think I wasn't destined to own a BMW.

Benson pressed his fingertips together and then his lips. He watched me for a moment in silence. "I've been thinking about what you said the other day, about Eddie getting money from your father."

I waited while Benson locked and then unlocked his fingers.

"I think I've got some idea what it might have been about. It's just conjecture, though, understand?"

I nodded.

"I don't even know whether I should be telling you this, but I suspect you've a right to the truth. Maybe it will help you make peace with the past."

I nodded again, this time in encouragement.

He dropped his hands to his desk and sat upright. "I think your father may have seen it as a way to get back at George Marrero. He told me, just a couple of days before he died, that he'd had a chance to, in his words, stick another burr under George's saddle."

I was confused. "I didn't think they even knew each other."

"Strictly speaking, they didn't. But your father blamed George for your mother's death. He blamed himself too, of course, but lately he'd become obsessed with the idea that George was ultimately responsible."

"I don't understand. Did my *mother* know George?"

Benson shook his head. "It's complicated." He hesitated before continuing. "I don't know if you remember, but your mother was in an automobile accident about a couple of months before she died."

I did remember, vaguely. "No one was hurt though, right?"

"Right. It was George who was driving the other car. He had been drinking and ran a stop sign. Your mother's car was a mess, but she escaped with only a few minor bruises." He paused and took a deep breath. "Soon after she became seriously depressed, ultimately taking her own life. Over the years your father became convinced that her depression and suicide stemmed from the accident. There was nothing he could do legally, but he took every opportunity to cause George trouble. It may not have been rational, but to him it was very real."

There was something about his tone of voice that brought me up short. I had the feeling there was more to the story than he'd told me. "You don't think her suicide was related to the accident though."

"Not directly." Benson ran his tongue over his bottom lip, then stared up at the ceiling. "This is the hard part, Kull." He took another deep breath. "Your mother was . . . well, I was in love with her. I guess you'd say we had an affair, although I don't like that word. It sounds so crass. And what we had together was . . . well, it was more about laughter and long conversations and picnics in the grass than sex, although I won't deny the latter was part of it."

I swallowed and struggled to find words. "Did my father know about this?"

"No. He knew she wasn't happy in their marriage, but I don't think he was aware she was involved with someone else." Benson lowered his gaze again and looked at me. "Your father was a good man, an honest man, but he lacked passion and imagination. Or at least he lacked the ability to communicate those qualities. And your mother was just the opposite—high-spirited, impulsive, temperamental. She used to complain that he never reached out to her, never sought to look into her soul, never, in some sense, really wanted her. Although, of course, he did.''

"And you," I said, "had passion and imagination?''

I didn't intend for the words to carry reproach, although I'm sure that's what Benson heard. His jaw tensed, and his eyes clouded over. "I loved her, and I think that, to a degree, she loved me. But had I been her husband, I doubt that I'd have made her any happier than your father did. I'm not sure, in truth, that any man could have.''

We were silent a moment, each lost in our own thoughts. Finally, I asked, "If the accident didn't precipitate her suicide, what did?''

Benson hesitated. "She was pregnant. She'd just found out and come to tell me. The accident happened on the way home.'' He cleared his throat, looked the other way. "She was pregnant, and she didn't know who the father was. The accident may have contributed in some way, but mostly it was guilt and despair. She felt suddenly the weight of her sins. It was a heavy burden.''

I found my eyes were wet.

"I'm sorry, Kali. I loved her, and in the end that wasn't enough. Your father loved her, too. Neither of us were able to give her what she wanted. And neither of us were able to save her.''

I called Tom to come pick me up. And then I called Jannine to tell her the news—all charges against her were being dropped. While I waited for Tom, out front under the vast velvet sky, I thought about love and happiness, and how it happened that one did not always follow the other. In fact, during this last week I'd glimpsed enough of the rough underside of love to make me wonder if it wasn't an overrated phenomenon.

I didn't have a chance to pursue the thought because Tom pulled up just then. Record time. He must not only have broken the speed limit, but thoroughly shattered it.

He got out of the car and greeted me with a loopy grin. "You sure have a knack for finding trouble," he said.

"Actually, I lead a very dull life."

He looked me over from head to toe, checking out the new scrapes and bruises. "Could have fooled me." He opened the door and helped me into the car. "Do I get the first scoop on this story?"

"Depends on what you're offering in return."

Tom raised an eyebrow in an exaggerated leer.

"Not that. I was thinking more along the lines of food."

"Oh." His face fell. "Well, I can probably manage that, too. How does pizza sound?"

"If you throw in a bottle of wine, I'll give you an exclusive."

"Deal," he told me, and leaned over to seal it with a kiss.

A warm, wonderful kiss that made me think once again about love and happiness. Only my thoughts this time around were very much brighter.

Please turn the page
for an exciting sneak peek
of Jonnie Jacob's newest
Kali O'Brien novel of legal suspense
WITNESS FOR THE DEFENSE
coming in hardcover in April 2001!

In general, I don't subscribe to the theory that unpleasant tasks are best confronted at once, but in this case I thought it necessary. I called Terri and asked if I could come by later that day.

"Is it important? We're kind of busy today."

"It's important. I won't stay long."

"More papers, I bet. Can you make it this morning? We're expecting friends in the afternoon." She laughed. "We can't help showing off Hannah."

My throat constricted. I swallowed hard. "I can be there in an hour. Is that too early?"

"It's fine."

Ted answered the door. He was dressed casually in a tee shirt and shorts. His shoulders were so broad, his arms so thick, I wondered if he had to have his shirts custom made.

"I'll let Terri know you're here," he said, ushering me past the large, formal living room into a smaller, more comfortable sitting area off the kitchen. He disappeared and I heard him calling Terri's name.

The mantel above the fireplace was lined with cards welcoming the new baby. A pile of baby gifts, largely unopened, was spread on the credenza. I sat on the beige chenille sofa, wishing I were somewhere else. Anywhere else. I hoped Ted and Terri didn't confuse the messenger with the message.

Terri came through the doorway followed by Ted.

"Sorry to keep you waiting," she said. "I was putting Hannah down for a nap. Can I get you some coffee?"

"No thanks."

Ted sat down, leaning forward with his arms on his knees. He tapped his foot impatiently. "Terri said you had some more papers for us to sign?"

"No, that's not why I'm here." My mouth was so dry, I was having trouble talking. "There's been a complication."

Terri had been standing. Now she, too, sat. "What do you mean? What kind of complication? Melissa signed the waiver of consent."

"Gary Ellis may not be . . . isn't Hannah's father. He's just someone Melissa worked with. The true birth father is a man named Bram Weaver. You may have . . ."

Terri let out a gasp and turned white.

"The guy with the radio show?" Ted stopped his foot-tapping.

I nodded. "And he says he's not going to agree to an adoption."

There was a moment of absolute silence, and then Ted exploded.

"What? Can he do that?" The vein in Ted's temple pulsed. With his bulky shoulders and powerful neck, he looked something like a bull staring at a red cape.

"He came to my office yesterday afternoon. I was in court so I haven't talked to him, but my associate did. And I talked to Melissa this morning. She confirmed that he is Hannah's father."

Ted slid an arm protectively around Terri's shoulder. "It's a little late for him to be getting involved, isn't it?"

"He claims not to have known about the pregnancy before now."

"What does this mean, exactly?" Terri's voice was so

soft it was a struggle to hear her. "Can he really stop the adoption?"

"I'm afraid so. We'll demand a paternity test. And maybe we can show that he did know Melissa was pregnant. If that's the case, and he made no effort to assert his paternal rights before now, then we may have a leg to stand on."

"And if not?" Ted asked.

"Then I'm afraid the adoption is in jeopardy. The law is clear."

"She's ours." Terri choked. Her eyes welled with tears. "We can't lose her. We can't lose another baby."

Ted squeezed her shoulder. "We won't, honey. We'll fight him on this."

"I have to warn you, your chances aren't good." It wasn't a pleasant role, being the bad guy. But I thought they needed to know what they were up against. "It might be easiest to bow out now rather than prolonging the ordeal."

"Roll over and give up? Not on your life." Ted was at the helm, ready to do battle.

"You may have to eventually," I cautioned. "And by then you'll be even more attached to Hannah, and she to you." I was sure I didn't need to remind them about Baby Jessica, whose adoptive parents fought to keep her for three years, only to eventually lose her.

Terri wiped her eyes, but the tears continued to come. "She isn't a piece of property, Kali. She's our daughter."

"Hit him with the heavy artillery," Ted bellowed. "Hell, nuke him if you have to. I don't care how much it costs or who gets hurt. We're not giving up our daughter."

Neither, apparently, was Weaver. Tuesday we received official documents from his attorney demanding that the

Harpers withdraw from the adoption and turn Hannah over to him.

I called to deliver the news.

"I've been checking into this guy," Ted said. "He's an ass."

"If you're looking for an argument, you're not going to get one from me."

Ted was breathing heavily into the phone. "Have you ever listened to his show?"

"The white male reigns supreme."

"Heck, I'm a guy, about as white as they come, and he makes *me* uncomfortable."

"If he's Hannah's father, though, all of that other stuff is irrelevant."

"How can the court choose a man like that over us?" Ted's voice sparked with indignation.

"It isn't the court's role to *choose.*"

"Someone's got to."

"This is different than contested custody in a divorce," I explained. "There the judge looks at what's in the best interest of the child. That's not a consideration here."

"Maybe it should be."

"I know how painful . . ."

"With all respect, Kali, you don't know. You can't know until you've been there yourself." His venom was directed at me this time.

"You're right. Whatever I imagine, the reality is probably a hundred times worse. But that doesn't change the fact that the rights of the biological father take precedence."

"Not this time," Ted said. "We're going to do whatever it takes to keep her."

* * *

I set Jared to work trying to dig up dirt on Weaver. I peppered Melissa with questions about what he might have known when. I called Weaver's attorney, who told me there was nothing to discuss unless the Harpers were willing to relinquish Hannah.

I held out hope that Weaver's interest in Hannah was a superficial one, like a boy with a new toy at Christmas, and that he'd lose interest when faced with the rigors of litigation—and the time to reflect on the challenges of child rearing.

Or that, in the alternative, he might care deeply about his daughter, and be swayed by the Harpers' sincerity. To that end, I'd tried to speak with him directly. But he never returned my phone calls.

Two weeks later we assembled in Judge Nye's courtroom for a preliminary hearing concerning the Adoption of Hannah B. Ted and Terri sat rigidly and silently, eyes straight ahead. Seated behind them, Melissa slumped, curling in on herself as though she were being pulled into the fetal position.

Bram Weaver's attorney caught my eye and started to approach. He looked to be in his mid-forties, ruddy-faced, and fashionably dressed in a European-cut suit of dark gray. I moved to meet him midground, beyond earshot of the Harpers.

"Bill Trimble." He winked at me as we shook hands. "Pleasure to finally meet you, Ms. O'Brien."

It was all I could do to keep from wiping my palm on my skirt.

He nodded in the direction of Ted and Terri. "That the couple who were hoping to adopt the child?"

I was sure his use of the past tense was intentional. *"Are* hoping," I said.

He gave me a supercilious smile and said nothing.

"Your client will be here today, won't he?"

"Any minute."

"I'd like to talk to him. We might be able to work this out ourselves, without involving the court. My clients are a warm and caring couple. They would provide a . . ."

"Save your breath, my dear. Bram wants his daughter."

Before I had a chance to argue further, the courtroom door flew open and a whippish, narrow-faced man with a cleft chin burst into the room. I instantly recognized Bram Weaver from the magazine photograph I'd seen, but he wasn't nearly as tall or devilish as I'd envisioned. His dark hair, trimmed close at the sides, was beginning to gray near the temples, and he wore silver-rimmed glasses, which had been absent in the picture.

Weaver strode to the front of the courtroom, took his attorney's arm and whispered something into his ear. Then he turned, casting a quick glance around the room.

As his eyes met Melissa's, she flinched and turned away. Terri by contrast, stared at him with a hateful glower. If her eyes had been lasers, Weaver would have been toast.

"All rise."

Judge Robert Nye entered the courtroom and took a seat at the bench. His face was pinched, whether from displeasure or habit it was hard to tell. He montioned for us to be seated.

"Bill, you're representing Mr. Weaver, correct?"

"Yes, Your Honor."

Not a good sign. The judge and Weaver's attorney were on a first-name basis.

Judge Nye looked toward the table where I sat with the

Harpers. I rose. "Kali O'Brien representing Edward and Theresa Harper."

"Is the natural mother here as well?" Nye asked.

Melissa stood, awkwardly, and then quickly returned to her seat.

"Is the child in court today?"

I took the question. "No, Your Honor. She's at home with her grandmother, Mrs. Cross."

Weaver tossed his head back. "She's not the baby's grandmother any more than those people"—he pointed to the Harpers—"are her parents."

Nye rapped his gavel. Trimble leaned over and said something to his client.

"I'll have no more outbursts in my courtroom, is that understood?"

Trimble nodded. "We understand, Your Honor."

Judge Nye folded his hands in front of him. "I've read the pleadings. Let me make sure I have the facts straight. The baby in question was born to Melissa Burke. She and the Harpers have initiated proceedings for an independent adoption, correct?"

"Yes, Your Honor," I said.

"And Mr. Weaver has just recently learned of the pregnancy?"

"Correct." This time it was Trimble who answered.

Nye stroked the corners of his mouth. "Go ahead, Bill, you may proceed."

Trimble rose and stepped out from behind the counsel table. "Bram Weaver is the father of the baby herein known as Hannah B. He was not aware that the baby's mother, Melissa Burke, was pregnant until several weeks ago when a mutual acquaintance caught sight of her on the streets of the city. When the acquaintance told my client about seeing Melissa, who was noticeably pregnant at the time, my client took immediate action to establish his parental rights. He tried to contact Melissa where she'd lived and worked at the time he knew her. When he determined that, she'd gone into hiding."

"Objection. She wasn't hiding."

Nye waved a dismissal my way. "This isn't a trial, Ms. O'Brien. It's an informal hearing."

Be that as it may, the casting of facts was often as important as the facts themselves.

Trimble continued as though he'd merely paused for a breath. "My client tried contacting her roommates, who claimed to know nothing about Melissa's departure. He tried by several other means to locate her. All to no avail. He checked birth records and contacted local hospitals several times a week. His efforts finally paid off when he found that Melissa Burke had given birth at California Pacific. He went to see her the very afternoon he located her. He wanted to assume his parental duties, to offer financial and emotional support. He wanted to meet his baby daughter."

Trimble paused, ostensibly for a drink of water, but more likely for effect. "You can imagine," Trimble continued, "how devastated my client was to learn that Melissa Burke had given the child away."

There we were with the casting of facts again. Trimble made it sound like Melissa was tossing the baby out with the recycles. I bit my tongue.

"Mr. Weaver immediately voiced his displeasure. He agreed to take on full financial and custodial responsibility and to raise the child himself. But Melissa Burke has refused to cooperate. He now seeks to establish his parental rights through the court of law."

Nye's features squeezed more tightly. "Ms. O'Brien, did you make any effort to notify Mr. Weaver of the impending birth and to obtain his consent to the adoption?"

I'd known this moment was coming, but that didn't make it any easier. I hated pointing a finger at Melissa, especially because it ended up making me look foolish. But there weren't a lot of options.

"I was operating under the belief that a different young man was the baby's father," I said, choosing my words carefully. "And that may yet prove be the case. Mr. Weaver hasn't established paternity."

Trimble was on his feet immediately. "He's more than happy to undergo a paternity test. The sooner, the better."

Nye pressed his knuckles into the furrows of his forehead. "Ms. Burke, perhaps you could help us out here."

All eyes turned in her direction. "I . . . I . . ." She swallowed. Her eyes held a look of panic. I'd warned her not to give away the store. If Bram wanted to establish paternity, let him take the lead and prove it. Melissa lifted her chin. "I'm sorry sir, I can't."

"Are you saying you don't know who is the father of your baby?" Nye came across like a stern and reproachful parent. I suspected it was a role that came naturally to him.

Melissa didn't look at him. "Right."

"Liar." Weaver's face turned red. "You know that baby is mine. I was your first, remember?" His tone was nasty, like a slap in the face.

But Melissa didn't falter. While she'd avoided looking directly at the judge, she faced Weaver squarely. She stood straighter and managed a haughty shrug. "You might have been first, but it's rather presumptuous to assume you were the *only* one."

Weaver's fist clenched into a ball. His eyes darkened, and he muttered under his breath.

Judge Nye banged his gavel. "Enough. Both of you."

He paused to let his words sink in. "Ms. Burke, why didn't you tell Mr. Weaver about your pregnancy?"

"I didn't want him involved." Melissa's composure surprised me.

"Is there something that makes you think he might be a danger to the baby?" Judge Nye asked.

"No, not exactly."

Nye leaned back and crossed his arms. "You don't want this child of yours, but you don't want Mr. Weaver to have her either?"

"I don't want him near her at all." Melissa's voice was filled with loathing.

"Yet you can give me no reason."

Melissa said nothing.

"You're coming from a position of revenge maybe?"

I'd had enough. "Your Honor. Ms. Burke is perfectly within her rights to place the child for adoption in a loving, two-parent home."

"Unless the natural father objects," Trimble added.

Nye sighed. "What's clear," he said, "is that we can't proceed in any direction until paternity is established. Let's get the testing done and then we'll reconvene. Until then, the baby will remain with Mr. and Mrs. Harper." He reached for the gavel.

Trimble was on his feet again. "If I may, Your Honor."

Nye raised an eyebrow.

"Mr. Weaver would like to visit his daughter. He hasn't even seen her except briefly through the glass at the hospital nursery."

Terri whimpered.

"Your Honor," I said, rising also. "We have nothing but Mr. Weaver's unsubstantiated contention that he is the baby's father. There may well be no blood relationship at all, in which case Mr. Weaver has no rights with respect to the child. We can't allow wide-open visiting privileges to every person who wants them."

Judge Nye made an elaborate show of looking around the room. "I don't see anyone else waiting in line to visit the baby, Ms. O'Brien. We're talking about one man, a man who willingly stepped forward to take on the lifelong and serious responsibility of parenthood."

Ted and Terri had clasped hands, holding on tightly to each other for support.

"She's only three weeks old," I said.

"If Weaver is the baby's father," Nye said, "he will be the one raising her. I think it would be beneficial for both of them, father and daughter, to spend time together early on."

"And if he's *not* the father," I pointed out, "visitation will have been granted to a complete stranger."

Trimble cleared his throat. "We're only asking for a short visit. Say, an hour or so."

"In the unfortunate event that this matter should become a legal battle . . ." Nye looked toward the Harpers at this point making it clear the ball would be in their court. "If it comes to that, you, Ms. O'Brien, will be the first to argue that the child has bonded with her adoptive parents, and that it will be detrimental to remove her from their home. I am only trying to anticipate your concerns."

Bullshit. But I kept the thought to myself. Instead, I said, "The welfare of a young baby is at stake, Your Honor."

"Precisely." Nye cleared his throat. "The court sanctions a supervised visit of one hour, to be arranged within the next week. This hearing is continued until such time as the paternity testing has been completed."

The whole thing took less than thirty minutes. Terri was shaking by the time the judge's gavel sounded. I could practically hear the outrage boiling inside her.

"Can he do that?" she sputtered. "Can he make us let that man take Hannah, even for an hour?"

"Yes," I said, "he can. But Weaver won't be alone with her. A third person will be present as well."

Terri was hyperventilating. "She's *our* baby. I'm her *mother*. I can't just leave her with strangers."

When we reached the hallway, I cupped Terri's elbow, pulling her and Ted off to the side. "This probably isn't the time for a discussion, but I'd like the two of you to think again about the wisdom of fighting Weaver."

Terri leaned back against wall, moaning. Ted shoved his hands into his pockets. "I understand what you're saying, but we just can't do—"

Terri let out a sharp wail. Suddenly she flew across the floor in a rage and began clawing at Bram Weaver, who'd stopped to get a drink of water from the fountain.

"No way in hell you'll get your hands on my daughter," she shrieked.

Weaver held up an arm to defend himself and Terri kicked him in the sins. "You're nobody in that child's life."

Ted pulled at Terri's arm. She fought him as well, broke free and pummeled Weaver with her fists.

"Fucking doesn't make you a parent," she screamed.

Trimble joined Ted in restraining Terri. Weaver stepped back and brushed himself off.

"In this case," he said with a smirk, "it did. You'd better get used to the idea."

"And you'd better watch your back." She spit at him. "I'd kill you before I let you have Hannah."

ABOUT THE AUTHOR

Jonnie Jacobs lives with her husband and two sons in northern California. Jonnie loves hearing from readers, and you may write to her c/o Kensington Publishing Corporation. Jonnie can also be reached via e-mail at Jonnie@netcom.com or you can visit her website: http://www. NMOMysteries.com

The Amanda Hazard Series
By Connie Feddersen

The Classic Mysteries of
Mary Roberts Rinehart

__The Album	1-57566-280-9	$5.99US/$7.50CAN
__The After House	1-57566-651-0	$5.99US/$7.99CAN
__The Bat	1-57566-238-8	$5.99US/$7.50CAN
__The Case of Jennie Brice	1-57566-135-7	$5.50US/$7.00CAN
__The Circular Staircase	1-57566-180-2	$5.50US/$7.00CAN
__The Door	1-57566-367-8	$5.99US/$7.50CAN
__Episode of the Wandering Knife	1-57566-530-1	$5.99US/$7.99CAN
__The Haunted Lady	1-57566-567-0	$5.99US/$7.99CAN
_ A Light in the Window	1-57566-689-8	$5.99US/$7.99CAN
__Lost Ecstasy	1-57566-344-9	$5.99US/$7.50CAN
__The Red Lamp	1-57566-213-2	$5.99US/$7.50CAN
__The Wall	1-57566-213-2	$5.99US/$7.50CAN
__The Window at the White Owl	0-8217-5794-6	$5.99US/$7.60CAN
__The Yellow Room	1-57566-119-5	$5.50US/$7.00CAN

Call toll free **1-888-345-BOOK** to order by phone or use this coupon to order by mail.

Name_____

Address _____

City_____ State _____ Zip _____

Please send me the books I have checked above.

I am enclosing $_____

Plus postage and handling* $_____

Sales tax (in New York and Tennessee only) $_____

Total amount enclosed $_____

*Add $2.50 for the first book and $.50 for each additional book.

Send check or money order (no cash or CODs) to: **Kensington Publishing Corp., Dept. C.O., 850 Third Avenue, New York, NY 10022**

Prices and numbers subject to change without notice. All orders subject to availability.

Come visit our website at **www.kensingtonbooks.com**.

Your Favorite Mystery Authors
Are Now Just A Phone Call Away

More Mysteries from
Laurien Berenson

"Berenson throws dog lovers a treat they will relish."
—*Publishers Weekly*

Mickey Rawlings Mysteries
By Troy Soos